EATS TO DIE FOR!

EATS TO DIE FOR!

MICHAEL MALLORY

A Dave Beauchamp Mystery

WILDSIDE PRESS

PROLOGUE

There are times when I wonder if becoming a private investigator wasn't the worst possible career choice for me.

My name is Dave Beauchamp and I live and work in the San Fernando Valley of Los Angeles. I'm a huge old movie buff and I became a P.I. simply because it seemed like the logical thing to do after getting dropped through the trap door of my former law firm. Why am I telling you all this? Because my life may end at any second and I'd like it if *somebody* remembered I was here.

At the moment I'm trapped underground in a place I never knew existed, a place, in fact, that I doubt most people know exist, and staring at a person who is holding a gun on me. I don't mind telling you that when I saw that gun appear, I nearly wet myself. It was not simply the sight of a gun being pointed at my chest, but also the identity of the shooter. Add to that the fact that, even before the gun came out, I really had to pee.

Looking down the barrel of the revolver was all I needed to assure me that the person I had pegged for the murders that had occurred over the past week was innocent.

Some detective I am.

A voice sounded in my head, one with which I was all-too-familiar. It was Humphrey Bogart, one of the chorus of old Hollywood film stars who have left Forest Lawn and taken up residence inside my skull. Bogie's voice often appears to comment on the situations in which I find myself, and sometimes he even offers good advice.

Don't bother asking me why this happens, because I have no idea, and yes, I do realize that in all the clinics in all the towns in all the world, I would be diagnosed as suffering from schizophrenia. But I prefer to believe it is simply my subconscious speaking to me in the voices of old movie stars. Perhaps that's two ways of saying the same thing.

If I live past tonight, I'll try to get myself booked on *Dr. Phil* and find out.

At this moment, however, I didn't have time to worry about it. All I could do was agree with what Bogie had just told me whole-heartedly: *Kid, you're really screwed.*

Somebody, somewhere once decided that your entire life passes before your eyes when you're about to die, but all I got was a montage recap of the past week and how I had gotten myself into this fine mess, which started when the tomato walked into my office....

CHAPTER ONE

"Are you Mr. Beauchamp?" the tomato asked, mispronouncing my name the way everyone does at first. It's *BEACH-um*, not *Bow-Champ*, though I find myself having to correct people so frequently that I've considered spelling it phonetically on the sign outside my office.

How about just Chump, Private Eye? a deep, sardonic voice said in my head. It belonged to Robert Mitchum, whom I knew from experience had very little faith in my abilities as a detective. Since my last case could be considered a success I had hoped that maybe Mitchum would give me a break. But here he was.

Maybe he was here to see the tomato.

She was about five-foot-seven, by my estimation, and had dark hair pinned up under a green cap that looked like a stem. Her long legs were encased in sheer green tights, which contrasted with the wide, round redness of her body. You see, she really was a tomato; at least she was dressed like one. Her tomato costume was so large that I wondered how she managed to get it into the elevator and up here to the second floor of the building.

"Are you certain you're a detective?" she asked. "You don't look old enough."

I sighed. I'm thirty-two years old but most people seem to think that I'm still in college.

"All detectives have personas," I said, trying to sound like Jack Webb, and failing. "Mine's that of a callow youth."

"It's very effective," she replied. "Well, I'll have to trust you that you're real. My name is Luisa Sandoval, and you're probably wondering why I'm dressed like this."

"It had crossed my mind."

She explained that she was done up like a simple fruit because she had been hired to promote the grand opening of a new Burger Heaven fast food restaurant just down the street. She was there along with other people dressed like hamburger buns, a patty, and onion and pickle slices, who were hired by the day to wave to the motorists fighting their way down Ventura Boulevard, the primary artery (or maybe *autory*) through the Valley, and hand out fliers to those hardy souls on foot, while chanting the chain's motto: *There's no hunger in Heaven.*

I, for one, was glad that Burger Heaven had decided to open up shop here in the Sherman Oaks stretch of the Valley where my office is located, since I had developed a real passion for their double burgers. Up until now I had indulged my habit mostly in the evenings or on the weekends, since there was a BH not far from my apartment in Studio City. Now with the grand opening, I could add lunch into the mix whenever I wanted.

"This isn't really what I do, though."

That seemed obvious. Given her looks, I assumed she must be an actress waiting for her big break, but in that I was surprised. Luisa Sandoval told me she was actually an investigative reporter with the *L.A. Independent Journal*, one of those freebie papers you find outside restaurants and bars all over the city.

"I've been working undercover investigating the Burger Heaven chain, but I'm afraid they're on to me," she said. "I think I'm going to need professional help. I came here because you're close enough to the Burger Heaven that I could safely sneak away and get back while on my break. By the way, do you know that you've been flamed on Yelp by someone who claims you turned her cat into a Democrat?"

"Mrs. Druxman," I sighed.

It had been a missing pet case. I found the cat in another yard and had photographed it for identification purposes, but included in the photo, next to the cat, was a lawn sign reading *Hillary 2016*.

"You can't win them all. But you haven't told me exactly why you are investigating Burger Heaven, Ms. Sandoval."

"You can call me Louie," she said, flashing a perfect, dimpled smile. "Everyone does."

Louie, I think this is the beginning of a beautiful friendship, Bogie said inside my head, and I hoped he was right.

"Very well, Louie. But as to Burger Heaven?"

"Right. Mr. Beauchamp—"

"Dave, please."

"Dave, you wouldn't believe what they're putting into their beef."

Putting into their beef? Burger Heaven? My favorite fast food chain?

"Soy?" I offered.

"All chains use additives. No, this is something else."

"What, then?"

"Well…I don't know, exactly," she hedged. "But I suspect it's something that shouldn't be there."

"Like what?"

"Mind if I take this thing off?"

I didn't mind at all, so she slithered out of the tomato costume to reveal underneath a red leotard that, when combined with her green tights, made her look more like an elf working at the North Pole Victoria's Secret outlet.

Not bad, Bogie said in my head, as ever, the master of understatement. Today, of course, one can't say things like that out loud.

"That's better," Louie said, sinking down into my guest chair. "I really hate this outfit, but it was the best way to get close to the organization. They don't seem to like reporters very much."

"You were talking about the meat at Burger Heaven," I prompted.

"Yeah. I don't know if you're familiar with the chain, but their hamburgers are widely regarded as being addictive. Some think that might not be a simple metaphor."

"You mean you think they're genuinely, literally addictive?"

She nodded. "When I started this investigation, I was operating under the assumption it was nicotine."

"Nicotine? In the hamburgers? That can't be."

"Why can't it be?"

"Well, because…"

Because I liked them too much to want to believe it.

"Why would they risk doing that?" I asked her.

"Doesn't it seem obvious? Sales. I've heard people say they simply can't get through the day without a Burger Heaven burger."

"Look, Louie, I don't want to sound like a paid spokesman for Burger Heaven, but their food is better than that of the other chains. Couldn't that be the reason for this so-called addiction?"

She leaned forward, her eyes locked on mine. "Okay, then what about the fact that they don't have a drive-thru like everyone else does?"

"I'm not following."

"There is no take-out. You can't remove their food off the premises, even if you want to."

"Are you sure about that?"

"Yeah. If you try, you're stopped."

"You'll have to excuse me, but that sounds a little…out there."

"Have *you* ever taken one of their burgers home?"

"No, I eat them there, but I think I read somewhere that their goal is to make the hottest, freshest food around, and they seem to feel that quality is compromised if you don't eat it right away."

"And you believe that?"

"Well, sure. Why not?"

She looked at me as though I was a third-grader who had just told her the dog had dined on his homework and started to laugh.

"Are you really that naïve or do you just think I am?"

"Um, really, I'm not trying to appear insincere."

"You're positive you're really a detective and not just answering the phone for your dad?"

As Robert Mitchum hooted in my head, I pointed out my framed license hanging precariously on the wall behind me, and tried like hell not to blush.

"Ms. Sandoval, how can I convince you that I have been around the block a time or two. Maybe I haven't walked the mean streets, but I've been on a few that were disagreeable. I've had people take shots at me and on my last case I barely escaped being murdered. I've even managed to feed myself on my own for the last ten years."

"Yeah, by going to Burger Heaven," she said, getting up and starting to wriggle back into the wire-and-fabric tomato outfit. "I guess I've wasted my time and yours. I'm sorry."

"Louie, please don't run off. Look, maybe if you actually told me what it is you want me to do for you, I'd have an easier time considering your case. But right now I'm a little confused."

She sighed. "My editor's always ragging on me, too, for not explaining the background of my stories thoroughly enough. Okay, here it is in plain language. I think there's something put in the meat at Burger Heaven that makes them addictive, but I can't prove it without a sample, and so far it's been impossible to get a sample. I took this stupid job with them to try and infiltrate the company, but I think they're starting to suspect I'm up to something. So I came here to ask for your help in getting a sample of Burger Heaven's beef so we could take it to a lab and have it analyzed, and finally find out what's really in it."

"That's all you want me to do?"

"That will be enough. I'll hire you at whatever your daily rate is."

"I charge fifty dollars an hour, but I almost feel bad about charging you money simply for going and getting a hamburger."

She smiled, showing me her dimples again. "Going and getting a hamburger and getting out with it."

"Still—"

"If you think I'm being silly or paranoid, Dave, go try it. Try to hide an uneaten Burger Heaven burger somewhere on you and leave the store. If you manage to do it, I'll pay you whatever you want."

She stepped to the edge of my desk and leaned over it as far as her tomato suit would allow. "And I mean whatever. Let me give you my number." She rattled off a phone number in the 323 area code. "If I don't hear from you in two days, I'll try another private dick."

I stood up, and thrust my hand out, which she took.

"All right, Louie, you've finally picked my dick. No, I mean pricked my interest! I meant *piqued*!"

"You're funny," she said through a wicked, dimpled smile. "Call me."

Then she squeezed her ripe, tomatoey hotness through the door, calling "Adios," before going down the hall.

Well, kid, that was smooth, Bogart reprimanded inside my head, *like stucco on a wet afternoon.*

He really puts the "shame" into "shamus," Mitchum seconded.

"Oh, shut up, both of you," I said to the empty office. "I'm still alive and you're not, so nyeah."

Yesss, but for how looooong, John Huston added.

My friends; my good friends.

I sat back down behind my desk and tried to think. I'd been directly challenged to take on a case that probably wasn't even a case by a gorgeous Latina who wasn't really a tomato, which might potentially prove damaging to my favorite fast food chain. I had nothing to go on except the challenge, since there was not much in the way of information.

What would a real detective do in this instance? And by "real," I mean one from the movies.

By gad, sir, that woman wants you to investigate an eatery, the psoriatic voice of Sydney Greenstreet said inside my head. *So go to lunch!*

"Great idea," I said to the now-empty office, and headed out.

CHAPTER TWO

Since the day was warm but not hot, my trusty Corolla, which had only recently become a teenager (a milestone I celebrated by buying it a full tank of gas and a professional wash) had not been turned into an Easy Bake oven. It started right up without an argument and in seconds I was off to Burger Heaven.

I decided not to go to the one having its grand opening down the street, the one Louie Sandoval was helping to promote, but my usual one, where the clerks knew me by sight. I drove past the new restaurant, however, and saw the happy ingredients, including Louie, playing broadly to the crowd of passers-by. They all appeared to be having a good time, at least as good as one can have out in public dressed like a strip of bacon or a slice of cheese.

I thought about rolling down the window, tooting the horn and waving to Louie, but then thought better of it. That's how accidents happened, men taking their eyes off the road momentarily to acknowledge beautiful women dressed like produce.

This is L.A.; there is probably even a statistic for it.

Traffic on Ventura was no heavier than usual, but it seemed as though the city had retimed the stoplights so that once your immediate light was green, the next one was red, and vice versa, making progress all but impossible. It took twenty-five minutes to travel from Sherman Oaks to Studio City, and not for the first time I wondered if maybe I should move either my office or my apartment to be closer to the other one.

I was actually starting to salivate as I pulled into the parking lot of my usual Burger Heaven.

Did I always? I suddenly wondered. Or had Louie planted her suspicions in my brain to the point that I was reacting to them?

Once inside I got in the line, which was quite long, even though it was a little past traditional lunchtime, and when I got to Amber, the young blonde clerk who usually takes my order, I got a special wink.

"Well, hi there, Mr. Beauchamp," she said. "You're early today. The usual?"

"You know, Amber, I'm feeling adventurous today, so I think I'll try…um…oh, heck. Yeah, the usual."

It wasn't that I *wasn't* adventurous, it's just that I knew exactly what I would be getting in the Twin Halo combo and didn't want to risk having something I might not like as much.

Amber gave me a look that perhaps wasn't intended to communicate that I was a pathetic, pattie-whipped dork, but a little of that came across. Someday I'd march right in her and order a Twin Halo with bacon, and then I'd show her!

But not today.

Burger Heaven prides itself on the speed of its service, and watching the workers behind the counter move, I'm always reminded of a silent comedy projected at the wrong speed, which makes everyone move abnormally fast. These folks really double-timed it to get the food to you as quickly as possible, and while I was always happy to be a customer, I was glad I didn't have to work here.

Your clients wish you did, though, Robert Mitchum said in my head, but I didn't care, because my combo tray was just about to be slid over the counter.

The feel of the hot hamburger through the paper wrap is part of the Burger Heaven experience, and I always take an extra second to hold it before tearing into it. The french fries here are always hot as well, unlike some other chains where they're allowed to become a little clammy. One of BH's carefully guarded trade secrets is how they keep the fries so hot without dumping them under a heat lamp.

I had just popped the last bite of my burger into my mouth when I remembered that the reason I had come here was to try and leave with a chunk of uneaten hamburger. Dang. I could always order another, but I wasn't hungry enough for another. Well, I guess it means I'll just have to come back again sometime. Now that I have a little cash in the bank, from my last case, I might find myself eating out more often.

Carole Lombard commented on that one, but I won't repeat it.

On the way out I was, as I always am, treated to a friendly "Have a Heavenly day" by the smiling security guard at the door. For all her dimples, legs and journalistic zeal, Louie Sandoval must be misguided; no place this friendly and cheerful could be engaged in shady activity.

Given that this particular Burger Heaven was within a few blocks of my apartment, it would have made sense for me to simply go on home, but I had left the lights on in my office, and it was only the middle of the afternoon anyway.

Even though I no longer had to worry about the DWP turning my lights off for me (at least for the next three or four months) there was no sense being wasteful, even if gas was perilously close to three bucks a gallon again, and the drive back to Sherman Oaks would probably drink up a half-dollar, minimum.

Three dollars...a GALLON? the voice of Jack Benny cried inside my head. *My CAR didn't cost that much!*

Yeah, well, times change, Jack.

When I drove back past the ingredient parade in front of the new-ly-opened Burger Heaven, I noticed that Louie was no longer there. Maybe she was in the bathroom. Even tomatoes have to squeeze out a little juice now and then.

I was sure after I'd closed up shop and was headed back home I would see her again, on the sidewalk gleefully shilling in customers alongside someone who had played Hamlet at their college to rave reviews, but was now searching for his motivation as a sesame seed bun.

Outside of my office building was a For Lease sign, which I knew to be relating to the double-suite space on the first floor that had once housed a porn movie operation, but was now sitting empty. Upon entering my very-well-lit office, the first thing I did, as always, was to check the answering machine on my desk to see if there was a blue flashing light indicating that a call had come in.

There wasn't, so I sat down and powered up my laptop, then went onto the Webfilms site to see if there were any new movies to download, or, more accurately, whether there were any old movies that were newly being offered for download.

People sometimes ask me how I can be such a fanatic over Golden Age Hollywood when at my age I should really be a fanatic of video games or role-playing endeavors. The truth is my father is to blame, though I hardly consider it blame. He is not simply a film buff but a genuine authority who has written scads of articles in magazines, mostly the ones catering to the hard-core movie freak. He is also a lawyer, but unlike my uneasy years at the bar, he is successful at it.

More importantly to me, he never told me that my preference for watching old movies over throwing around a baseball was not normal. I had to find that out on my own, in school. As a result, while Sammy Sosa and Barry Bonds are just names I've heard somewhere, Cuddles Sakall and Mischa Auer are old friends.

I was only a few minutes into a post-war gangbuster epic titled *The Street with No Name*, which featured a personal endorsement from J. Edgar Hoover himself, when my stomach became very unhappy. It wasn't the Twin Halo, which was lying easy with the tide; it was the sudden realization that something was wrong.

It was the phone machine.

Even though the blue call-indicator was not flashing, there was a digital "1" on the screen indicating that I had an old message. Except I shouldn't have an old message because earlier today I had cleared two overnight messages, which were nothing but misdirected fax tones. There were no old calls remaining, I was sure of that. Since no calls had come in while I'd been here in the office, there was only one other possibility: someone had phoned while I was out at the Burger Heaven. But were that the case, the blue light would be flashing.

That left only one possibility: somebody had called and left a message, and someone else had listened to it while I wasn't here, relegating it to "old message" status.

Which meant somebody had broken into my office while I was gone.

Had it been the landlord? I couldn't imagine why, since I'd actually paid my rent three months in advance last week. Even if he had come in, I doubt he would have listened in on my phone messages.

Then I noticed the picture on the wall.

It was a painting of a moody, rainy street scene that I'd picked up at a thrift shop. An appraiser would probably judge it the fine art equivalent of an Ed Wood, Jr. movie, but I liked it. Staring at it, I could imagine myself in a trench coat and fedora, cigarette in hand, walking down that wet street.

You don't smoke, kid, Bogie reminded me, *you're allergic*.

Details.

But something was wrong with the picture, and it took another couple seconds before I figured it out. Up until now that picture had been hanging at a slight angle. It was one of those things that I had intended to fix for a long time but never did, meaning I had not only become used to its tilt, I appreciated it for aesthetic purposes, like a "dutch" camera angle in a film.

But now the painting was perfectly straight. As I approached the picture, I tried to figure out why somebody would mess with it in the first place. Did they think I had a safe hidden behind it, like in the movies?

Taking the picture frame with both hands, I turned it back to its usual angle and heard a scratching sound, like something was abrading the wall. Lifting the frame off its hook, I turned it over and saw a tiny black box affixed to the backing. While I'm certainly no expert on high-tech spy gear, I can recognize a bug when I see one.

So while I was out enjoying a hamburger, someone had entered my office, listened to a phone message, and planted a bug. I'm sure if I looked around more I would find even more evidence of their presence. But what were they looking for?

And who were "they" in the first place?

Amateurs, obviously, said New Jersey-flavored voice that I recognized it immediately as belonging to Sheldon Leonard.

All right, Sheldon, I'll bite: why amateurs?

It came to me a second later, prompting Sheldon and I to answer in unison: *Because a pro would have noticed the picture was askew and re-hung it that way.* Actually, Sheldon had said *dat way*, but I knew what we meant.

I peeled the device off of the backing, where it had been attached with a strip of medical adhesive tape, and fumbled with it until the back popped off. Inside was a SIM card like the one my cell phone used, so I presumed that removing it would deactivate the bug.

I knew I should call the police and report this, but there was one problem: I had no actual verifiable proof that someone had broken in. Sure, I was holding a bug, but I'm a private investigator, so it would be perfectly logical for me to have such equipment lying around. It would only be my word that I'd discovered it, having been planted by someone else.

And as for the phone message clue, it was my word against my phone's, and given my past experience with the police, they would be more likely to believe my phone.

Speaking of my phone, I realized I had not yet listened to the message. While I doubted it would reveal a voice saying something like, "Oh, hi, I broke into your office earlier and planted a listening device, and now my keys are missing, so could you look around for them and call me back?" it might reveal something.

Stepping to my desk I jabbed the playback and was told the call came in at 2:47 p.m., which was maybe ten minutes after I'd left.

David, it's J.D., a familiar voice said from the box. *You are out ridding the streets of miscreants, I imagine, or else looking through the sale DVD bin at Best Buy. In any event, when you return, call me. Cheers.*

While "J.D." sounded like an old time Hollywood studio executive, it was short for Jack Daniels—yes, that's his real name—a friend of mine who was a mystery writer. He wrote under a pseudonym, one you would immediately recognize if you've browsed through an airport newsstand in recent years, but off the page he was always Jack, or else "J.D."

A Brit by birth, Jack lived in Santa Monica, Raymond Chandler's "Bay City" and currently home to a large English émigré population, and he called every so often to grill me about investigative procedure for one of his stories. I in turn called upon him during my last case and asked him to use his writers' imagination on an overabundance of facts, leads and clues that I could not conform into one solitary picture.

So it was his turn.

I dialed his number back and when he answered, said: "Jack, it's Dave Beauchamp."

"David, m'lad!"

He sounded soberish, so I went on. "Are you in need of someone to help you spend all that cash you're making again?"

"Oh, yes, right!" he laughed. "These days most publishers think an advance check is a chess move. No, I called with a question. You have a second?"

I knew this was going to take longer than a second, but said yes anyway.

"You have a mobile phone, right?" Jack asked.

"A cell phone? Sure. I don't know anyone who doesn't."

"Right, so here's my problem. I need to get Tory into a situation where he's abducted and he has to stay locked up for a big chunk of the book."

Tory Poacher was Jack's series character.

"But these days, like you say, everybody has a mobile. Anyone who's trapped somewhere can simply call for help, or text for help, or go online and Facebook for help. So I have to get the phone away from him."

"Well, have whoever's abducting him take the phone away."

"Cliché, my boy. In the old days, the bad guys always took the detective's gun. These days they take the phone. I'm looking for something different."

"How about he drops it somewhere and can't reach it?"

"How many movies have you seen where the good guy loses his gun during a chase, while the bad guy retains his? All you're doing is substituting a phone."

"Hmmm. Well, then, there's no service available where he's being held. That's endemic to a phone."

"Yeah, but the bad guys are there too, and they have to call people, so there has to be service."

"I never realized what a difficult job you have, Jack," I said.

"I'll tell you David, the ubiquity of mobile phones is the worst thing that's ever happened to the plotting of a mystery. Even if you can figure out how to get rid of the damn things, it has to be for a logical reason or else you get a thousand-word two-star Amazon review explaining how a real person in the real world would have gotten around that problem. I think that's why so many TV crime shows these days are done with period settings."

"I suppose having the battery run out is too convenient."

"Oh, come on. Have you ever run out of juice while working a case?"

I almost hated to confess that yes, I had. I had forgotten to charge my phone so when I needed it the next day, it was dead.

"Crikey," Jack said, after hearing my confession, "you should get two."

"Two phones?"

"Yes, so while you're carrying one, the other's always charging, and…oh, bollocks! I've just made my problem twice as bad, haven't I?"

"Only if you've already established that Tory Poacher has two phones precisely for that reason."

"I haven't, but it's such a good idea that I've got to do it at the end of this book, after he's gotten out, just so he can make certain this never happens again. I'm dying, David, naked to mine enemies. Please help. Is there never really a time when you don't carry your mobile phone?"

"When I'm in the shower or in bed."

"No good. He's accosted in a crowded movie theatre."

"A movie theatre?"

"His client is a big director and Tory's been invited to a screening of a movie the guy's made because the director is anticipating trouble from one of the producers, and don't bother telling me that you have to power down the mobile once inside the theatre, because I know that. You can always power it back up later, so he still has the damn thing."

"Jack, is this a pre-release screening?"

"Yes, like a sneak preview, but with a lot of people in attendance. You know how much I like the idea of somebody disappearing from a crowd."

"Then you've solved your own problem, Jack."

"How so?"

"Have you ever been to a sneak preview?"

"Only movies made from my own books, though the last one was quite some time back. Why do you ask?"

"Because if you go to a screening or preview today, you can't take in your phone or any other device that could record what's shown on the screen. The studio's are paranoid about film piracy, so if you're packing, so to speak, they literally confiscate your phone and put it in a little plastic bag and hold it until—"

"That's brilliant!" Jack shouted. "Tory goes to the screening, has to surrender his phone, and is abducted before he can get it back! Then it becomes a question of who has it! David, my boy, J.D. owes you a lunch, with gratitude."

"I'll take it. But in the meantime, I have a return question for you."

"Make it quick. Now that I'm back on track, I have to get typing."

Oh, I do hope I'm not inconveniencing you, the mordant voice of Vincent Price said in my head.

"Jack, someone broke into my office today and planted a bug."

"A bug? Who'd want to spy on you?"

A thought bulleted through my mind: it might be someone from the legal dream team defending a certain killer I had brought to justice, who had threatened to crucify me in court when the trial finally occurred. But if so, they would probably have been more professional about it.

I didn't wish to tell Jack any of this.

"I've no idea," I said instead. "What would Tory Poacher do?"

"Well, Tory would look out the window, see a strange van with tinted windows, deduce that's where the listener is, and run down to the street to confront it, only to have the van speed away from the curb, leaving Tory in a cloud of exhaust, which serves to obscure his view of the rear license plate. But then he would look down and find something, like an Irish Sweepstakes ticket from 1957, lying on the ground where the van had been."

"What's the Irish Sweepstakes got to do with it?"

"I haven't the foggiest. I'm making all this up. It's what I do."

"Look, at least tell me how I can trace this device. Maybe where it was bought. I know there are commercial spy shops in town, so could I go in and ask who purchased one of these?"

He laughed.

"David, this is L.A. Not only are there commercial spy shops in town, there are so many of them that you might as well go into a Whole Foods market and ask who bought the organic eggplant. These days, you probably don't even have to go into a spy shop, just go to one of those sex stores and find microphones and perv cameras on the same aisle as the handcuffs. Or go online and get your spy gear delivered by a drone, thank you Mr. Bezos. I think you're looking at a dead end."

"Yeah, well, at least I know where to buy handcuffs now."

"That's so twentieth century," Jack said, laughing. "These days the cops are likely to use nylon cable ties instead of bracelets."

"Nothing is the way it used to be, is it?"

"Only rejection. That is the one fixed point in a changing world. Now, if you'll excuse me, the voice of my muse is screaming in my head. I have to get back to work."

You're lucky, I thought. *You have only one voice. I have dozens.*

"I'll let you know about lunch," he said, and then hung up.

"Great," I said to the dead line, and replaced the receiver. Since my window didn't face the street, I didn't bother to get up and go look for a van, but I still did not know what to do with the bug. Stomping it to bits didn't seem like a good idea, since it was possible the thing could still bear a clue as to its planter, but just sticking it in my desk drawer wasn't a good idea, either, since I only assumed I had deactivated it by removing the card.

Now would be an outstanding time for one of my friends to chime in and give me a suggestion. Bogie? Any ideas? Mitch? Basil Rathbone? Lloyd Nolan? George Sanders? Heck, Johnny Weissmuller? Anyone?

While I didn't hear Johnny's voice, which would likely have consisted of little more than "Me, Tarzan; you, stupid," it was simply thinking of the former Olympic swimming champion that gave me the solution. Swimming…water…tank of water.

Going to the small kitchenette that came with the office, I grabbed a food storage bag, the kind with the zipper closer, from the cupboard and put the bug and SIM card into it. Then I took my only two spoons and put them in as well (I'd bring some more from home). When I was done I squeezed out all the air I could and zipped it shut, and took it to the equally small bathroom that came with the office, took the lid off the toilet tank and dropped in the baggie. If the thing was still working, whoever was listening would be getting some mighty interesting sounds.

There was little left for me to do but lock up and head home, because in my experience, nobody contacts private investigators after four in the afternoon.

It was another successful day at Beauchamp Investigations.

After powering down my laptop, I closed up and headed out.

Driving down Ventura toward my apartment, I fought down an urge to stop at the brand-new Burger Heaven, not because I was hungry already, but just to see Louie and tell her how I was progressing on the case.

But'cha aren't Dave, ya aren't! Bette Davis was nice enough to point out.

Well, I could still check in with her, couldn't I?

As I drove by, I saw the tomato waving alongside all the other ingredients, and rolled down my window to wave. Then I stopped.

The tomato was there, all right, but it was not Luisa Sandoval. It was a young African-American woman wearing the same costume. Well, maybe Louie's shift had ended.

You really think it's that simple, kid? Bogie said.

Until he had piped up, I was certainly hoping.

CHAPTER THREE

I made a flash decision to turn into the Burger Heaven. I was not particularly hungry, having eaten a Twin Halo only a couple hours ago, but damned if I wasn't also drooling at the thought of having another one. Could it be that Louie was right?

Pulling into the first parking spot I saw, I got out and went inside. There was a line for the order counter—there always is—and I waited patiently until I got up there. A very young, fresh-faced, overly made-up woman smiled effusively at me and said, "Hello, welcome to Burger Heaven, how may I help you?" Her voice had a Midwestern twang, which probably meant she was on last month's bus from Iowa or Missouri or Indiana, one of a thousand wannabe actresses ready to take their shot at the big time.

"Oh, just a regular burger, I guess."

"Not the combo?"

"No, not the combo."

"Our fries are awfully good."

"Yes, I know they are, but I'm not hungry enough for a full meal. Just a regular burger."

"All righty," she said, grinning, and calling the order into a microphone. The burger was wrapped and on a tray within thirty seconds, and I carried it over to the first vacant table. Sitting there, munching the burger, I looked through the front wall of windows to watch the ingredients dancing and skipping about outside the restaurant. I may not be much as a PI, but I didn't have to dress up as a pickle to earn bed and board.

I was about to pop the last, rather large piece of burger into my mouth when a voice said, *You're not going to finish that, are you?* It was Lauren Bacall, and she arrived just in time. The point of my being here was to bring home a leftover. Looking longingly at the aromatic six-ply of buns, meat, tomato, lettuce and onion, I forced myself to wrap it up inside a napkin. After carrying my tray to the stack above the trash can, I started for the door, cupping the still-warm ort in my hand, thinking that whatever I decided to charge Luisa Sandoval for the patty chunk was the easiest money I ever made.

I was just about to go through the door when someone suddenly touch my elbow from behind. Turning, I saw a very tall woman in a security guard uniform, which bore a shoulder patch containing the Burger Heaven logo, holding a clipboard. "Thank you for coming, sir," she said. "If you can spare a moment, we'd like you to take a survey."

"A survey?"

"Yes, regarding how often you come to Burger Heaven, what you order, and so on."

"Oh, well…"

"It will only take a minute or two, and in return for you time and information, we will give you a gift certificate for your next visit."

"Really?"

"Absolutely." She smiled broadly, which made her look very unlike a security guard.

"All right," I said.

"Excellent, let's just step out of the doorway." She led me a few steps away to an alcove, and handed me the clipboard. "It's just a few questions."

Since taking the clipboard and writing on it took two hands, I had to set the napkin-wrapped burger bite down on the counter. The survey questions were pretty basic: Do you live in the neighborhood? How often to you visit Burger Heaven? The prices are competitive; Agree, Disagree, Don't Know…that sort of thing. It did, in fact, take only a minute to complete, including jotting down my email to receive further coupons. I handed everything back to the grinning guard who thanked me so emphatically one would think I'd just donated a kidney to her, and handed me the gift certificate.

I glanced down at it and saw it was for ten bucks! "This is very nice," I said, but when I looked up again, she was gone.

And so was the wrapped up bit of burger I'd set down to take the survey.

Okay, all right; somebody thought it was trash and picked up like a good employee. That's all.

You're certain *of that*, the voice of Raymond Burr intoned in my head, phrasing as a statement, not a question.

Well…even if I was not convinced, with a ten dollar gift certificate, I could try it again sometime.

Right now I thought I have a word with the new tomato. Going outside, I sidled up to the happy group on the sidewalk, only to be told to get out of the shot by a woman taking a picture of them with her phone. Once the woman was done, I went to the tomato and said hi. She smiled without really looking at me, handed me an ad flier and said, by rote, "There's no hunger in Heaven."

"Got a second to talk?" I asked.

"Sorry, but we're not suppose to fraternize, just perform," she replied.

"Well, I was really hoping to talk to Luisa anyway, you know, the tomato who was here earlier today?"

The tomato handed a flier to a middle-aged Japanese man, whose expression indicated that he was wondering on what planet he had suddenly found himself.

"Don't know any Luisa," she said, "and I've been here since nine this morning."

"But—"

"Sir," another voice said, and I turned to see the happy security guard, only now she wasn't quite so happy. "I'm very sorry, sir, but we can't really allow you to interfere with the duties of the Heavenly Host."

"The Heavenly Host?"

"The performers. Please, sir." Taking my arm, she started pulling me away gently but firmly—firmly enough as to imply that if I became a problem it would no longer be gently. "It's an insurance problem, you see."

I didn't, really, but I decided not to press the issue. "I am sorry. They're just so…"

"Heavenly," she finished for me.

"That's the word. Well, thank you again for the gift certificate. Goodbye."

"Have a heavenly day, sir. Come again."

As I walked back to my car, I attempted to make sense of what had gone on today. The new woman in the tomato suit was plainly lying, because I had seen for myself Louie Sandoval standing out in front of the restaurant, but what was the point of lying? Nothing made any sense.

I drove down Ventura toward home, but while stopped at a light, I made another decision. Louie had wanted me to get a burger sample, and I had failed. Even though I still found it a little hard to swallow that it was impossible, I had failed. So I decided I was going to go get a piece of hamburger or die trying. I made a quick left turn at the next street, went around the block, and headed back toward the same Burger Heaven. Pulling in to the lot, I parked and got out of the car, and then noticed a woman walking to the back of the restaurant. Even though she was no longer wearing the awkward tomato costume, I recognized her; the green stem hat was the tipoff. I watched her as she trotted through the parking lot and stopped by a large brown dumpster, where she lit up a cigarette.

As unthreateningly as I could, I strolled her way. When I got close enough, I said, "Hi, there."

She reacted as though she'd been burnt.

"Shit!" she cried, stubbing out the cigarette. "What do you want?"

"I want to talk to you, just for a second."

"You won't tell them I was smoking, will you?" she asked, sounding like a six-year-old who had just gotten caught standing over a broken vase. "I'm supposed to have quit, but it's so damn hard."

"I don't even know who they are," I said. "I just want to ask you a few questions about your life as a tomato."

"And suppose I don't want to answer any questions?"

"Then I guess I'll find them and tell them you were smoking."

A look of panic crossed her otherwise beautiful face. "No! I mean…shit, mister, what is it you want to know, and why?"

"Well, why, because I'm a private investigator."

Her eyes narrowed. "For who?"

"For Luisa Sandoval."

"I don't know any Luisa Sandoval. I told you that already." Even Oedipus at the end of the play could have seen she was lying.

"So you have been here playing a tomato since nine this morning."

"I never said that."

"You told me you've been here since nine."

"I have, but I wasn't playing a tomato." She started to pull out another cigarette and then glanced at me and thought better of it. "Shit, I hate this! I want a damn cigarette! Look, whoever you are, I'm the director of the little pageant we've got going out on the sidewalk. I'm a dancer, so I was brought in to tell the people how to move. You know, what kind of body language an onion would have, that sort of thing."

"Wow, Burger Heaven really takes this seriously."

"Oh, yeah!" she said. "We did have a girl playing the tomato, but she left, so I had to take over. Her name wasn't Luisa Whatever, though, it was Maria. Maria Ramirez, I think."

And a more stereotypically artificial Mexican name you will never hope to find, mi amigo, Ricardo Montalban said in my head. But I had already beat him to that one. As pseudonyms went, *Maria Ramirez* was as convincing as Jane Doe.

"What's your interest in all this?" the woman asked.

"I really am a private investigator," I said, "and the name's Dave Beauchamp. I'm looking for her is all."

"Well, she left. They had to get rid of her."

"Why?"

"She wasn't very good, for one thing."

"That all?"

"Look, I don't have to talk to you, you know." Apparently she had decided by now that I was not going to tell "them" about her smoking.

"I'm done, I guess, though I would like to know your name."

After a few seconds deliberation, she said, "Regina."

"Thanks, Regina. And your cigarette habit is safe with me. But simply out of curiosity, how do you get a gig directing people dressed as hamburger ingredients on the street?"

"Thinking of changing jobs?"

Something you might want to think about, I heard. Shut up, Mitch.

"I'm just curious," I said.

"Well, I guess you just find yourself in the wrong place at the right time, that's how." Regina walked past me, across the parking lot, and entered the restaurant, only to emerge a few moments later in full tomato regalia. She then went to join the others.

She didn't even wave goodbye.

I could have gone in and ordered another burger, but Regina's obvious fear lent a little bit of credence to Louie's claims, making me think that maybe she had been right in her suspicions that she had been under scrutiny and suspected of something.

Just because you're paranoid doesn't mean they aren't out to get you. If I showed up so soon after trying to sneak out a burger bit, they might think I was onto them, too, so I got back in the car and headed home.

Once there I decided to give Louie Sandoval a call and see if I could find out what had happened to her career as a love apple. Fishing out the number she gave me, I dialed it and listened to four rings, before it went to a machine. *Hello,* her recorded voice began, *this is Luisa. I'm not here, so leave a message. And if you're a tele-marketer...* She went on to describe an action that I doubted could actually be done, even by professional contortionists.

After hearing the beep I left a message asking her to give me a call, or come by the office again, if she had the time.

Obviously, I was not hungry for dinner, which coincided quite nicely with my having little food in the refrigerator. It wasn't that I could not afford to pack the fridge, at least this month, it was that I hadn't bothered going to the store this week.

Figuring there was no time like the present, I headed out for the local Ralph's and filled up the cart with basics—milk, bread, eggs, orange juice, coffee, hamburger meat (of course, my burgers wouldn't be as good as Burger Heaven's), frozen french fries, a bag of salad, some quick frozen dinners—and a DVD copy of *Pomeranian Springs*, a made-for-cable neo-noir that was one out of dozens of remaindered titles relegated to a $5.99 dump bin in the main aisle. At that price, I almost bought two.

By the time I headed back to my car with my groceries, which were tucked into three paper sacks, each of which cost a dime, dusk was starting to blanket the city. Maybe that was what affected my vision. *Something* had to be affecting it, because it just didn't seem rational that the woman standing by the front of the store, appearing to look straight at me was the Burger Heaven security guard who had given me the gift certificate, now out of uniform. Once I noticed her, she turned and went inside the store.

It wasn't impossible, of course, but the odds that I would see the same person on the same day at my usual grocery store had to be astronomical. But what were the odds that she was actually tailing me? No, I wasn't that paranoid. It was someone other woman, it had to be.

If you say so, kid, Bogie chimed in, and I could tell he didn't believe me.

CHAPTER FOUR

It had been two days since the tomato had walked into my life. Two days without a new case or client, or even the promise of one. Two days of coming to the office and downloading movies on my laptop while waiting for something to happen. Two days of realizing that even at $5.99, the DVD of *Pomeranian Springs* was a waste of money. At least I knew why they named it after a dog. I saved the jewel box for future use and put the DVD itself on my desk to use as a coaster.

Two days without hearing so much as a word from Louie Sandoval.

By eleven-thirty, I called Louie's number again and left another message. It was the fourth. Either she was hot on the trail of a story, or had decided I wasn't worth the money either, or something had happened to her. I didn't want to think about that last *or*.

Picking up my well-thumbed copy of the Leonard Maltin Movie Guide, I went into my closet-sized bathroom. I once had a girlfriend who ascribed a more kinky connotation to my taking a movie guide into the john, but I swear, it's only to pass the time. After finishing, I took the lid off the tank, fished out the bug in the baggie, and said into it: "Thank you for listening to station KRAP, Los Angeles," and then flushed, after which I returned the bug to its place of honor. I doubted if anyone was still listening or recording, but it made me feel better.

Knowing who had planted it would make me feel better still, unless it made me feel awful, depending on who it was.

By one in the afternoon, having zapped a frozen box of mac-and-cheese for lunch (and yes, I *did* want to go back to Burger Heaven, but I was forcing myself not to until I talked with Louie), I was ready to do some detecting.

Going online I found the homepage for the *L.A. Independent Journal*, and after plowing through all the layers of offers to subscribe, join or donate, I found an office phone number. Dialing it led me to a mechanical voice, because all business telephones lead to a mechanical voice. I waited for the company directory and took a chance that the first name would be the person I wanted to talk to, since the most important people in a business were usually the first named, and since the first name was *Zareh Zarian*, I figured it wasn't alphabetical.

Pressing the code, I waited until a real voice answered, "Zarian, make it quick."

"Hi, Mr. Zarian, my name is Dave Beauchamp and—"

"Beauchamp," he interrupted, "Beauchamp…aren't you the guy who cracked that twin murder case?"

"That's right, but now I'm—"

"Yeah, I remember. We did a few inches on it. Hey, can't you see I'm on the phone?" he suddenly yelled.

"Uh, I'm here with you. On the phone, I mean."

"Not you, Beauchamp. One of my staff is talking to me and…oh, right. Sorry. I just got a new headset, and he really can't see I'm on the phone. I hate these things. Now, what were you were saying?"

"I hope I'm not interrupting your day, but I was really trying to get a hold of Luisa Sandoval."

"You know where she is?"

"No. I've been trying to contact her."

"So have we. She's nowhere to be found. It's like she's disappeared."

The word *disappeared* lodged in the pit of my stomach like an ice block.

"What's your interest in Sandoval?" he asked.

"She came to see me to get me to help her with a story she was working on."

"The hamburger thing?"

"That's right."

"What did she need a dick for?"

That's private *dick to you*, the voice of Dick Powell said in my head.

"This might sound a little funny, but she wanted me to sneak a hamburger out of a Burger Heaven."

"I'm not laughing. Look, can you come down to the office so we can talk in person?"

"Sure."

"Okay, two o'clock. Don't be late."

With that he hung up.

Since he hadn't bothered to give me the address of the *Independent Journal*, I had to check the website again. The offices were on the west side of Los Angeles so I decided to give myself plenty of time to get over the hill from the Valley, particularly since today was one of those overcast days that seem to confuse L.A. drivers almost as much as actual rainfall.

Because of slow traffic on Coldwater Canyon Avenue over the hill and the perennial automotive quagmire known as Beverly Hills on the downside, it was not much before two o'clock when I arrived at the nondescript building on Pico Boulevard. There was a call box on the front door, and I hit the O button. A woman's voice soon answered, "Can I help you?"

"I'm here to see Mr. Zarian," I replied. "My name is Dave Beauchamp."

Instead of a verbal response, I heard a loud buzz and click, and went inside.

The offices of the *L.A. Independent Journal* were as unprepossessing as the building's exterior, consisting of concrete walls and floor. The lobby area contained a front desk inhabited by the young woman who had buzzed me in and a sofa, and not much else. Before I had a chance to approach the desk, an Armenian guy, probably late thirties, with uniformly short hair and a beard stubble and dark, probing eyes under a unibrow, appeared from the back. He was wearing chinos and a loose white shirt, and a phone headset with the cord tucked into his shirt pocket.

"You Beauchamp?" he asked.

"Yes. I'm a few minutes early."

"S'all right, come on back."

I was expecting to be led into a private office, but instead walked into a large open space with a desk in the middle—at least I think there was a desk under the simulated skyline made from stacks of papers—and shelves and file cabinets all around.

Pushed against one corner was a smaller desk at which sat a young man pounding away on a computer. Overhead were banks of fluorescent lights and, most peculiarly, at the rear wall was what looked to be an abandoned freezer case.

"This building used to be a grocery store," Zarian said, following my puzzled expression. "We never bothered taking it out. The *Journal* is a no-frills operation. Every cent we earn goes back into the quest for truth, not fancy decor. Sit down."

The only place to sit in the room was a folding chair, so I slid it closer to his desk and sat.

"Okay, Beauchamp, tell me what you know about Sandoval going MIA."

What did I know? Not a great deal, which I proceeded to outline.

"So the last time you saw her was in your office?"

"That's right. Well, no, actually, the last time I saw her was a short time after that when I drove by the Burger Heaven where she was doing her tomato act. She was still there. But when I went back later, another woman was in the suit."

"And she came to you because she wanted you to steal a hamburger."

"No, not steal, I was to buy it, but I was supposed to take part of it out of the restaurant and give it to her for testing. She said that Burger Heaven doesn't allow that, and I have to say that I've had more difficulty than I imagined I would, though that's partially my own fault. I keep compulsively eating the things so there's nothing left to take with me."

"Yeah, strange, isn't it?" Zarian said, leaning back in his chair. "She's been working on this story for several weeks and not getting very far, and if you knew Sandoval you'd know that just makes her more tenacious."

"Not the quitter type, you're saying?"

"Hell no. I'd force her off of a story if it was tanking, but she'd never quit."

"So there's no way she would have abandoned this story?"

"Absolutely not."

"Could her disappearance mean that she's simply gone deeper undercover?"

"You're never undercover to your editor," Zarian snapped. "What are you thinking?"

"Am I thinking?"

Not from where I sit, Robert Mitchum said. Who invited you into this meeting, Mitch?

"You look like you're thinking."

"It's just that if you didn't take her off the story, and she doesn't quit on a story, and she never fails to check in, then that leaves only one conclusion."

"You're saying she was abducted?"

"Believe me, I hope I'm wrong. I hope there's a perfectly innocent explanation for her disappearance."

"Shit," Zarian muttered, "I don't like this. Hey, did she offer you money?"

"We didn't really have the chance to get into details, but she said she'd pay whatever it took for me to get the evidence."

"*She'd* pay it, sure. Whenever Sandoval treats, I end up writing the check. What do you charge?"

"My usual rate is fifty dollars an hour."

"Shit! I'm in the wrong business!"

"But it doesn't always take a lot of hours," I added.

"I guess it would be worth it if you find out what happened to Sandoval."

"Would you happen to have her address?"

"Yeah, hold on." Opening a drawer, he pulled out an old-fashioned Rolodex and flipped through it until he found the proper card, then transferred the information onto a sheet of paper.

"That's not very high-tech," I said, eyeing the phone headset that was still plugged into his pocket.

"Index cards can't be hacked."

He handed the paper to me. The address was in the Palms area of L.A. abutting Culver City, which some seventy years ago was a concentrated center of film production within the city, housing the MGM, Selznick and Hal Roach studio lots. I tucked the paper into my pocket.

"I suppose you want some money now," Zarian said.

"Is that a problem?" I asked.

"A little, yeah."

Since I was, at least for the time being, flush (my definition of such being that I could actually afford new clothes instead of coloring in the threadbare seams on everything in my closet with Sharpies), I decided not to push it.

"Tell you what," I said, getting up from the chair, "I'll keep track of my hours and bill you when I have something to report."

"Great. Oh, and Beauchamp? While you're out there looking for Sandoval, keep trying to get one of those hamburgers and bring it back here. I'd rather have that than your invoice."

Taking the address that Zarian had given me, I headed out for Palms, which wasn't all that far away from the *Independent Journal* offices by L.A. standards. Louie's apartment was on Lawless Street, which sounded like the perfect place for a Western shoot out.

Sign me...up, Gary Cooper requested inside my head, but I ignored him.

Lawless was right off of Motor Avenue, one of the main drags through the Palms area, and a thoroughfare of particular interest for film buffs, since it starts at Twentieth Century-Fox studios on the north end, and runs straight into what was once MGM at the south end, passing through Hillcrest Country Club on the way.

Hillcrest was almost as important to the history of Golden Age Hollywood as the studios themselves, since in an era when most country clubs were exclusive Gentile, Hillcrest was exclusively Jewish, and boasted as members practically all of the major studio moguls as well as the town's top film and radio comedians, who formed their own "Round Table."

But judging from the looks of the apartment building that I pulled up in front of on Lawless, the building in which Luisa Sandoval lived, few, if any, of the residents had the status to join Hillcrest.

Louie's apartment number was 216, but when I punched the button on the front directory and waited the allotted time, I got no response or buzzing to let me into the building. I tried again with the same result.

It was pretense time.

Pretense is basically creative lying, or maybe acting, done on the part of the investigator to gain information.

Usually it's done over the phone, such as the old, "Hi, I'm from UPS and I have a package to deliver, and I have to verify your address," gag. Pretense in person is usually reserved for the movies, like when Bogie as Philip Marlowe turns effeminate and goes into Geiger's book shop in *The Big Sleep*, pretending to be looking for a rare first edition.

Or like your doll pretending to be a tomato to get information, Bogie reminded me. *And I wasn't doing a swish act, kid. I was being eccentric.*

I buzzed the manager's button and waited. It took two more buzzes before a man's voice came on. "Yah?"

"Hi, I'm here to pick something up from Luisa Sandoval in 216," I lied. "I'm from the *Independent Journal*."

"Then buzz Luisa Sandoval in 216," the voice slurred.

"She's not there," I replied. "She's on assignment, but she left a file with her story for this week's edition outside her apartment. He phoned me and told me to come and get it."

"Come and get it!" the guy shouted, then laughed. He was definitely drunk, and it was barely mid-afternoon.

"Please, we're on deadline."

"Aw, Chrise…"

The door then buzzed and I entered. A few moments later a man lurched out. He was about sixty, grey, unshaven, with a bushy moustache and glasses, and was dressed in sweatpants and a muscle shirt so old he might still have had muscles when he bought it.

"Hi, thanks for coming out," I said.

"Coming out, bullshit. I'm straight as a goddamn arrow."

"What I mean is, thanks for letting me in so I can get Louie's story."

"Who the hell's Louie?"

Apparently not *everyone* called her that. "Luisa Sandoval, in 216."

"You said she was gone."

"She is, but I need to go up to her apartment so I can get her copy for the story she's working on. She told me it was in an envelope labeled Burger Heaven."

The truth was, of course, I had no idea what kind of file she might have left or in what format.

"I don' know anything about what she does," the manager drawled. "Burger Heaven, huh? Owned by the damned church."

Sure, whatever.

Since I knew Louie had not actually left an envelope outside her apartment, at least I'd be extremely surprised to find that she had, I had to get inside her place. It was time for phase two of the pretense.

"Hey, my cell phone's vibrating," I told the manager.

"Lucky you."

I pretended to take a call: "Beauchamp…Louie, hi! Yeah, I'm at your place. Oh, okay. Yeah, he's right here. Yeah, sure, I'll ask him. Great. Okay, thanks." Turning back to the drunken manager I said, "That was Louie. She forgot to put the envelope in the hallway, so she asked if you could let me in to her place. It's on her dining table."

He leveled a bleary look at me. "You really think I'd open up the apartment of a tenant for some asshole I never met?"

"But I've already introduced myself," I countered, even though I hadn't, fully. "So how about it?"

"Depends."

"On?"

"On whether you're willing to make it worth my while."

I sighed and reached for my wallet, and found that Andrew Jackson made the case much better than I could have.

Even he's a better lawyer than you, Mitchum said in my head.

The manager led me to the elevator and once confined inside with the guy the booze fumes were nearly overpowering. By the time we got off on the building's second floor, I was practically gasping for clean air.

Taking me to apartment 216, he managed to open the door with his passkey on the third try. Before pushing the door open, though, he turned to me and attempted to give me the Robert DeNiro "I'm watchin' you" gesture, but managed instead to give himself a Three Stooges eye poke with his own fingers. I tried not to laugh.

"I'll only be a second," I told him, entering the room and turning on the light.

At first I thought that Luisa Sandoval, for all her personal charm, must be an unmitigated slob, because the place was not simply a mess, it was a catastrophe. Then I realized that I wasn't looking at a messy apartment, I was looking at one that had been tossed. Just like my office had been broken into.

Except the person or persons here had clearly been searching for something.

Was it the same person or persons?

"Gonna be all day?" the manager called from hallway.

I didn't reply, just in case there was a bug planted in here, too. Instead I scooped up a bunch of papers that were strewn all over the floor and neatened them into a stack. I had no idea what they might be, but the fact that they were still here strongly implied they were expendable.

Finding a large envelope in the pile, I stuck the papers inside and quickly scrawled "Burger Heaven" on the outside. I then rejoined the manager in the hallway. "Got it," I said, waiving the envelope in front of him.

"'Bout damn time," he said, closing the door and locking it.

We were back to the elevator when I heard footsteps running down the hall. A tall, impossibly thin, gawky young man appeared and hollered, "Hold the door, okay?" The manager made no attempt to, but the guy managed to slide in sideways through the narrowing gap of the closing doors. That's how thin he was.

"Thanks," he said, guilelessly.

Down on the ground level the manager lurched back to his unit, presumably to continue his regimen of emptying bottles and ignoring requests for maintenance, while I headed for the front door.

Halfway there, I noticed Mr. Skinny following me. "Why were you looking in Luisa's apartment?" he asked.

I turned around and faced him, smiling. In my experience, smiling often diffuses a confrontation, except for those rare times when you get punched. "Why do you want to know?"

"Because I'm her neighbor. We're friends. I haven't seen her in a couple days, which is unusual. Do you know where she is?"

"No, not really. I was asked to come here by Louie's boss."

"Louie?"

"That's what's she's called. You didn't know that?"

"Well, we haven't really talked all that much, outside of hi."

Suddenly I got the picture. This poor, wormy *naïf* was stuck on Luisa Sandoval, and probably waited in his apartment for the sound of her door opening so he could pop out and say hello. He harbored in his heart the impossible dream that they could someday be a couple, and so was not simply puzzled by her disappearance but distressed by it.

What's more, he now appeared crushed at finding someone who knew something so basic about his precious Luisa, which he did not know.

There but for the grace of Us go you, Bogie sneered, truthfully, unfortunately.

But since we were on the subject of truth, I decided maybe I'd better come clean to the beanpole. "Look, I'm a private investigator. Louie came to me about a case, and that was the last I saw of her."

"What were you looking for in her room? What's that stuff you're holding?"

"First things first. What's your name?"

"Avery."

"Well, Mr. Avery—"

"No that's my first name. My full name is Avery Klemmer." He stuck out a hand, which I took. It was like weighing a filet at the fish market.

I dropped the damp, dead hand. "Dave Beauchamp, but as to what I'm looking for, I'm afraid that's confidential to the case."

"Are you going to keep looking?"

"I got your charming building manager to let me in today, but I don't think he's going to do it again."

"I can get you in if you're brave."

"Brave?"

"Our apartments have balconies," he said. "If you're not afraid of heights, you can jump from one to the other. I can let you into my place and you can get to her balcony."

"And you've done this?"

He looked down at the floor and uttered, "No. I'm afraid of heights."

"You'd let me into your place?"

"If it will help find Luisa. I mean, Louie."

"Let's go."

We went back up the elevator and he opened up his place to me. Avery Klemmer's apartment was the opposite of what I had found in Louie's: it was immaculate. It was also largely empty, with just one thrift-store sofa, a battered table and mismatching chair by way of furniture, but with an enormous plasma television, a gaming console, and a shelf packed with video games shoved against one wall.

"Do you game?" he asked.

"You mean play video games? No, I'm afraid not."

"It's my job. I review new ones." He sounded very proud.

"Is this the balcony?" I asked, rather redundantly, because if it wasn't, the wall-sized sliding door led out to a two-storey drop to the ground.

Stepping out, I saw what he was talking about: there was only about a three foot gap between the edge of his narrow stucco balcony and the edge of Louie's, which had a few potted plants scattered around on it.

It looked easy…at least until I climbed up on the ledge. Now it looked terrifying. Those three feet had suddenly turned into a mile. But I knew this was the only way to reenter Louie's apartment and continue snooping.

"Wish me luck," I called back. Deciding I couldn't actually step over, I tried lunging head first, figuring I could catch the ledge and balance myself on it with my hands, while I vaulted my legs over.

Boy, was I wrong.

CHAPTER FIVE

The good news was that I did not fall two storeys in my attempt to jump from balcony to balcony. The bad news is that I took a direct belly-splat onto the rough stucco surface of its side wall. I managed to pull myself over until I was safely on the balcony of Louie's apartment, and tried to retain my wind, which had been knocked out of me.

Popping up again, I faced the nerdy kid next door.

"Wow, that looked like it really hurt," Avery Klemmer said.

"Yeah, it hurt," I assured him through gritted teeth, "but it's all part of the P.I. game."

"Tell you what," Avery called back, "why don't you open the front door and I'll in that way."

I was about to refuse, but then realized that if not for him I wouldn't have gotten this far, so I felt that I owed him something.

"All right." Stepping inside the darkened apartment, careful not to disturb the ransacked clutter, I first lifted my shirt to make sure I was not bleeding. My stomach was a little red, but miraculously there were no abrasions.

When I opened the front door, Avery was already standing there.

"This is so cool," he said, grinning like a jack-o-lantern.

"Come on in, but don't touch anything," I replied. "Technically, we're both trespassing."

"That's what's so cool. It's like I've made it to the hidden level."

No one said anything in my head, but I did hear the *Twilight Zone* theme music.

I glanced both ways down the hall to make sure we were not being seen by the sodden manager or anyone else, and once satisfied on that score, I closed the door and turned the lock again, then switched on the lights.

"Wow, what happened here?" Avery asked.

"Someone's gone through the place, in search of something."

"In search of what?"

"I don't know."

"Maybe that stuff you found earlier."

"Yeah, maybe."

I'd actually forgotten about the folder I'd taken, which was probably still in Avery's place. I was pretty sure that wasn't the object of the search, or else it wouldn't have been left behind, but I didn't bother explaining that to him.

Instead I started looking around myself. There were not a lot of things hanging on the walls of Louie Sandoval's apartment, just a large clock, a framed poster from a Leonard Cohen concert, an unseasonal wreath, and a photo of a young man, stripped to the waist, and in a lot better shape than I ever was. A boyfriend? It had to be.

I looked behind each hanging object; the bug had been placed behind the Cohen poster.

"Did you find something?" Avery Klemmer asked.

"Mm-hmm," I uttered, pulling the bug off the backing and carefully stepping through the mess on the floor to the bathroom, which had also been ransacked. Hair stuff and a few pill bottles were strewn around the counter, including one for birth control pills.

The bare-chested guy in the photo was a lucky dude, and had I known who he was, I'd contact him immediately to see if he had any insight into Louie's disappearance. As for the bug, I didn't bother putting this one in the toilet tank. I simply flushed it down the stool.

Except for the fact that the place was trashed, this had the same M.O. as my break-in, which meant the burglar had probably picked the front lock to gain entry, and while I had no proof that it had been the same person who had broken into my office, it argued so. What's more, the fact that my place was left neat—neater than it had been before, in fact—while Louie's place was a mess, argued that the burglar knew she wouldn't be coming back. Like maybe the burglar was the one responsible for her disappearance.

Not so fast, kid, Bogart chimed in. *Something doesn't add up.*

"What?" I asked aloud.

"What?" Avery responded.

"Oh, I was just thinking out loud. I do that sometimes."

"Yeah, the people in my games do that, too."

Swell. I was about to phrase my confusion over Bogie's comment in the form of a mental question when it finally hit me. If the burglar knew Louie was not going to be coming back, why did he bother to plant a bug? Unless the bug had been planted some time earlier, but had yielded no information, so whoever is listening was forced to go to the next level, breaking in and turning the apartment over…and possibly taking Louie.

"Do you know who this is?" Avery was asking, as he stared at the photo of Louie and Mr. America.

"Joe Six-Pack Abs? No, I have no idea. You live here, have you ever seen him?"

"No, but I hate him. He probably hates me, too."

"If he knew you existed, he might," I said before I could stop myself, and immediately the voice of Sabu said: *You must not damage your Karma, master*. I'll try to remember that, Sabu. I'll try to be nicer to those few individuals in the world who are worse off than me. But what do you care anyway? You were Muslim, not Hindu. You didn't know from Karma. Still, the Elephant Boy had a point.

As I moved toward the bedroom, the door of which was hanging open, Avery said: "You're not going to search her bedroom, are you?"

"There might be evidence in there."

"But that's an invasion of privacy. I mean, it's her bedroom. You can't just go in and search it."

"I'll leave a chocolate on the pillow when I'm done. That'll make it all better."

Not bad, kid, Bogie said in my head.

Switching on the bedroom lights I saw an even bigger, more concentrated mess than existed in the living room. Every bit of clothing from the closet and dresser must have been pulled out and tossed into a variety of piles. Kneeling, I peered under the bed, but found nothing. I'm not sure what I'd been expecting to find, but it was the cleanest under-bed space I'd ever seen. There weren't even any shoes.

If there was some indication as to the disappearance of Louie Sandoval in this room, I wasn't getting the message.

Message.

That had been my own voice inside my head, clueing me into what a dope I was being. Message. I had called Louie several times and left a message on her phone machine, which had to be here somewhere.

Going back out to the living room, I began searching again.

"What are you looking for now?" Avery asked.

"A telephone with a phone answering machine. I left messages for Louie, so she has to have one."

"Unless it's the message box in her cell phone," Avery said. "In that case it wouldn't be here. She'd have it with her."

He had a point, though not a waterproof one.

"If she has her cell phone with her, why hasn't she used it to call out to anybody?"

He shrugged. "Battery ran down, maybe?"

"Yeah, maybe," I said, smiling at the thought that Jack Daniels would never stoop to including such a thing in one of his novels.

"You know, there's only one way to find out."

Pulling out my wallet, I retrieved the slip of paper containing Louie's number and used my own cell phone to call. A second later a muffled ringing could be heard in the direction of the kitchen.

"I think it's here," Avery said, pointing to a pile of dish towels that had been torn from a drawer and tossed into chaos atop a counter that separated the kitchenette from the living room. We both heard her recorded voice leave the same message I'd heard the other day.

I began removing the towels, fully revealing the phone right at the point the recording announced what telemarketers could do with their heads, the description of which made Avery gasp.

I cut off the call after hearing the beep.

"Jeezo-peet," he whispered, "I'm glad I'm not a telemarketer."

The message light was blinking and the read-out announced that there were seven new messages. Using a corner of one of the towels to prevent leaving fingerprints, I punched the playback button and soon heard the voice of Zareh Zarian asking where the hell she was. After that came the first message I had left for her, two days ago.

Zarian and I alternated the rest of the new messages, after which the device announced an old message.

That was the call that chilled me.

At first I thought it was a telemarketer who hadn't gotten the memo, because initially there was nothing but empty air, but then a man's voice said: "You should know better than to fuck with us," before the call cut off.

Avery Klemmer was staring at me with wide, frightened eyes, and was breathing heavy. "We should call the police."

"Yeah, I think you're right," I said, trying to coax the hairs on my arms and the back of my neck to be nice and lay back down again.

I had just pulled my cell phone out to call the cops when I became aware of the sound of footsteps in the hallway, footsteps that stopped right outside the apartment door. Then came the sound of a key being inserted into the lock.

CHAPTER SIX

"Hey, she's back!" Avery cried.

"Shhh!" I commanded, grabbing him by the arm and dragging him out to the balcony.

"Jump!" I whispered, pointing at his adjoining balcony.

"What? I can't!"

"Yes, you can!"

I practically lifted him up onto the balcony wall and then shoved, and he soared over the distance like a paper airplane, catching himself with his hands and then swinging his feet around like an experienced practitioner of the parallel bars.

I followed a second later, making the leap and landing far more gracefully than I did the first time, which means I only banged my knee on the side of the balcony wall instead of doing a full belly-flop on top.

"Inside!" I ordered, and limped back into Avery's apartment.

"What was that all about?" he asked, panting.

"Think for a minute! What if it isn't her?"

"Whoever it was had a key."

"Right. But we don't know who might have a key. Maybe it's the guy in the picture, or maybe it was whoever had broken in the first time and trashed the place."

Then a thought hit me: what if they were the same person?

"I think you're wrong," Avery said. "It has to be her."

"Okay, fine, it's her," I sighed. "How do you think she would react if she came home and found her place tossed and the two of us standing in the middle of it all? She'd be the one calling the police, and we'd be the ones trying to convince them not to arrest us. Even if it is her, we had to get out of Dodge."

"I hadn't thought of that."

"Now we can simply stroll over next door and knock on the door and talk to her, and she never knows we were invading her privacy."

"And if it's somebody else?"

"Well, if it's somebody else, they're not supposed to be there either, which means they probably won't answer the door. In that case, we call the police."

"You're pretty smart, you know that?" Avery Klemmer said, though inside my head Robert Mitchum made a rude sound.

"Thanks. Let's go over and see who's there."

The two of us slipped through his door and into the hall. The door to Louie's apartment was hanging open and Avery rapped on it.

"Hello," he called. "Someone here?" It was casual enough.

A man yanked the door fully open so quickly it startled both of us. It was the fellow from the photograph, only this time fully clothed and looking much bigger.

"Who are you?" he demanded.

"Avery Klemmer, I live next door." The mooncalf held out his hand, but the man didn't take it. "I, uh, heard some noise and wondered if everything was okay."

"How about you?" the man asked, turning to me.

"My name is Dave Beauchamp and I'm here at the request of Louie's editor at the *Independent Journal*," I said. "He hasn't heard from her in a few days, and he's getting concerned."

"Aren't we all."

"Are you a friend of Louie's?"

"I'm her brother, Ricardo Sandoval."

"Her brother!" Avery all but squealed.

"What, she can't have a brother? You guys know what the hell has happened here?"

I shook my head.

"All I know is I came by to pick up some paperwork from her and she didn't answer the door. Did something else happen?"

"See for yourself," he said, stepping inside and allowing us in.

My performance at seeing the ransacked place for the "first time" was more convincing than Avery's, who badly overplayed it, but Ricardo Sandoval did not seem to notice.

"You said you were here to pick something up from her about a story?"

"That's right. We're on deadline."

"Is it an important story?"

"I can't really reveal what it's about before it appears in print," I said.

"Hmm. The reason I'm asking is because Louie called me a few days ago and said she wanted to see me to discuss something, and I think it was about her assignment, which is unusual."

"How so?"

"Luisa was the brains of the family," he said. "She was always into politics and news reporting and everything. I work security at a nightclub. So it's rare our paths cross except on family occasions. I couldn't even tell you who the hell the mayor of Los Angeles is, but she probably knows him personally. I don't have a clue why she would have wanted to talk to me about one of her stories, but I said fine, hell yeah, let's get together and talk. I'd be happy to offer whatever I could."

"Do you think she might have wanted to ask about securing protection?" I ventured.

"Protection…you mean like a bodyguard?"

"Possibly."

"You think she's in trouble?"

"I wish I could answer that."

"Play the phone message!" Avery blurted out, and both Bogie and myself thought in unison, *Smooth move, junior.*

"What phone message?"

"What he means," I began, turning to shoot as murderous a look at Avery as I could muster, "is that he heard the phone ringing several times over the last few days through the walls, and going unanswered. So he assumed that somebody must have left a message. At least that's what he told me."

"Well, I tried calling her several times," Ricardo said, "but I never left a message. I figured there was no point if she wasn't there to hear it."

I opened my mouth to respond, and then shut it again. Ricardo Sandoval's assessment that his sister had gotten all the brains in the family appeared to be quite accurate.

"Louie was always neat, even as a kid," he said, looking around and the well-rummaged apartment. "She wouldn't have left the place like this."

"Did anyone else have a key to her apartment?" I asked him.

"I dunno. I doubt it, but I dunno. Think we need to call the cops?"

Now it was my turn to say I didn't know, but only because I was trying to think this thing through.

Finally, I said, "Mr. Sandoval, how is it you have a key to Louie's apartment?"

"Oh, she had it made for me. I bunked here for a while when I was in between places of my own, and you can call me Ricky."

"All right, Ricky."

"Louie was always great that way, helping me out when I needed it. Why?"

"Well, I don't want to alarm you, Ricky, but if you call the police and they know you have a key, you might become a suspect."

"A suspect in what? Messing up my sister's place?"

"They might think you had something to do with her disappearance."

"That's loco talk!" he said.

"Yes, I know, but I'm trying to think like a policeman."

"*Are* you a policeman?" Ricky asked, suddenly suspicious. "I thought you said you worked for the newspaper."

"What I said was that I was doing a job for Louie's editor, which I am." I fished out a business card and handed it to him. "I'm a private investigator."

"Really?" the big man asked, inspecting the card. "I didn't think there really were private eyes. It thought they were only in movies and TV shows."

"The real job isn't the same, but we're still here," I told him. "It's probably not that different from what you do as a security guard."

"Well, I'm not really a guard. I'm more of a bouncer. I work at the Tropico Room on the Strip."

I knew that the Tropico Room was the current incarnation of a nightspot owned in the 1950s by a hugely popular entertainer with underworld ties.

"Pretty classy."

"Last week I had to carry Lana Loncraine to her limo. She was a little…" He made a drinking gesture.

Lana Loncraine was a former child star who had lived the high life before falling on hard times, and had just recently blown her six-hundredth chance at rehabilitation.

"Managed to cop a feel while doing it, too. They aren't real. Her chichis, I mean." Just in case we didn't get it, he held his hands out in front of his own impressive chest.

"They look real on TV," Avery said.

"I know. I was surprised too."

"Guys, can we please forget about Lana Loncraine's boobs for a moment?" I broke in. "We need to concentrate on a plan here."

"What kind of plan?" Ricky asked.

"First, I think you're right, Ricky, you should call the police and report Louie as missing. But they don't need to know you have a key, and frankly, they don't need to know that you were here today."

"Isn't that like lying?" he asked.

"It's *like* lying, but only if they ask you point blank, 'were you there, did you have a key?' and you say no. What I'm suggesting is that you don't offer the information that you were inside Louie's apartment and saw its condition. Just call the police and report her missing, and let them handle it. If they show up here, the manager can let them in when they come."

"So he has a key?"

"Of course, he's the manager," I said, but then realized that Ricky had managed to make another good point. The drunk downstairs *did* have access to the apartment. I would have to figure out how that fitted into the mix later, though.

Right now I thought we should not be standing here with Louie's door hanging open, just in case someone else came by.

"Ricky, I'll tell you what. You give me your key for safekeeping. That way you don't have to lie to the police about having a key."

"Wouldn't you be taking a risk by keeping it?"

"Risk taking is part of what I get paid for."

You're a devious bastard, Lauren Bacall said inside my head. *I like that.*

"If you say so," he said, handing the key over to me.

"Okay, so here's what we do, guys," I began, feeling less like the brains heavy of a crime drama delivering instructions to his henchmen, than Moe hatching a doomed plan for Curly and Larry to follow.

"We leave here and I lock the door. Ricky, you go home and call the police. You haven't seen Louie in days, you're worried, so you're going to ask what you should do. Got it?"

"Haven't seen her, worried, what do I do?" he repeated.

"Good. Avery, you go to your place, but keep an eye and an ear out for anything. If the cops do show up, let me know, okay?"

"How?"

"Oh, right." I fished out another business card and gave it to him. "So we're all agreed, right?"

"Right," the two said in unison.

Ricky then left the apartment and strode down the hall toward the elevator. I started to leave, too, but Avery stopped me.

"You really think something bad happened to Luisa?" he asked.

"I really don't know. I hope not. But I do know that if the police get in the way I won't be able to investigate anything. Now come on, let's get out of here before someone else shows up."

In the hallway I looked both ways to make sure no one else was there, then closed the door and locked it, pulling out my handkerchief to wipe the knob clean.

"If the police talk to you, tell them everything you know about the last time you saw Louie, but don't tell them you were in her apartment. And whatever you do, Avery, don't tell them about the balcony trick. Call me if you need me."

"I will," he said, sticking out the dead halibut he wore at the end of his arm for me to squeeze. "Should I tell them about the messages on the phone machine?"

"If the police are any good, they'll find those themselves."

And unless they're stupid, they'll realize they've been listened to, I thought.

"Avery, I think you might have just saved our butts," I said, explaining the fact that now that the messages had been reviewed and reclassified by the machine as "old," it would be clear that someone else had been in the apartment after Louie's disappearance.

It might not be ethical, in fact it might even fall under the category of withholding evidence. But better safe than sorry; the messages had to go.

"Will that get us in trouble?" Avery asked.

"You? No. Because you're not going to do it. Go home and shut the door, and don't think about it. If anyone asks you if I erased the messages, you have no direct knowledge of that."

"But you told me you were going to."

"That's called hearsay. Trust me, I used to be a lawyer."

"I think I see why you're not one anymore."

"Just go home. Leave the worrying to me. I'm good at it."

"Okay."

I waited until he disappeared inside unit 214, and then quietly unlocked the door again and entered Louie's place. Going to the machine, I ran down through the messages, hitting the delete button at the start of each one.

When I got to the threatening message, I considered deleting it as well, but decided against it. Suppressing evidence to keep oneself out of the interrogation room is one thing, but suppressing genuine evidence that might lead to the solution of a potential crime was another. And the police would likely conclude that Louie herself had listened to it prior to disappearing.

After reclosing, relocking, and re-wiping down the door, I slipped the key into my pocket. I decided not to risk the elevator, where I might be seen, and instead found a stairwell and took it down. I didn't feel like I had to hide or slink as I walked to my car, though once I had arrived there, I rather wish I had been more discrete, because standing across the street, about a half-block down, was someone I recognized.

It was the female security guard from the Sherman Oaks Burger Heaven.

CHAPTER SEVEN

Or maybe it wasn't, maybe I'm just nuts.

(*Maybe*? Robert Mitchum shouted, but I had anticipated that.)

Maybe I hadn't really seen the same woman following me around Los Angeles. This was, after all, the facelift capital of the world, and it was pretty amazing how many women one ran into on the street or in stores or in offices who looked like they were sculpted from the same prototype face by the same doctor.

If, on the other hand, I was not crazy—

(Shut up, Mitch.)

—and it was all the same person who had been assigned by someone to tail me, she was pretty poor at it. Then again, Sheldon Leonard and I had already agreed that the break-ins had been the work of an amateur, so it stood to reason that if I really were being tailed, it was also by an amateur.

But *why*?

No matter from which direction I approached the problem, all roads seemed to lead to Burger Heaven, and it was close enough to dinner time for a combo. Since I was still carrying around that coupon for a free meal, it wouldn't even have to go on my expense report.

The question was, did I have the strength to leave a bit of it so as to try and sneak it through the doors again.

Oh, oh, if you need someone strong, I-I-I'll help you...sure I will! the voice of Lon Chaney, Jr. said in my head. Thanks, Lennie, but I think I can do this.

While my intention was to jump back on the freeway and head over the Sepulveda Pass back into the Valley, then go to the newly opened one, I spotted a BH on Pico Boulevard, half-way to the on-ramp of the 405 freeway.

This was truly miraculous, since in my experience the only quick eating places to be found anywhere throughout the West Side were frozen yogurt shops or that ubiquitous sandwich chain whose stores smell a thousand times better than the polystyrene food they serve up tastes.

There's a rumor that a pizzeria exists somewhere on this side of L.A., but I've chalked that up to urban legend.

I pulled in to the spacious restaurant parking lot—another miracle on this side of town—parked and went in. While standing in the predictably long line, I fished the gift certificate out of my wallet, and upon getting to the counter, where I was greeted by a young blonde who actually looked too happy to be working in a fast food joint, I ordered a Twin Halo combo. When I presented the gift certificate, though, she looked at it as though she was uncertain how to handle it. Frowning slightly, she turned and flagged down a fortyish man wearing a tie, presumably a managerial type, and showed it to him.

"Well, congratulations, sir!" he beamed, pulling out a pen to initial the coupon before calling the order into the back. He he asked me to initial it too, which I did.

It seemed to take a little bit longer than usual for my order to be prepared, but once I received it, I decided that it was the result of waiting for a fresh batch of fries to come out of the grease. They had to be fresh because they were nearly too hot to pick up.

The hamburger was equally hot and good, but I actually managed to force myself to leave a bit of it uneaten. It wasn't easy; in fact, it was so difficult that I wrapped it in a napkin so as not to have to see it, and got up to go get back in line at the counter.

All right, I'm weak! But it's a hamburger, not a fix of heroin! It's my reward for actually saving a piece to sneak out.

"Are you finished with your tray, sir?" I heard a voice ask, and turned to see a kid with a wet wipe rag in one hand, while half-way reaching for my tray with the other.

"No, I'll be back," I said, reaching for the wrapped burger ort as casually as I could and palming it. "Please don't take the tray away, I'm coming back. You're food is so good I'm going for seconds."

"Excellent," the kid said, grinning, and then moving on.

I got a single burger this time, which turned out to be as much a masterpiece of hot, juicy goodness as its big brother the Twin Halo. When I was finished, I piled everything onto the tray, except, of course, for the wrapped piece of my first burger, which I could feel was leaking secret sauce through the napkin in my pants pocket, then carried it to the trash bin, and then started to walk out.

And I made it.

I made it all the way to through the door, into the patio dining area, which was filled with cement tables and benches and halo-shaped sun umbrellas, and into the parking lot. And then into my car. And then out of the lot and onto the street.

Nobody tried to stop me, nobody tried to hassle me, nobody said a word.

So much for the rumor that Burger Heaven would go to any lengths to prevent their food from being taken off the premises. The first time I tried this stunt, only to be stopped by the security guard, who imprinted her image so firmly onto my brain that I see her everywhere now, it must have been a coincidence.

As I got closer to the 405 freeway, I could not help but notice that the lane for the on-ramp was backed up several blocks. This was not a good sign. Even with recent widening efforts, the 405 could be a nightmare, so I needed to avoid it for a while.

The answer was simple: since I was not far from the offices of the *L.A. Independent Journal*, and since I had the piece of evidence I had been charged with obtaining, I decided to drop it off on the way back. Maybe traffic would have lessened by the time I finished.

And maybe giraffes can fly, hoo hoo hoo! Hugh Herbert said inside my head.

Okay, then maybe Zareh Zarian would realize that I can accomplish what I set out to do.

About twenty minutes later I pulled up to the *Journal* offices, parked and went in, telling the receptionist, "I don't have an appointment, but I need to see Mr. Zarian. I have something he wants."

Zarian popped out of his office a few minutes later and waved me in.

"What have you got?" he asked, and I dropped the burger fragment on his desk. "Just like that?"

"Just like that."

"Hot damn! I'll get it to the lab right away. Sit down, Beauchamp." I did so. "Did you find anything out regarding Louie?"

"Someone broke into her apartment, ransacked it, and left a bug in it."

"A listening device?"

"Yes. I found it and flushed it."

"What do you suppose they were hoping to hear?"

"You're in a better position to say that. Had she been working on a story other than this Burger Heaven one that might be considered dangerous in some quarters?"

"Her last assignment was looking into a billionaire developer who's got the building-and-safety supervisor and half the city council eating out of his trough enough to get waivers on everything, and rip down any historic building that gets in his way. But that story went to press, and while a few sabers were rattled, nothing much came of it."

"Who's the guy?"

"Nick Bandini. He keeps threatening to run for mayor of L.A., but that would really be redundant since he controls the damn city anyway. Why, what are you thinking?"

"Someone left a threatening voice mail on Louie's machine. It said, 'You should know better than to eff with us, sister.'"

"*Eff* with us? You mean 'fuck with us?'"

"I'm trying to be polite. The point is, *us* implies an organization or a company, not just one man, no matter how rich."

"So you're thinking *us* is the Burger Heaven corporation."

"Based on the reason she came to me, that has to a consideration."

"Have you gone to the police about any of this?"

"Um, no, I haven't. I want to do a little investigating myself first without police interference."

He nodded. "Good move. We've been keeping tabs on the LAPD for some time, even before every other black teen in South L.A. began sprouting a target on their back. The heat doesn't like being on the receiving end of investigations very much. If they were able to trace you back to me, things wouldn't go so smoothly for you."

I didn't bother informing him that my relationship with L.A.'s finest wasn't that flowery to begin with.

"What about you?" I asked. "Won't they try to shut you down?"

Zarian smiled, and his teeth were alarmingly small, straight and powerful looking. "They can harass and shoot people all they want, but even they know better than to take on the free press. So, Beauchamp, what's your next step?"

"Well—"

Think fast, kid, Bogie said.

"—there was a woman at the Burger Heaven, Regina, who said she was the one who put on that little show with the people dressed up like food, though she claimed she had never heard of Luisa Sandoval, because Louie was operating under an assumed name."

"Our people do that sometimes."

"Right. But this woman claimed that Louie, or whatever name she gave, was fired because she wasn't performing up to par."

"And you don't think she was leveling with you?"

"Well, it's not like you have to be Meryl Streep to play a tomato. But more to the point, if that's all there was to it, then where is she?"

"You tell me."

"I think Louie already had already discovered something about the Burger Heaven chain, something concrete and damaging, and believe me, it pains me to say this, since I love their food, but having gotten the goods on them, I think she had to disappear for her own safety."

"That makes more sense. I was never sold on the abduction theory."

"Either way, my gut is telling me that something bad is going on, and this Regina might know more about it than she's saying."

Always trust your gut, young man, I heard Sydney Greenstreet chortle.

"When I talked to her before," I went on, "she acted skittish, like she was afraid of someone or something. If I can figure out what she's afraid of, I might able to get her to spill."

He grinned. "Is that a technical term, spill?"

"It's an old movie term, actually."

Zarian smiled. "How would you like to keep working for me?"

"You mean in regards to finding Louie? I plan to do just that."

"No, I mean any time we need an investigator. I'd like to put you on permanent retainer."

"Oh, well—"

Well what, stupid? Robert Mitchum asked. *You got something against money?*

"That might impugn my independence a little," I answered both of them.

"Shit, man, we're the L.A. *Independent Journal*!" Zarian cried. "You can't get much more independent than us!"

"What would this permanent retainer amount to?" I asked.

Zarian shook his head. "I'll put you on the payroll for three-hundred a month. In return, whenever I need you to look into something for us, you're there. You give me first dibs on your time, no matter what else you're working on. If I don't need anything that month, then take the three hundred and go to a Dodger game. It might cover it."

"I think that could work," I said. I still had a few vague, unformed reservations about the deal, but those might be chalked up to the fact that I've never had to consider an offer like this, being Paul Drake to someone's Perry Mason.

"Great. Send me an invoice with all your information and I'll put it in the system. Say 'Retainer Contract Termination date TBD,' or something like that. No need to get too technical. I'll know what it is. Checks are cut at the end of the month. You got anything else for me?"

"No, but you might be able to do something for me," I said. "Do you have a picture of Louie?"

"Why? I thought you met her."

"I did, but I want something to show to Regina when I talk to her. She can waffle about the name, but she can't about the photo. It might loosen her up."

Zarian nodded and then shouted, "Ashley!", which startled me. A few seconds later the young receptionist walked in.

"Print out a picture of Sandoval, would you?" Once she had turned and gone, Zarian said, "All our files here are digital."

"I thought you only dealt in files that couldn't be hacked."

"You want to work for me or you want to be a smartass?"

Can't I do both? Cary Grant asked inside my head.

"I'll work for you," I said.

But his comment had set a little bell off in my mind. If the *Journal* used all digital files, then there was little use in looking for Louie's notes on paper. They would more likely be contained on a disk or a flash drive.

I also realized there was no reason to go back to her place and look for it, since Ricky Sandoval had likely called the police already, which meant they might be sniffing around the place, and even if they weren't Avery would be.

I didn't particularly want to see any of them right now.

Ashley returned with a still-warm printout of Luisa Sandoval's headshot and handed it to me. Surprisingly, as attractive as Louie was in person, she did not photograph well. Some people are like that. In Hollywood, they're called stand-ins.

"Thanks," I said, rising, "I'll let you know what I find out."

I left the building wishing I could be as skeptical about the notion that Louie had been abducted by someone as Zarian was.

I'd covered a lot of miles today, with the only result being that I'd finally made off with a scrap of hamburger and delivered it, and part of me just wanted to go lock up the office and head home.

But the other part, the one with the promise of a retainer, said that it would be better to try and talk to Regina Fontaine sooner rather than later. If she wasn't in tomato drag today, maybe I could talk to some of the other ingredients.

Once on the freeway, which was slow, but not a parking lot, I turned the news on the radio, but learned nothing other than the serious drought that was crippling California was expected to last until it rained. I've always been a sucker for a well-reasoned argument.

I soon switched over to the CD function and joined Miklós Rózsa's portentous theme for *Double Indemnity* in progress. By the time the grandly opened Burger Heaven came into view, Miklós was on to "Parade of the Charioteers" from *Ben Hur*, and I was on my way to realizing I'd been carried away by my expectations.

There were no costumed ingredients outside the restaurant.

Pulling into the lot, I parked and went inside and got in line, purely to ask after Regina.

Since I had eaten nearly an entire Twin Halo combo, followed by a single burger within the last hour, there was no reason to order any food. I wasn't hungry, so despite the aromas coming out of the restaurant and my knowledge of what these things tasted like, hot and juicy, with tangy sauce and crisp lettuce, tomato and pickles, there was no reason on earth that I would—

"I'll have a Single Halo combo," I heard myself telling the young man at the register, whose fresh-scrubbed face was a map of Iowa.

You're weak! a piercing voice sneered inside my head. *You've always been weak and you'll never be anything but weak*! Thank you, Joan Crawford.

"And I'd like to speak to the manager," I added.

"Is there a problem?" the clerk wanted to know.

"Not at all. I just have a question."

He looked warily at me but relayed my request nonetheless. When my order was ready, a thirtyish, soccer-mom type with a different colored shirt picked up the tray from behind the counter and walked out to see me.

"Hello, sir, I'm Gloria, the manager," she said, "and I understand you have a question?"

Well, yes, actually," I said, taking the tray from her, "but I also wanted to say how nice it is to have a BH so close to my office now."

"Oh, that's terrific, thank you. Do you patronize Burger Heaven often?"

"I do, yes. I love the food here."

You've eaten enough of it, Lauren Bacall cracked.

"And we love to hear that," Gloria replied, unable to hear Baby.

"Good. Now, as for the question, I was wondering if I could talk to Regina."

"Regina?"

"She's the one who was directing the group of performers you had out front, the ones dressed like ingredients. That's a great idea, by the way."

"Oh, yes, the Heavenly Host," Gloria said, smiling. "Each new Burger Heaven restaurant has a Heavenly Host promotion."

"I met Regina a couple days ago, and I'd like to see her again."

Her smile froze a little. "I see. Well, that is something that is handled at the corporate level. You know, your food's going to get cold."

"So you don't know how I can get a hold of Regina?"

"I'm afraid not. Sorry. Look, I hate to see a customer eat less than perfect food. Would you like me to take your combo back and bring you a hot, fresh one?"

"Oh, no, it's all right. Well, thank you for your help."

"Sorry it couldn't have been more."

The bloody hell you are, Jack Hawkins growled inside my head. You remember Jack Hawkins? *The Bridge over the River Kwai*; *Lawrence of Arabia*? Even if his face doesn't ring a bell, you'd remember the voice.

While I was convinced Jack was right, I didn't press the issue. Instead I slid into the nearest empty table and unwrapped my burger. Zarian already had his sample; this one was mine.

If only Orson Welles have lived long enough to experience Burger Heaven.

When I was finished I headed back to the office. I checked my phone machine but no one had called; no one cared. Aye, me.

Given the fact that nothing was going on, I'd be justified in simply locking up and heading home, but there was something I wanted to try first. The less-than-helpful manager at the Burger Heaven had told me Regina had been brought in at the corporate level, but she had not offered any information on how to contact someone at corporate level.

I was pretty sure Burger Heaven was headquartered locally, and I didn't know where. But I had every confidence that my partner, Joe Laptop, would be able to tell me.

I typed in *Burger Heaven* but got nothing but ads and customer rating sites. Surely the thing had a website. I tried *www.burgerheaven.com*, and was informed that such a domain name was up for sale, if I was interested. One would think it would at least have a website. Maybe it did under a parent company, that route went nowhere as well.

This was starting not to make much sense.

"Joe, you've let me down," I said. *Why not try to find the girl herself?* the unmistakably twangy voice of Harry Morgan said in my head.

"All right." I typed in *Regina* and *Dancer* and found a half-dozen listings for women named Regina Dancer, none of whom seemed to be my Regina, who worked as a dancer. I tried *Regina Dancer Choreographer*, and found someone named Regina who taught dance classes in Reno.

Finally I tried *Regina Dancer Choreographer Los Angeles* and this time, after some searching, I found the link to a site that featured a professional-looking headshot and resume.

Bingo!

Her name was Regina Fontaine and her resume noted that she had been featured on the television shows *Bunheads* and *Glee*—each time playing a character named "Dancer"—and had staged a dance number for something on cable called *I Hate My Teacher and Want Him Dead*, which so far had managed to escape my attention.

The rest of her resume consisted of work at something called the Star Stage Center Theatre in Hollywood. Her photo made her look about nineteen, which I assumed was what one's photo had to do these days for one to get work. The Regina I'd met had already crested Mt. Thirty.

Fortunately, there was a number attached to the resume, which I tried calling.

And got a machine.

"Hi, Regina," I said after waiting for the tone, "this is Dave Beauchamp. We met a day or so back at Burger Heaven. I'm the private investigator. I found your number online and I'd like to ask you a couple more questions if I could when you have a moment. Could you please give me a call back?"

I left my number and hung up, wondering if I would really ever hear from her, given that she had acted like someone was stalking her during our first encounter.

I hoped my message had sounded more professional than creepy.

Why not both? Peter Lorre asked innocently inside my head.

Great.

I was also wondering if I should have given her my cell number instead of my office number. I could always call back and...naw. That *would* be creepy. I'd wait to hear from her tomorrow.

Packing up my laptop, I switched off the lights and headed out. What I really hoped was not so much that Regina would call back as that Louie Sandoval would simply turn up safe and sound, wondering why everyone was so stressed over her absence.

Was that really too much to ask?

Yes, someone said inside my head, but I didn't catch who it was.

CHAPTER EIGHT

The next morning, there was a knock on my apartment door a little after seven-thirty.

Fortunately I was already up and clean and dressed and ready to greet the day. I'm not always at a little after seven-thirty, unless there is something to get up for, but I had awakened very early, despite not having slept all that well, largely due to an extremely realistic dream in which I was bitten in the leg by Lassie. I woke up wondering if Robert Mitchum had put her up to it.

The knock came again, more insistent this time, and while I hoped it would turn out to be Louie, I figured it was more likely either the building manager or a neighbor, given the time. Worst case scenario was that it would be some kind of salesman that someone else had let into the building, who was now going door-to-door.

As soon as I opened the door I realized that I was wrong. This was much worse. I was staring into the cold, disdainful eyes of LAPD Detective Hector Mendoza.

"Remember me?" he asked with a smile that was like the last thing a hamster sees in a snake cage.

I was not likely to forget Hector Mendoza, whom I had not seen since the resolution of my last case, and was hoping to never see again.

You see, Mendoza hated me. I don't mean disliked me or thought I was an idiot, I mean he *hated* me; the kind of hate no amount of therapy could fix. It was the sort of hate Chief Inspector Dreyfus holds for Inspector Clouseau in the *Pink Panther* movies, only nowhere near as amusing.

I had come to find out that he had a free-flowing hatred for all private investigators since his mother's affair with one had broken up his parents' marriage when he was young. And since I was the only P.I. with whom he had actually associated, he took all of his generalized, abstract hatred for the breed and focused it like a laser beam exclusively on me.

Well, that and the fact that the guilty party in said last case had kicked him in the crotch so violently during an interrogation that he had to undergo surgery to repair his *cojones*.

"Why are you here, Hector?" I asked.

"Official business."

He walked past me and into the apartment, making certain that he managed to brush me out of the way in the process.

"C'mon in," I said.

It was then that I noticed someone else was standing in the hall, a young blonde kid, dressed in a suit and tie. He flashed me a badge, which identified him as Officer Bruce Willford, after which he walked inside as well.

"Where's Colfax?" I asked. Detective Dane Colfax had been Mendoza's partner during our last waltz. He was older, fairer, a little bit stoic, but a policeman who did not come with enough baggage to fill a rail car. I don't think I'm exaggerating that without Colfax to stop him at various moments, Mendoza would have either done serious bodily damage to my person, just for the hell of it, or would have railroaded me into prison for the very murder I had managed to solve.

I could only hope that Officer Bruce Willford had an similar leavening effect on him, but I doubted it.

"You want to know where Colfax is?" Mendoza sneered.

"I did ask that, yes."

"Transferred downtown to Robbery/Homicide. I wanted to go too, but you know what? My injury kept me back."

"Wow, sorry, Hector. That must be a real crotch for you to bear."

I meant to say *cross*, of course, though I doubted I would have been able to convince Hector Mendoza of that were I given a hundred years to try. He spun around and took a step toward me, only to have Officer Willford quickly step in between us.

"Maybe we should tell Mr. Beauchamp why we're here," the younger cop said, and maybe I'm imagining things, but I thought I caught Willford struggling to stifle a laugh.

It was a ray of unexpected sunshine inside my apartment.

"Fine," Mendoza said, stepping close enough to allow me to see the patches he missed while shaving. "Your girlfriend is dead."

"My girlfriend?" *Jeez, please don't be talking about Louie San-doval!* "What girlfriend is that?" I asked, trying to keep the shake out of my voice.

"Regina Fontaine."

"Regina? Good god. Hector, I'm shocked, but Regina was hardly my girlfriend. I'd met her only once."

"But your voice was on her answering machine, and don't call me Hector. It's *Sergeant*, asshole."

"*Sergeant Asshole*," Robert Mitchum chimed in, *I remember reading a script by that name back in the fifties.* You're a lot of help, Mitch.

"You're right, I did leave a message on Regina's machine last night. I wanted to talk to her in reference to a pending case."

"What pending case?"

"I'm afraid that's confidential."

"Bullshit. What pending case?"

"Sergeant," Detective Willford broke in, "maybe if I were to speak privately with Mr. Beauchamp—"

"Stay out of this." Mendoza stepped so close I had to lean backwards. "What... pending...case?"

"You know, Hector, a private investigator can't betray a client's confidence," I said. "I'd have thought you would have learned that from your mother."

Had that been out loud? my mind screamed a second later. Had I really thrown a *Yo mama!* into the face of a policeman who already wanted to kill me, and would probably get away with it if he did? What was wrong with me?

Maybe you're getting sick and tired of being pushed around, Bo-gie said forcefully. Great; that will be a huge comfort as my head is being beaten into cranberry sauce.

I swear at that moment Mendoza's eyes turned crimson, like a horror movie special effect. He was not simply close now, he was doing that chest-bump intimidation move where you try and force the other guy to back up.

He didn't have to force. I backed up.

"I should take you in right now," he growled.

"On what grounds?" Willford was asking.

Mendoza's fists clenched. "Resisting arrest."

"But sergeant—"

"Fine, take me in," I told Mendoza. "I have a feeling I'd be safer down at the station than I am here with you. And while I'm there I can tell your captain what a charming and pleasant conversation we've been having."

I genuinely thought Mendoza was going to hit me, maybe even pull out his gun and shoot me. But Detective Willford once more stepped in and deflected the pending violence.

"Maybe you should tell us about your relationship with the dead woman, sir," he said in an even voice.

I used the opportunity to turn and move away from Mendoza without making it look like a retreat.

"Well, like I told you, there really wasn't any relationship. I only met her one time. I barely knew her at all."

"Then why did you have her phone number?" Mendez snapped.

"I found it online. She was a dancer, and her resume and contact info is all there for anyone to see. I didn't even know her last name until I found it on the Net. How did she die, detective? I'm assuming foul play is suspected or else you two wouldn't be investigating."

"Yeah, foul play is suspected," Mendoza said in a sing-song, mocking voice. "And I've got an assumption of my own."

"Actually, Mr. Beauchamp, it's going to take an autopsy to determine the exact cause of death," Willford broke in. Either he was naturally polite or I was the birdie in a game of Good Cop/Bad Cop.

"I see. So she wasn't shot, stabbed or strangled."

The two detectives exchanged a glance, and Willford asked, "How did you know she wasn't shot, stabbed or strangled?"

"How else?" Mendoza said. "Because he did it. He's just confessed."

I directed my response to the younger, more reasonable detective.

"I haven't confessed to anything except having a sense of logic. Had Regina been shot or stabbed or strangled it would have been obvious, you would have seen it right away. An autopsy wouldn't be required to determine cause of death."

"Unless she'd been all three," Mendoza spat, "and we'd need the autopsy to find out which of those assaults proved fatal. Ever think of that, Einstein?"

I hadn't.

"Was that the case?" I asked.

Since neither answered immediately, I had to assume that it was not.

Willford broke the silence by asking, "Care to tell us where you met the victim, sir?"

"It was at a Burger Heaven, the one they just opened on Ventura Boulevard in Sherman Oaks. She'd been hired to choreograph a bunch of people playing hamburger ingredients out on the street."

"You want to give met that again?" Mendoza said.

I explained the restaurant promotion as best I could, but even as I heard my words coming back it sounded pretty dopey.

Finally, I said: "Look, you know those people you see on street corners who flip around a big arrow-shaped sign to announce the opening of a new business? Sometimes they're even in costume? Well, it was a little like that, except instead of spinning signs, they were dressed up like burger patties and buns and lettuce and onions and tomatoes. Regina was the one in charge of their act."

Mendoza smiled. "So, realizing that playing a vegetable comes naturally to you, you went to see her for a job, huh?"

"I've already told you, I wanted to talk to her for a—"

"Pending case," Mendoza interrupted. "What kind of case?"

"And as I've also already told you, I can't—"

"*What is it?*" he thundered, lunging at me, and even Willford jumped.

"Missing person," I squeaked, fighting to keep my legs from buckling.

Mendoza backed off. "There. Was that so hard? Who's missing?"

"A mutual friend."

"Give me a name, Beauchamp."

"I can't. She's also a client."

Mendoza exhaled like a dragon whose pilot light had gone out, which allowed Willford to jump in.

"Did Ms. Fontaine seem troubled to you when you spoke to her?" he asked.

"Troubled? Well, she seemed nervous. She was smoking a cigarette, and acted like I had caught her doing something naughty on the playground and was going to tell the teacher."

"Sure it was tobacco?" Mendoza asked.

"Positive," I said. "Maybe I don't look like it, but I have been around long enough to know what marijuana smells like."

You're right, you don't look like it, Mitchum said, and I knew better than to argue with him on the subject of marijuana.

There was a tense, half-minute lull in the interrogation, after which Willford asked: "Mr. Beauchamp, have you told us everything you know?"

"Well...maybe not."

"So you've finally decided to come clean," Mendoza said. "Okay, Beauchamp, what are you holding back?"

"For one thing, I know that *Citizen Kane* was not Orson Welles' first Hollywood movie. *Swiss Family Robinson* in 1940 was."

Glancing over to Willford, I added: "Well, you did say *every-thing*."

Mendoza turned a shade of purple that I did not think was possible in a human being.

"That's it," he growled. "Turn around."

"So you can shoot me in the back in my own home?"

"Turn...the fuck...around."

I turned around, waiting for the cold feel of the handcuffs.

"Sergeant—" Willford began, but Mendoza cut him off with a snarl. "Sir," the young detective tried again, "Are you certain we have cause for this?"

I had to give the guy credit. He had a spine.

"Are you counteracting my authority, *officer*?" Mendoza countered.

"Look, fellows, there's no need to fight on my account. I have told you everything I know about Regina Fontaine. I'm very sorry to hear that she's dead, but I had no involvement with that whatsoever outside of that one chance meeting. Cross my heart and hope to die."

"That makes two of us."

"Can I turn back around now?"

Mendoza violently spun me around and shoved a finger in my face. "This isn't over, asshole," he said, then pushed me out of the way so he could march out of my apartment.

"Thank you, Mr. Beauchamp," Officer Willford said on his way out.

"Thank you, officer."

After they'd gone I sat down and tried to control the delayed-reaction shaking.

You did okay, kid, Bogie said, encouragingly. *But where does this leave you?*

Where did it leave me? Regina had been my only lead into Louie's disappearance. Could her suspicious death have any connection to it? It didn't seem to scan because Regina didn't even know Louie's real identity and purpose.

Unless she found it out and that's why she got iced, a tough, gravelly voice told me. It was either Lawrence Tierney or Charles McGraw.

"We don't know for a fact yet that she was iced," I said to the empty apartment.

About the only thing I did know for certain was that as far as leads went on this case, I had just run into a brick wall. The only option I had left was to go to Louie's apartment and do a more thorough search for a flash drive.

For a brief second I thought about calling Avery Klemmer to ask if there were any police hanging around, but I didn't want him "helping" me in my search. I'd have to take my chances.

After stopping off at the office to check for messages (or signs of further burglary), and finding none of each, I went to the nearest hardware store, which wasn't all that close, and had a duplicate key made for Louie's apartment. I figured Ricky Sandoval would want his back at some point; even if he didn't, a spare never hurt.

Then I headed down to Palms.

It was of course too much to ask that Louie's apartment key also opened the front door of the building. About the time I was ready to admit defeat and buzz Avery, or the manager again, I saw someone coming through the lobby. Taking the key that didn't work, I pretended I was about to unlock the door right when the woman opened it from the inside.

"Oh, thanks," I said.

"Sure." She was short, fortyish, and dressed in running sweats. A headband held back her blonde bangs as she darted outside and then turned back, jogging in place.

"I don't think I've seen you here before," she said.

"Right, well, I'm still in the process of moving in," I lied.

"I hope you're not one of those who blocks the parking garage with your moving truck."

"Wouldn't dream of it."

"Good. Have a nice day." She then ran down the steps to the sidewalk and disappeared down the street.

"Thanks," I called after her.

Riding the elevator up to the second floor, I made certain that no one was in the hallway, particularly the cops, before walking down to 216 and stopping at the door.

After one last check each direction in the hall, I grabbed the doorknob and turned it slowly to see if it might possibly be unlocked, which would indicate that the police were here, but inside the apartment.

It was locked.

I carefully inserted the key, unlocked the door, and pushed it open, then stepped inside. The place was pretty much as I had last seen it, maybe straightened up a little bit, but showing no signs of present habitation.

Had I been thinking I would have brought gloves with me, but I hadn't. Carefully making my way into the kitchen, I opened the cabinet below the sink, using a handkerchief, and looked around until I found some rubber cleaning gloves. They were a bit tight and not very comfortable, but I made do.

Switching on the lights, I walked through the entire apartment, first to make absolutely sure that no one was there, either dead or alive (though if someone had been dead, I think my nose would have detected that fact by now), and second, to try an examine every place where a flash drive might logically be kept.

The most obvious place, of course, would be the desk, though I also examined the nightstand drawers and the top of the dresser in the bedroom. I did not relish searching the dresser drawers, knowing I would probably find her most personal items, but it had to be done for the sake of thoroughness. I desperately tried not to imagine what Louie would look like in the sheer, pink bra I found in the top drawer and the matching panties in the second one.

It turned out I didn't have to imagine it, since there was a photo of her in very similar underwear at the bottom of the third drawer.

There were a few other photos in there, which I peered at purely to see if they might contain some kind of clue.

Oh, suuure, Robert Mitchum needled.

Most were nothing but tease shots, the sorts of things that these days end up on people's phones and photo sharing accounts, but the last one I looked at was the one that made me drop all the others.

My mouth fell open as I stared at it.

It wasn't simply that Luisa Sandoval was posing naked in bed.

It wasn't simply that Luisa Sandoval looked pretty incredible naked.

It wasn't simply that another naked figure was cuddled next to her.

It was that the naked person cuddling Louie was Regina Fontaine.

CHAPTER NINE

I put the photos back in the drawer while swallowing my heart and forcing it back into my chest.

It wasn't like I had any claim on Louie, or even any real reason to hope that a relationship might result. It was merely an uncomfortable reminder of my college days when the girl I was most stuck on in my sophomore year and I turned out to have a lot in common: the same taste in women.

Beyond that it was the strong suggestion, if not outright verification, that Louie's disappearance and Regina's death were somehow intrinsically linked.

Upon grim reflection, it made sense: how else would a journalist be able to infiltrate the corporation she was investigating without the help of someone inside?

Maybe Regina had been Louie's first contact, the one who informed her that there was something unsavory being added to the burger meat. That would mean that Regina's denial of any knowledge about Luisa Sandoval had been nothing more than a ruse, which in turn explained why she had appeared so nervous.

Maybe she thought I had been hired by Burger Heaven to find out what she was passing on to a reporter.

That was a lot of maybes, but in my experience maybes tend to count for quite a bit in lieu of actual facts.

But it wasn't a smoking gun.

I went back into the front room where Louie had her desk and began a more thorough search. There were lots of papers, quite a few notebooks, filled with illegible scrawl, and post-it notes plastered here and there as reminders of things that bore no significance, so far as I could see.

But there was no flash drive.

Something I found in the bottom drawer of her desk that did surprise me was a brochure for the Temple of Theotologics.

Known around town simply as "The Temple," it was a Hollywood-based pseudo-religion that had been started in the mid 1950s by a former B movie actor named Palmer Hanley.

Sixty years later, what had apparently been started as a self-help system had grown into a major corporation, operating out of a modern-day castle built in the wacky twenties up in the Hollywood hills. The Temple might actually have a basis in religious belief or it may simply have pulled enough legal strings to maintain a tax-exempt status, but regardless of whatever existed at its core, it made money.

Lots and lots of money. Stories abounded that it was nothing more than a cash-cow cult, preying on the weak who had day jobs and could pay for the Temple's classes, stories that were invariably disputed and discredited by the Temple hierarchy and the handful of Hollywood stars who were adherents, such as Vince Cranna, the action film hero.

But what was Louie Sandoval's connection with the Temple? Maybe it was research material for a future story. I hoped that was all, anyway.

But what about the other doll? Bogie asked me. *The dancer. Maybe she was a member.*

Now that made more sense. It even explained the panic that Regina Fontaine had shown when I saw her smoking.

One of the primary boasts made by the Temple is that their process of "Adjusting" (insert registered trademark symbol here), or getting rid of all the bad stuff in one's life, can cure any kind of addiction, problem or obsession. Charges by former members of the Temple that their rehab programs were based on a regimen of mental and physical abuse continued to dog the operation.

If those charges were true, and Regina had indeed been a member of the Temple and was using their program to break her cigarette habit, then her paranoia at being spotted backsliding would indeed be justified.

But this was still nothing more than speculation.

I continued my search through Louie's apartment, opening and rummaging through every drawer in every piece of furniture that had one, but found nothing.

That left me with three possibilities: whoever had ransacked her apartment in the first place had found it and taken it; Louie had hidden it in a place I'd never find; or wherever she was, she had taken the flash drive with her.

Unless she had sent it to someone else or destroyed it.

The only really useful bit of information I had uncovered was the realization that finding pertinent clues in someone's apartment might look easy in the movies, but it wasn't in real life.

I was about to leave when I heard a thump against the wall that Louie's place shared with Avery Klemmer's apartment. That was followed by another thump, like someone was hitting the wall.

Maybe he was taking online dance courses.

Then I heard a muffled cry, some banging, and a crash.

Rushing out into the hallway, I listened against Avery's door. It was now quiet. Maybe I was just being ridiculous; maybe he was rearranging the furniture and something fell and broke. I waited another few seconds before knocking.

"Hi, Avery?" I called through the door. "It's Dave Beauchamp."

For several more seconds it was completely silent, after which I heard the sound of a lock being turned.

Yet the door remained closed.

Taking the knob, I slowly turned it and then stepped inside. "Avery? Hello. It's Dave Beauchamp."

There was no answer.

Something's wrong, kid, Bogie said, needlessly. I could figure out that much on my own.

I was about to call his name again when something hit me squarely on the back of the head and I went down.

The visual metaphor is always an array of shimmering stars, and that's not far off, though for me it was more flashing lights than anything in a particular shape. I kissed the carpet and heard movement behind me, which I prayed would not lead to another hit. It didn't. Once the explosion in my head settled, I rolled over and looked, but it was too late.

The apartment door was wide open and from the end of the hallway I could hear the faint sounds of the elevator door closing. I could try running for the staircase and hope to make it down before the elevator got there, but I knew that would be futile, mostly because I was not yet certain I could get up off the floor. There were no windows in the elevator area for me to look out and see who was running down the sidewalk, either.

Whoever had coshed me in the back of the head was going to get away scot free.

I managed to force myself into a kneeling position and now saw a large collectable bust of Batman, the kind that nerds spend fortunes on in comic book shops, lying on the floor next to me. That must have been what my assailant had used to hit me.

It's too bad the flashing lights weren't accompanied by the word THWAP! If this were a movie or TV show, I could take the bust and have it tested for fingerprints, and a few would actually show up. But even if there were fingerprints on the statue, the chances that they matched those of someone who was already in the system were remote.

Pros don't leave prints and amateurs aren't in the system.

Now the headache was starting. Again, in the realm of the movie or TV detective, getting hit over the head is as much a part of the job as billing for expenses.

But in the real world, it was as miserable as it was rare.

"Avery, are you here?" I called out, fighting nausea. I was hoping he was hiding in a closet. Even more, I was hoping he had not been the one who had tried to dent the back of my skull with Batman.

That was when I smelled it, and my stomach turned cold.

Okay, let's back up: every movie mystery that's ever been made and every murder mystery novel that's ever been written leaves out one important fact regarding a dead body. They stink.

Not just after a few days' worth of decomposition, but immediately, because life and breath are not the only things that leave a person at the moment of death. The bowels and the bladder also release. This unpleasant little fact belies the notion that a body can stay hidden inside a trunk, which is kept in plain sight, until Jimmy Stewart or some other Hollywood sleuth catches on through the nervous reactions of the killer. You might be able to hide a body from view, but you can't do it olfactorily.

And what I was smelling now was not encouraging. Not at all.

I found Avery Klemmer in his bedroom, on the floor, a wet stain on his pants. He was motionless, as befit his status among the dead.

A string of cable ties linked one to another cinched his neck, cutting into his flesh.

Something crunched underneath my shoe, and I saw that the ceramic base of a lamp lay on the floor in pieces, which must have been the smashing sound I'd heard.

Why did this have to happen? What did Avery know?

Pulling out my cell phone, I checked the time. It was a little after noon, but eating lunch was the furthest thought from my mind.

If, as I assumed, the bumping and thumping I'd heard coming Louie's apartment minutes earlier had been the sound of Avery Klemmer being killed, the actual time of death might prove to be important.

To fake an alibi if nothing else, Bogie said. Yeah, to fake an alibi, because while I knew I hadn't killed Avery, convincing the police of that would be a harder sell than claiming I could cure cancer.

What's more, I couldn't help but think that my assailant, Avery's murderer, realized that, which is why he left me alive.

Or why she *left you alive*, Lauren Bacall's voice said in my throbbing head.

Right. Or she.

There was nothing I or anyone else could do for Avery now, except find his killer.

Having decided that reporting the murder was the proper thing to do, I had *nine* and the first *one* already pressed when I heard the siren.

Sirens were pretty commonplace in Los Angeles, but this one was getting closer and closer, and pretty soon it was joined by a friend. Then two more friends. Within seconds it was an entire chorus of sirens, which became deafening before they suddenly wound down.

That meant one thing: they were stopping here.

Somebody had already called the police, and I had a feeling I knew who.

I had to get out of this apartment.

I could chance running down the hall and hope nobody saw me, or I could be sneakier about it.

Operating on the assumption that the drivers of those emergency vehicles were already on their way up, I decided to take the back route. Rushing out to Avery's balcony, I crawled on top of the ledge and then leapt over to Louie's, managing to clear the balcony wall without injury, though when I landed, the jolt made my head feel like a railroad spike was being driven through it.

Checking her balcony door through the pane, I was relieved to find it still unlocked, so I let myself in, crawled to a corner and sat still…at least until I noticed that I had never closed Louie's front door! Racing to it, and hearing the sounds of people approaching from down the hallway, I shut the door as silently as possible and turned the lock, then dashed back to my hidey-hole.

Voices now filled the apartment hallway, including a woman's who asked: "What's going on here?"

A man's voice answered, "We don't know yet, ma'am, please go back to your apartment and close the door."

I could hear people entering Avery's apartment, and after a few more seconds heard a voice shout, "In here!"

For a while the only sound I heard was my heart beating, which sounded like Eleanor Powell tap dancing on a gigantic drum, and then was able to make out the distinct sound of Avery's balcony door being opened.

Then a voice called, "Anybody down there?"

I could only barely make out the reply from the ground below: "I don't see anyone."

Clearly, escaping by jumping off of the balcony was out, though I can't say it had ever rated very high on the option list.

Then from the hallway I heard a voice, presumably that of the policeman in charge, say, "All right, get statements from the neighbors, see if anyone saw or heard something."

Someone was going to be knocking on Louie's door at any moment. Sure, I could pretend no one was home, but with a dead body next door, there was going to be no shortage of policemen for quite some time.

I knew enough about real police investigations, as opposed to filmed ones, to know that a crime scene was sequestered for far longer than it took to deliver a few snappy, cynical lines of dialogue. The cops could be next door for days, a week even, and I would have to leave at some point during that time.

My sudden appearance and emergence from an "empty" apartment would not make me look innocent.

If any of my interior brain mentors had an idea…any idea… this would be an excellent time to bring it up.

Anyone?

I think your best course of action would be to come clean, Dick Powell offered.

Did he mean give myself up? That hardly seemed helpful. Then a moment later I got it.

Rushing to the bathroom, I turned on Louie's shower and stripped off all my clothes, then jumped in, unfortunately before the water was fully warm.

That, however, was not as bad as the fact that the water from the shower felt like buckshot on my aching head.

After wetting myself, I stepped back out and listened for the front door. The knock came about three minutes later, by which time I had to re-immerse myself under the water.

At the second knock I called, "Just a minute!" and then turned the shower off and wrapped a towel around my waist. I put another one on my head, wincing as the weight of the towel came down on the bump on my head.

Dripping my way to the front door, I unlocked it and cracked it open, just enough to let the officer, a policewoman, outside see that I had just gotten out of the shower.

"What is it?" I demanded.

"Oh, sorry, sir," the policewoman said. "There's a situation next door and we're talking to the neighbors."

"Next door, with Avery? What's going on."

"Well, sir, we need to ask if you've seen or heard anything unusual this morning."

"Um…could you come back in a few minutes, maybe? I was in the shower."

"Yes sir, take your time, Mr…" she said, fishing for my name.

"Sandoval," I said, "Louie Sandoval. Thanks."

Then I closed the door.

Drying off as I ran back to the bathroom, including drying my hair as much as my bump would allow comfortably, I put my clothes back on and waited.

If only Louie's tomato outfit were here somewhere, I could have put it on and run out, and if anyone happened to see me, all they'd report to the police was the suspect was about five-eleven, very round, and red ripe. But it was not here in the apartment, or else I would have discovered it by now.

Moving back to the front door of the apartment, I listened until the voices had abated, and then cracked the door open again and peeked out. I could see the back of a uniformed officer standing in the doorway of unit 214, but not his face. Nobody else was visible.

Now was my chance.

Taking a deep breath, I exited Louie's apartment as quietly as I could and ran like hell for the elevator, pressing the down button. Making it down to the lobby unnoticed, I got out and saw a group of people, presumably tenants, collecting in the lobby. Walking through them, I headed for the front door.

Once outside, I counted four police cruisers, two fire trucks and a yellow paramedic's vehicle, which unless one of the other tenants had fainted from the shock, was redundant.

I almost made it past them when a man standing on the sidewalk stopped me. "Hey, what's going on?" he asked.

"I have no idea," I replied. "All these vehicles just showed up, so I guess someone is sick, or had an accident, or something."

"You look a little sick yourself, buddy."

"I do?"

"You're all pale."

Yes, well you try getting hit on the back of the head with a statue of Batman and then trip over a dead body and see how you react to it, a voice said in my head, and strangely enough, it was my own.

"That's why I'm on my way to the doctor," I said, leaving the guy and walking, but not running, to my car.

Sliding behind the wheel, I sat there for a moment, thinking about what had just happened. I had touched nothing in Avery's apartment, except for the doorknob, and I did not see that as a problem since the prospect of isolating one specific set of prints from a frequently used doorknob seemed daunting at best.

As best as I could tell, I was in the clear. The real question at this point was, what do I do now?

Despite my lack of actual information, I felt it might be best to keep Zareh Zarian at the *Journal* apprised of the fact that this seemed to be turning into a highly complex problem. I reached into my pocket for my cell phone to call him, but it wasn't there. I checked my other pocket and found nothing.

I checked every pocket I was currently wearing: nothing.

Where the hell was my cell phone?

The last time I had seen it was when I checked the time and then started dialing 911 to report Avery's death, and…

"Oh, *jeez,*" I moaned, lowering my aching head onto the steering wheel. I must have set down my cell when I first heard the approaching sirens. It was still inside Avery Klemmer's apartment, waiting to be found by the police.

And when it is found, I become the prime suspect in Avery's death.

"If I'd been a character in one of Jack Daniel's novels," I told the steering wheel, "this never would have happened."

CHAPTER TEN

I actually ran a red light driving back to my office, something I never do.

Normally I never even run a yellow light unless stopping in time means excessive tire damage, but I was preoccupied. Fortunately there was no cross traffic coming, and even better, no cops around to pull me over. Because of my sudden vehicular crime spree I slowed down to a grandpa-crawl for the rest of the way.

It was nearly two by the time I arrived at my building. After parking in my spot, I went up to my office, finding that it took me three tries to get the key into the lock on my door, my hands were shaking so badly.

Take it easy, kid, Bogart told me.

"Hey, don't you give me any guff," I said, finally opening my door. "Your hands shook, too, in *The Maltese Falcon*. Remember?"

Must have been Huston's idea, he argued, and then disappeared.

Maybe I was overreacting. Maybe I hadn't dropped my cell phone in Avery's apartment. Maybe I had put it back in my pocket and it had fallen out in Louie's bathroom when I peeled my clothes off to do the shower pretense.

Naw, you gotta expect the worst on this beat, sonny, Charles Mc-Graw said in my head.

Swell.

I flopped down in my desk chair and started searching through my top drawer where I was pretty sure I had a bottle of Advil, which I desperately needed right now. Finding it, I popped three of the remaining five pills in my mouth and then went to the kitchen sink to wash them down.

Returning to my desk, I decided to take score. I had one vanished client and two dead witnesses, my cell phone was probably in the hands of the police right now making me a prime suspect for at least one of those murders, while Detective Mendoza desperately wanted to frame me for the other one.

And I had no leads.

I tried to think on the bright side: at least no one had kicked me in the crotch so hard I required surgery.

The Advil were beginning to work to the point where I could probably withstand the sound of another real voice without my head splitting open, so I picked up my desk phone and put in a call to Zareh Zarian.

"Hey, Beauchamp, what've you got for me?" he asked.

"An expense report for a crate of Advil," was the best I could come up with.

"That's it? How about Sandoval's notes?"

"Sorry. She either hid them so well no one can find them, or she has them on her, or someone else has them, or they've been destroyed, I just don't know. Look, Zarian, I have a rather awkward question to ask. Would Louie go to bed with someone just to get information from them?"

He laughed. "You think it's going to be that easy getting in her panties?"

"I'm serious. Would she sleep with someone in return for information?"

There was a long pause before he answered, "She is a very dedicated reporter."

"So that's a yes?"

"Why are you asking?"

"I'm just curious, is all."

"Look, you're not hearing this from me, okay? That story I was telling you about, the exposé of the developer, well, for that one she did what she had to do to get close to someone who works in the city permit office. I should say used to work in, since he got canned when they found out he was the source of an information leak."

So somebody wanted to get even with her, William Demarest's voice barked in my head.

"I don't know," I absentmindedly responded. "It doesn't fit."

"What doesn't fit?" Zarian asked.

"Hmm? Oh, uh, what I meant was, opening herself up like that is kind of a dangerous business practice, isn't it?"

"You don't know Louie like I do. She has a little bit of a jones for getting into danger."

"She should be having a field day right now, then."

"Why, what have you learned?"

I quickly laid out everything that had happened since we had last spoken, but left out the business of finding the picture in her apartment.

"Holy shit, two murders?" Zarian said. "This is big!"

"Big and serious. But getting back to Louie's method of gaining information, would she ever go so far as to…"

"As to what?"

"Well, might she ever trade herself to the other team if that's what it took?"

"Are you asking if she's a lez?"

"Well, maybe, or would she go to bed with a woman even if she wasn't a lesbian just to get information out of her?"

"Look, Beauchamp, I really don't know where you're going with this, but I don't have to answer these kinds of questions about my staff."

"It might be important."

I heard a sigh at the other end of the line, and then Zarian said, "Sandoval is a dedicated reporter, the best I've got. Sometimes I wonder myself how far she'd go for a story. That's all I can tell you. Now, if there's nothing else, hang up and let me get the hell back to work."

"There is one other thing. Whatever is going on might have something to do with the Temple."

"The temple?"

"The Temple of Theotologics."

"Oh, Jesus."

"You didn't assign Louie to investigate them, did you?"

"Hell no!"

There was a pause and I heard him yell off into the distance, "Ashley, go someplace, would you?"

After another moment, he came back on.

"You're not wearing your headset any more, are you?" I asked.

"My headset? No, I couldn't get used to that frigging thing. What difference does that make?"

"None, I guess. It's just that I heard you move away from the phone, which means you're using the receiver."

What it really meant was that I was relieved to discover the deductive reasoning portion of my brain was still functioning after the blow to the head.

"Whatever. You want to hear about the Temple or not?" he asked. I did.

"Okay. I don't want my staff to hear this, but I won't touch the Temple of Theotologics. I won't go anywhere near them."

"Why not?"

"Because their belief system doesn't include freedom of the press, that's why not. You try to investigate them and you find yourself shut down."

"How can they do that?" I asked.

"They own an entire law firm here in town. They even own a few judges who are all too willing to sign off on a warrant so that all your computers and files can be confiscated."

"You know this for a fact?"

"A couple years ago I wanted to run a story on an enterprising little theatre here in town that somehow attracted big name actors and directors despite its size and location, and got citywide attention, the kind usually reserved for the Mark Taper. It wasn't even a controversial story. It was supposed to be a nice little puffy feature about a playhouse with a real can-do attitude, with quotes from actors, directors, stagehands, management, all about the little stage that could. I assigned our second-string theatre critic to do the piece and he started researching it. He did too damn good a job."

"What do you mean?"

"Jonathan was part of the L.A. theatre scene so he knew how things were supposed to work," Zarian went on. "Back then acting unions had agreements and rules that governed these little places based on the number of seats, and everyone is supposed to be making a little bit of money. These days the union's got even greater control over them, but in those days you were supposed to get something, even if it wasn't much. Yet this place was paying nothing to anyone, not the actors, not the crew, not anybody. They were working with the absolute best, but nobody got anything. Well, Jonathan smelled a rat somewhere and he started digging around, and before we knew it the piece had changed. It became an exposé about a place where something really fishy was going on."

"Like what?" I asked.

"Like the fact that some people who worked in the theatre were never seen again."

"Maybe they took the bus back to wherever they came from."

"Not everybody moves back to Springfield, Beauchamp. Then there was an instance involving an actor who was killed when a light fell on him. Our guy started digging and found out it took three tries before it was successful."

"Murder? Why didn't you run a story on it?"

"Because, and here's the point I'm making, Jonathan found out the theatre was owned and operated under the table by the Temple of Theotologics."

"Oh. Well, maybe I should talk to Jonathan, then."

"You'll have to wait for visiting day."

"What?"

"He's up in Chino serving fifteen to twenty-five."

"What did he do?"

"Discovered the truth. The Temple made sure that story never saw the light of day by implanting kiddie porn on his computer and making sure he got caught, tried, convicted and imprisoned."

"You've got to be joking."

"Think? Want to drive up to Chino and tell that to him? When you go tell him I said hi."

"You know for a fact that the child porn was planted?"

"I know it for a fact, because the day he was sentenced I got a phone call from some guy telling me that if I tried to resurrect the story, or think about doing any other story that involved the workings of the Temple, I'd find myself in the cell next to him. So the only time you're ever going to see the word Theotologics in the *Independent Journal* is in one of their paid ads."

I felt chilled. Could this sort of thing really be going on outside of a movie or thriller novel?

Then something struck me. "What was the name of that theatre your guy was writing about?"

"They call it the Star Stage Center Theatre."

Right. The same theatre that Regina Fontaine had done so much work for.

"I have to tell you, Beauchamp," Zarian went on, "if you're dragging the Temple into this, I'm going to have to cut you off."

"But you do want to find Louie."

"Of course I want to find Louie, and I still want her notes. I just don't want to hear the word Theotologics mentioned again. Now get off my phone, I'm busy."

"I'll be in touch," I said.

"Yep." He hung up.

At least the call had given me a positive connection between Regina Fontaine and the Temple of Theotologics, but that was cold comfort from any direction. I doubted I'd get very far going down to the theatre and saying, 'Hi, folks, anyone here know anything about a dead dancer?'

Though if Mendoza had anything on the ball, he would have already done that.

Mendoza.

Oh, the idea that just came into my head was a diabolical one, and it was my own creation, not one from the Hollywood Victory Caravan, and it might even alleviate my other, bigger, immediate problem, the one involving my cell phone.

Maybe the bonk on the head back there at Avery's apartment had sharpened my wits!

Opening my desk drawer, I pulled out the stack of business cards I keep rubber banded together and flipped through them until I saw the one for Detective Dane Colfax at LAPD's Northwestern station. I knew from Hector Mendoza that Colfax was no longer there, but I hoped the phone number still worked.

I dialed it and on the second ring a voice answered, "Yee."

"Yee what?" I said.

"This is Detective Dylan Yee, who is this?"

"Oh, I was looking for Detective Willford," I said. "I'm sorry if I got the wrong number."

"No, he's here, hold on."

A few seconds later, Bruce Willford identified himself.

"Hi, detective, this is Dave Beauchamp. We met a day or so back."

"Right, hi. What can I do for you?"

"Well, this may make you laugh, too, because it's so ridiculous, but someone stole my cell phone."

"Someone stole your cell phone?"

"Yeah, I was standing on a corner waiting for the light to turn so I could cross, and someone bumped into me," I lied. "I felt something in my pocket, like a hand, and then my phone was gone."

"But not your wallet?"

"Um, no, because see, I keep my cell phone in my back pocket, where most guys carry their wallets. He probably thought that's what he was getting."

"Where did this happen?"

"On the West Side, around Palms."

"That's not our jurisdiction, Mr. Beauchamp," he said.

"Yeah, I know, but, I thought maybe you could tell me what to do."

Then I heard a voice in the background shout, "Did you say *Beauchamp*? Gimme that!"

A few seconds later, my old friend Detective Mendoza came on the line. "Beauchamp, what the hell do you want?"

"Oh, hi, Hector. Well, my cell phone got stolen, and I thought I'd call in and report it."

"Your cell phone? Your goddamned *cell phone*? Do you know how many cases we have open right now? Your CELL PHONE?"

After screaming out a suggestion that would have made Lenny Bruce blush, Mendoza slammed down the receiver at the police station, breaking the call, and likely the phone.

Even though the sound did nothing to help my still-aching head, I had to smile. Now, thanks in large part to Detective Mendoza's tirade, which could have been heard in Santa Barbara, an alternative explanation for my cell phone turning up in Avery Klemmer's apartment, other than my having been there, had been established.

It might not get me off the hook entirely, since I was known to have been inside Avery's building, but it should raise enough reasonable doubt to knock me down a few places on the suspect list.

Not bad, kid, Bogie said in my head, *you're learning*.

Now if I could only figure out who had murdered Avery Klemmer.

It didn't take Philip Marlowe to figure out that it had been the killer who hit me over the head before fleeing. Nor was it much of a leap of logic to assume that on the way out the killer had made an anonymous call to the police to report the murder, which is why they arrived so quickly. Conclusion number three was that Regina Fontaine was not just the link between Louie and Burger Heaven, but she also connected Burger Heaven and the Temple of Theotologics.

It was then that I remembered something else, a passing reference made by the inebriated manager of Louie's apartment building. When I mentioned Burger Heaven, he'd drawled, *Goddamn Church owns 'em*.

At the time I assumed he was confused by the pseudo-Biblical terminology and iconography used by the chain, but now I wondered.

If the Star Stage Center Theatre was owned by the Temple of Theotologics, couldn't Burger Heaven be as well?

Opening up my laptop, I powered it up to see what, if anything, I could find online that might confirm that supposition.

At the same moment, I heard through the window the telltale sound of the mail truck pulling up outside. It's the mailman putting on the parking break for each stop that makes it so identifiable.

While my computer went through its prolonged booting process I went downstairs to get the mail in person.

It was a typical mail day: two bills, an offer from an internet provider, some grocery store fliers, and another missive from Front Row Video, a movie rental chain that had was supposed to have gone out of business, but was somehow still sending me threatening letters over a dispute that had been cleared up years ago.

But stuck within the fliers was something unexpected: a small padded envelope addressed to me but with no return address. Ripping it open as I walked back to my office, I saw it contained a flash drive.

"Louie, I love you!" I said excitedly.

Dashing back inside, I took the flash drive and plugged it into a port in my laptop, and waited. I did not have to wait long.

It only took a few seconds for all my desktop icons to disappear, followed by my screen saver, which had been a shot of the Hollywood Sign. Everything went black.

"Oh, no, no no no no no..." I droned, trying to find the curser to shut off the program, but failing because my keyboard no longer worked.

For all intents and purposes, my laptop was dead.

Even though it was probably too late, I yanked the flash drive out and threw it across the room. But even without it, words began to appear, scrolling up the screen from the bottom, like the back-story crawl at the beginning of a *Star Wars* movie:

Congratulations! it read, *You've pissed us off*! *Here's your reward: we have disabled your computer and erased your hard drive. The only files that remain are the ones we have put on. Care to see what they are...?*

A photo then slowly faded up, eventually filling the screen. It showed an adult man, whose face was carefully hidden, with a girl of about eight, whose face was not. Both of them were naked.

Suddenly I felt sick. I could only pray for humanity's sake that it was PhotoShopped, not that the authorities would much care if any of them found it on my machine.

The words *Have a nice day!* then appeared, after which they burst into a bouquet of flowers, which animated away, leaving only the picture.

Clearly, the laptop was gone for good, but given the fact that the keyboard had been disabled, I couldn't even turn it off. I would have to wait until the battery ran out, or maybe I could simply take a hammer and smash it to bits.

That seemed like the better idea, but I would first have to get hold of a hammer, since I didn't keep one at the office.

My head hurt like the devil. I closed my eyes.

"Guys?" I said to the empty office, "Bogie? Even you, Mitch? Anyone? Can someone tell me what to do?"

It was Dana Andrews who drew the short straw. *Sorry, we're out of our league here*, he intoned. *In our day, all we had to worry about was getting beat up and shot at.*

I couldn't take the hideous picture any more. I started to close the laptop when I heard a knocking sound at the door, which, because I had run in so quickly with the mail, was standing open.

Looking up, I actually moaned and closed my eyes.

"What's the matter, Dave," the man standing in my doorway said. "You don't look happy to see me."

Happy? At this particular moment in time the sight of Detective Dane Colfax in my office was causing my life to pass before my eyes.

CHAPTER ELEVEN

"You look like you just swallowed a rock," Colfax said. "You okay?"

"Fine," I croaked. "How are you, Detective?"

"Can't kick."

"I hear you're with Robbery and Homicide now."

"Where'd you hear that?"

"I ran into Mendoza a day or so back."

"How is he? Still limping?"

"Physically, no. Emotionally, I think he needs a crutch."

"Oh, Hector's all right. Maybe a little uptight."

Saying Mendoza was maybe a little uptight was like saying Marilyn Monroe was maybe a little sexy.

"Why are you here, Detective?"

"Know anyone named Avery Klemmer?" he asked.

Play it cool, kid, Bogie told me.

"Avery Klemmer…I've met him. Why?"

"How did you meet him?"

"A client of mine lived in his apartment building."

"Really? Hmm. That might explain it."

"Explain what?"

"Why your cell phone was found in Avery Klemmer's apartment."

"My cell phone? Really?"

You're over…acting, Gary Cooper cautioned.

"But my cell phone was stolen a day or so back, at least I thought it was. I wonder if it fell out of my pocket inside the building? I already reported it as stolen."

"Are you leveling with me, Beauchamp?"

"Why would I not level with you?"

"I can't imagine, but if you don't mind my saying so, you look a little like a dog who made a puddle on the carpet when he knows he's not supposed to. You hiding something?"

I sighed. What I was contemplating was pretty counterintuitive, and probably a huge risk, but Colfax had always treated me fairly, and letting him in my problem might be a good thing in the long run.

Don't do it, kid, Bogart advised.

On the other hand, honesty is the best policy, Clifton Webb countered, though it was hard to tell if he was being sarcastic or not.

I had to make the decision myself, so…

"Are you here alone, Detective Colfax?"

He looked around. "I'm the only one I can see outside of you."

"What I mean is, shouldn't you be with a partner?"

"Oh, yeah, but she's trying to find a place to park the car. Why? What's so important about me being here alone?"

"Because I like to think that we had established a pretty good relationship on that last case we were on," I said.

"I like to think I look like George Clooney," he deadpanned. "Where is this going?"

"I have a problem, a potentially big one. I think I might be able to explain it to you, but maybe not someone else whom I've never met before."

His eyes narrowed.

"Whatever it is, Dave, don't forget that I'm still a cop."

I sighed again, then said, "Come over here and look at this."

I stepped away from my desk as he walked over and looked at the photo on my laptop.

"Jesus jumping baldheaded Christ on a pogo stick!" he cried, with uncharacteristic force. "Why the hell are you showing this to me?"

"Because I think it's the only way I can prove to you that I'm being set up. Over in the corner there you'll find a flash drive. It was sent to me in the mail, and I thought it was some material from a client, but when I put it in my machine, it ate all my files and put on this picture. It also disabled the whole system, so I can't get rid of it or even shut it down."

Colfax hit the Escape key a couple times, to no avail.

"You believe I'm telling the truth, right?" I asked.

"Either that or you've become a 33rd degree moron. You have any idea who's doing the setting up?"

"No." And that was the truth, since I did not *know*, even though I suspected.

"You think it was the same person who stole your phone and put it in the murdered man's apartment?"

"I don't know, it might—"

You don't know he's dead, you don't know he's dead, YOU DON'T KNOW HE'S DEAD! Laurence Olivier shouted maniacally in my head.

"—Wait, what did you say?" I blurted, and thank you Sir Larry! "Avery's been murdered?"

"That's why I'm here," Colfax said. "Robbery and homicide, remember? What, you think he was stolen like your cell phone?"

"I…I'm shocked."

Oooh, you're such a liar! Joe Besser whined inside my head.

"You said that flash drive came in the mail," Colfax said. "You still have the envelope?"

"Right here." I handed him the envelope, from which he appeared to deduce nothing.

"Is there anything you're not telling me?"

"I've told you all I know. I'm on a case, and I'm starting to get the distinct impression that someone, somewhere, doesn't want me to be pursuing this case. That's about it."

At that moment a young woman entered the office. She was short, African-American and attractive.

"Beauchamp, you were asking about my partner, well here she is, Detective Waters," Colfax said. "What took so long, Angie?"

"You don't know what it's like to park around here!" she declared.

"Actually, I do," I acknowledged, "so on behalf of Sherman Oaks, let me apologize."

Colfax closed my laptop.

"Thanks for the use of your computer, Beauchamp, I got what I needed," he said, and at that moment I could have kissed him.

"Angie, it appears that Mr. Beauchamp's cell phone was stolen a day or so back, so we're at a bit of a dead end."

"Did you know Avery Klemmer?" she asked.

"I met him once," I said.

"I have his story," Colfax said, "I'll fill you in on the way back."

Turning to me he said, "Good to see you again, Beauchamp."

"Good to see you too, and thank you."

"If you think of anything that might be pertinent to this case, you'll contact me, right? Right?"

His eyes bored into mine.

"Give me a card and I'll keep it handy," I said.

"Oh, right, my new number."

He fished out a business card and handed it over. "If you talk to Hector again, give him my regards. I still keep tabs on him."

"I will."

The two detectives started to leave, but then Colfax stopped and turned back.

"When did you say you saw Mendoza?" he asked.

"A day or so back."

"Right. And when did you lose your phone?"

"A day or so—" I instinctively shut up.

"A day or so back was a pretty eventful day, wasn't it?" Colfax asked. "So eventful I'm surprised you can't remember it more clearly."

"Um, well, days all kind of run together when you work alone," I uttered.

"Mm-hmm, and rocks go down hard when they're swallowed. See you, Beauchamp, we'll be in touch."

They filed out of my office and as soon as they were gone I had a decision to make: do I faint, or do I simply vomit?

I did neither. I simply sat down at my desk, gazing at my now-dead, now dangerous laptop. I could get another computer, of course. I even had the money to do it. And there was really nothing on the laptop that couldn't be reloaded. Even the loss of my email address book wasn't that big a crisis.

Oh, you think not, huh? Robert Mitchum chimed in, cynically.

Okay, Mitch, I'll bite; why is the loss of my email…"Oh, jeez," I muttered aloud.

What if the virus had also sent copies of that horrific photo to everyone on my email list?

I would have to go to the library to check my email on the one of the public computers, but I would have to do it very, very carefully.

Better yet, I could drive down to the *Independent Journal* offices and ask to use one there, since if anybody understood what might pop up, it would be Zareh Zarian, who would be less than thrilled that I was involving him in Theotologics shenanigans yet again.

But that was the chance I had to take. I switched off the lights and locked the door behind me.

It felt strange leaving without my laptop.

My office is one of those with a parking court in the back, underneath the building, which someone at some point in time had labeled "dingbat" architecture. Usually it applied only to apartment buildings and not commercial structures, but I guess I just got lucky. What one forfeits in any sense of security that your building will not tumble like a Jenga tower in an earthquake, one gains in having a place to park in the city of Los Angeles.

All of this was somewhat academic, however, since I never made it to my car. A hand was suddenly clapped on my shoulder from behind, which caused me to jump nearly to the second floor.

Spinning around, I saw Ricky Sandoval.

"Good lord, you scared me half to death," I moaned. "What are you doing here, Ricky? How did you find me?"

"You gave me a card, remember?" he said. "Look, can we go inside?"

"Well, I was actually on my way out—"

"This is more important! I've got a problem! C'mon, man."

"Fine, we'll go inside."

"Hurry, man!"

"Why, is someone chasing you?"

"No, I really have to take a crap!"

"Great."

I rushed him inside and he practically ran up the stairs, and then danced in the hallway until I unlocked my door, after which he ran to the bathroom and stayed there for several minutes. When he came back out, a look of relief was on his face.

"You were almost out of paper," he said. "I had to get another roll from the cabinet."

"Does this sort of thing happen to you often?"

"Sometimes I get surprised. It's my high-fiber diet."

"Everything's okay now, though?"

"I wish it were," he said, flopping himself down in my guest chair. "I think I'm in trouble, Mr. Beauchamp."

He pronounced it *BEE-chump*.

"It's Bee-*chum*," I corrected. "No P."

"No pee? Shouldn't I have done that when I was in the bathroom? I thought it would be okay, even if I didn't specifically ask."

I rubbed my forehead.

"Why are you in trouble, Ricky."

"The police, they think I killed the Klemmer guy."

"How do you know they think that?"

"Because they told me."

"They *told* you? Ricky, if the police really think you've killed someone, they usually take you into custody."

"I know, and they probably would have if I hadn't run away."

"You ran away from the police?"

"It was all I could think to do! See, I went to Louie's apartment and there was this commotion next door, and then I saw the police, and they wanted to know why I was there, and I said it was none of their business why I was there, and then they got aggressive, and said that maybe I should come down to headquarters, and I said screw you and pushed the policeman who was talking to me and turned around and ran. Since I knew the building better than they did I was able to outrun them to my car, and then I drove here."

"Ricky, this is important. Did they at any point start reading you your rights?"

"You mean about remaining silent and all that? They started to, but that's when I ran out."

"Oh, jeez."

"I figured that it didn't really count until they got all the way through and then asked if you understood and agreed. You know, like a 'cancel' button on a computer if you change your mind. Is that wrong?"

"Honestly, I don't know," I replied. "It's a question that I suppose could be tried in court, but for the time being, let's just say it wasn't the best thing you could have done."

"Oh, man. How much trouble am I in?"

Enough to make Matlock shoot himself, I thought.

"Before I answer, Ricky, I have just one question for you, and I want you to answer it truthfully. Did you kill Avery Klemmer?"

"No!" he protested, looking hurt that I would even think such a thing.

"All right. I'll see what I can do to help you. Why don't you go on home and let me think about this."

"What if the cops are there waiting for me?"

"Do they know where you live?"

"Well, one of them asked me where I lived so I told him."

Now I was holding my head in my hands.

"So, you gave them your address, and then you fled?"

"Not a good idea, huh?"

How come Robert Mitchum never chimed in to comment on the stupidity of other people?

"Let's just say that if you do return home, you will almost certainly be arrested."

"So I won't go home," he said, easy as that. "How about if I stay with you?"

"Ricky, I live in an apartment that is not really equipped for guests. It's barely equipped for me."

Lifting my head to look at him, I said from the heart: "If there was only some way I could make you disappear."

Then I had an idea. "I wonder…"

"What?" Ricky asked eagerly.

"I have an idea. Just sit tight for a minute while I call a friend."

"Can he help me?"

"Possibly."

Picking up the phone, I punched in the number for Jack Daniels.

"You have such perfect timing, David," he answered after the third ring, without the benefit of *hello*. "I've just saved today's work, of which I'm rather satisfied, and was on my way to the pub. Were you to join me I could repay your contribution in saving my story from the mediocrity bunny."

"Quick question, Jack. Let's say I'm suspected by the police, even though I'm completely innocent, but I made things even worse by foolishly escaping their capture how could I make myself disappear from view?"

"Ah, this is an old one. The answer is sign with the William Morris Agency. You will never be seen or heard from again."

"Jack, please…"

"Are you writing a novel yourself?"

"No. Why?"

"Because this sounds like something that would never actually happen."

"So does most of my life. But humor me, Jack, how would one do it?"

"Well, wear a disguise, obviously, and stay away from one's usual places."

"How about leaving town?"

"Perhaps, though I've always liked the concept of hiding in plain sight, which goes back to the disguise. I'll tell you what. Meet me at the *Hound and Badger* in one hour and I will outline it for you. My treat."

"I'll be there," I said.

"Excellent. I will even bring something that might be useful to you. Ta ta."

Then a thought came to me. "Wait, Jack, don't hang up yet."

"My boy, Mr. Fuller's casked ambrosia is already calling to me."

"I know, but could you check and see if you've received an email from me today? And if you have, for God's sake, don't open it. I think it's a virus."

"Oh, dear, hold on."

I could hear keyboard tapping for a few seconds, then his voice came back on.

"No, nothing from you."

While it was still too early to stop worrying altogether, the fact that no emails had been sent through my system was a good sign.

"If something does comes in, delete it immediately," I said.

"I shall. Don't be late."

Jack hung up.

An hour would be plenty of time to make it to the Santa Monica location of *The Hound and Badger*—a place that always sounded to me like it was run by a collection agent—and even though I was not addicted to pubs in the way that Jack was, or at all, his offer to pay simply could not be refused. The only problem was…

"So what's the story?" Ricky asked.

"I'm meeting a friend who says he can help you out."

"Oh, am I going to stay with him?"

"No. For the time being, why don't you just stay here? There's a little bit of food in the kitchen, but not much, and the bathroom, as you already know. I even keep a cot here for emergencies."

"Like if your apartment gets flooded?" he asked.

No, like that time a few years ago when I was so far behind on my rent that I was evicted, I thought, but didn't say so.

"Something like that. I have a spare set of keys in my desk you can use. Hopefully it won't—"

Then came one of those moments when seven times thirteen equals twenty-eight. Like the old Abbott and Costello routine, things weren't adding up.

There was one key question I had overlooked up to this point... and I mean *key* question.

"Ricky, where were you when the cops tried to arrest you?"

"In Louie's building. I was going up to Klemmer's place, and they were already there."

"How did you get in?"

"What do you mean?"

"You gave me your key to her apartment, remember? I still have it. But that key doesn't work on the front door of the building, so how do you get inside?"

"Well, in the past I always buzzed Louie and she let me in, but when she's not there I either wait for someone to come out or I try other apartments until someone buzzes me in. Since I'd already met Klemmer, I buzzed him today and he—"

He stopped talking and, after a three-count, frowned. "Wait a minute, how could he do that if he was already dead?"

Ah, now we are getting somewhere! Inspector Clouseau said in my cranium.

CHAPTER TWELVE

Unfortunately, we weren't really getting somewhere. We were only sinking deeper in the mire.

"You look like you don't believe me," Ricky Sandoval said.

"Well, here's the problem I'm having. You buzzed Avery Klemmer's apartment and someone let you in, but it couldn't have been Avery, because he was dead. And it couldn't be the killer, because—"

CEASE! W.C. Fields bellowed in my head, cutting me off mid-sentence, before I blurted out that it couldn't have been the killer because I believed the killer had fled the apartment some time earlier, after bashing me on the head in Avery's place, which I was not yet willing to let Ricky, or anyone else, know.

"Why couldn't it have been the killer?" he asked.

"Because the killer would never have buzzed back. He would have run," I ad libbed. "So it had to be the police who let you in. But there's a problem with that, too. You wouldn't be buzzing for Avery unless you thought he was still alive enough to let you in, so why did the cops make you the prime suspect if you believed he was still alive?"

"Maybe they didn't know I believed he was still alive."

"Did you say anything like, 'Hi, Avery,' when they answered the call?"

"No. I pushed the button, and then the door buzzed open. That was it."

"And then you went upstairs and the police were there."

"Right." His brow furrowed as though he was thinking very, very hard, and it hurt him. "You know, maybe I'm wrong. Maybe they didn't try to arrest me for killing Klemmer. Maybe they tried to arrest me for punching that officer in the face."

"You punched an officer in the face?"

"Hey, I don't like being hassled!"

"So you belted a cop and then ran away?"

"Yeah, I guess so."

I wondered how stupid each of the hundred-million sperm who *didn't* make it to his egg had to be.

"Okay, let's start over again, Ricky," I suggested. "At any time, did the police ever identify you?"

"What do you mean?"

"Did you give them your name or your ID?"

"No. All I told them was where I lived."

"So all they have is your description, and address?"

"I guess. Unless I left a knuckle-print on that one cop."

"Okay, fine."

I dug through my desk until I found my spare keys. Tossing them to him I said, "I'm leaving now, after which I'm going straight home. You'll be here alone. But you should be all right. Go out if you need to, but try to stay inconspicuous. There's a little market down the street if you need something. I'll be back tomorrow morning. Okay?"

"You don't have a TV, do you?"

"I'm afraid not."

"Do you have any games on your computer there?"

"Um, no, and it doesn't work anyway." I picked it up and stuck it under my arm. "I have to get it fixed."

"Well, I guess I could go see a movie. I mean, I've still got my car."

"Fine," I agreed. Anything that could keep him in the dark and unrecognizable for a few hours would be a good thing. "I'll be back about eight-thirty tomorrow."

"All right, Mr. Beauchamp." This time it came out *Boo-SHAM.*

"You can call me Dave, Ricky."

"Thanks. And you can call me Ricky."

I said nothing. I just left.

My delay in getting away from the office plus the usual problem parking in Santa Monica meant that I was a few minutes late getting into *The Hound and Badger.* Jack, who was seated at a front table with a half-empty pint glass on the table before him, waved me over.

"Sorry I'm late," I said.

"Not a problem. I've already opened a tab, so order whatever you like, David. Not only that, but I come bearing gifts."

He put a book on the table. "My new one, not even in stores yet."

The title was *Double Agent, Double Death*, and upon opening it up I noticed that it was also double the price of the last book of his that I had actually bought.

"This is really great, Jack, thanks," I said. "I'll start it at once."

"And here's to your finishing it at once as well," he toasted, then took a large gulp of his British-brewed bitter, which I knew from experience was his beer of choice. I had tried it once, and while it wasn't particularly bitter, neither was it a taste I was anxious to acquire.

"Now then, my boy, what kind of trouble have you gotten yourself into?"

"It's not me, Jack, it's someone involved in a case I'm working on."

The English-accented waitress (who was either genuinely from England or a very skilled actress) came over to the table and I ordered a bowl of the *Hound and Badger*'s excellent clam chowder and a glass of cider, which was more to my taste, while Jack got the Happy Hour bowl of banger bits and chips, and another bitter.

When she was gone I went on: "Someone involved in the case has…what's that phrase you like…really stepped in it? Anyway, he's in trouble and has to hide from the police for a while."

"What has he done?"

"Nothing except punch a cop."

"For most people, that would be enough."

"Yeah, well, that's probably still going to come back and bite him in the butt, but for some strange reason, I'm trying to save his butt until then."

"And I might have something that will help you," Jack said, reaching down and grabbing a book-sized box, which he set on the table with a flourish.

Opening it, I thought for a brief second there was an animal inside. Instead it turned out to be a wig. There was also a moustache, a beard, a jar of theatrical spirit gum, some sponges, a tube labeled *Nose Plastic* and a lot of small discs of color.

"This looks like a makeup kit," I said.

"That's because it is," Jack said. "I've had it for years, but never used it."

"I never knew you were an actor."

"An actor? Good god, no. I have enough problems as it is."

The waitress returned with our drinks and food, and I closed the box and set it down under my chair.

We ate in silence for a minute—and however this place made its clam chowder, it was spectacular—before Jack went on:

"As to that kit, many, many years ago, right after I had completed my first novel, I managed to acquire an agent who told me that I was going to be huge."

"I guess he was right," I said.

Jack smiled. "Lee Child is huge, David. James Patterson is huge. Michael Connolly, John Grisham, huge and huger. The best I can claim is slightly overweight, but I'll gladly accept it. The point is, I believed this fellow, and thus went out and bought that kit, assuming that if I ever went out in public I would be mobbed."

"And were you?"

"No, but it turned out the agent was… mobbed up to his hairline, in fact. Before he had the chance to sell my book he took a business trip to New Jersey from which he never returned. I think he's feeling *pier* pressure. Under an actual pier."

"You mean swimming with the fishies?"

"If not feeding them. Anyway, the short version is I got a new agent who eventually sold the book, and it did well, and here I am today, but the very idea that I would become so famous that I needed to go down to the corner liquor store in disguise is now almost embarrassing to admit. That only happens to writers on television, like Jessica Fletcher, who could go to North Korea and be recognized on the street."

"So you think this will work for my guy?" I asked.

"Without a doubt. Instant disguise, just add sunglasses."

"Really?

"Absolutely, because the two most distinguishing characteristics of a face are eye color and the philtrum. You do know what a philtrum is, don't you, David?"

"Yes, I know what a philtrum is," I replied, tracing the vertical indent between the bottom of my nose and my upper lip with my finger. "I do know a few things."

I was expecting Mitchum to weigh in, but instead I got Bogie, not chiming up to insult me, but to chuckle that the only reason I knew what a philtrum was is because his costar from *In a Lonely Place*, Gloria Graham, was so obsessed with hers that she underwent multiple plastic surgeries to make it more pronounced, only to end up looking like she had an ashtray groove under her nose.

Jack went on: "The philtrum can be covered by a moustache and eye color can be disguised by contact lenses, or if one is cheap, sunglasses."

"What about the ears?" I countered. "I thought Sherlock Holmes once said that the shape of the ear was the only feature that could not be disguised."

"He never said that to Leonard Nimoy, did he?"

"Point taken."

"*Touché*, David. If not *toupee*. Wait, that was the other fellow, wasn't it? No matter. Tell me about this friend of yours who's in trouble."

"He's the brother of a client who might also be in trouble, so it's in my client's best interest to keep him out of jail."

"Wasn't your last client murdered?"

"Yes, and I really don't want to see that happen again."

"And you don't think this fellow, the brother, can keep out of trouble on his own?"

I sighed. "Jack, left to his own devices, this fellow is capable of accidentally starting a nuclear war with Canada."

"If it would keep them from exporting teenage pop stars, I'd be all for that," Jack said, signaling the waitress with his empty pint glass.

We continued to chat for another half-hour or so, by which time Jack was on his sixth pint, though I was not particularly worried about him, knowing that he lived close enough to the *Hound and Badger* to walk home, or if that proved difficult was well off enough to hail a cab. After thanking him for the dinner, the book, and the silly makeup kit, and bidding him goodnight, I got up and left.

The scent of the ocean permeated the cool darkness that had descended on Santa Monica. I liked the city at night, but I doubted I could live here. That's the aspect of L.A. that its haters simply don't understand: no matter what environment you want, it's out here somewhere. You only have to find it.

As long as you're searching for what's yours, see if you can find your brain, Robert Mitchum said.

I really should know better than to attempt thoughts.

Despite my original plan to simply head home, part of me wanted to go back to the office to check in on Ricky Sandoval. But I fought it. I was not Louie's brother's keeper. I'd worry about him tomorrow.

But after a predictably long, congested drive from Santa Monica, I suddenly had another idea. Changing course slightly, I headed to Edendale Video and Poster, which is to old movie buffs what Rick's *Café Americain* was to European *émigrés*.

It was named after the small, hilly, one-time suburb of L.A. that housed the first movie studios in Los Angeles, including Mack Sennett's Keystone operation, one building of which still stands today as a storage facility. Countless people stashed their skis in the exact location where Charlie Chaplin twitched his first moustache, without realizing it.

As a suburb it is long gone, having been absorbed into the voracious city of L.A. as the northern extension of Echo Park. Its namesake, Edendale Video, however, remains a thriving business, even in the wake of the download age.

When I walked into the store I saw the owner, Brian McLiamore, a sturdy, balding guy known to everyone as "Mac," behind the counter.

"Hey, Mac, how's it going?" I asked.

"Still here, though I'm toying with the idea of changing the name of the place to 'Download Be Damned'. What'll you have tonight?"

"I need to check out the pre-Temple Palmer Hanley."

"Palmer Hanley? Boy, you really are slumming."

"How can you know what's good if you don't experience the bad?"

"I should have a poster made up with that. Let's see, Palmer Hanley…"

He typed the name into his computer.

"We've got *Zombie Castle* on disc"

I was already familiar with *Zombie Castle*, an old Monogram epic from 1949 featuring Mantan Moreland, a moonfaced, bug-eyed, African American comedian who was so naturally funny he could have gotten laughs laying a wreath at the Tomb of the Unknown, but whose career was effectively over by 1950 because society had become less tolerant of his specialty, frightened black servant roles.

I just hadn't realized Hanley was in it.

Mac was also able to produce a videocassette of an old *Kraft Television Theatre* episode which contained Hanley's last appearance as an actor. Since the show was cribbed from a broadcast and not commercial available, Edendale couldn't charge for the tape, but offered it as a "loaner."

"That's all we've got listed under his name," he said, "'cause you know he'd usually just pop up somewhere in a film, a lot of times uncredited. Have you looked him up on IMDb?"

"Oh, my computer's broken," I said.

"Want me to?"

"No, these two are fine."

After paying for the disc and tape, I stayed to talk movie shop for a little while and then headed out.

Once home, I made some microwave popcorn, grabbed a can of A&W, and put *Zombie Castle* in first. The print of the film etched into the disc was pretty bad, but I doubted if a pristine copy would have made much difference.

The film's story was Poverty Row Plot horror movie plot number five: a group of people find themselves stranded on a strange island inhabited by a mysterious doctor living in an old, creepy cast. The doctor was played by Henry Victor, a sort of road company Bela Lugosi, and the captain of the boat who shipwrecks there was played by an obscure B-movie actor named Dennis Moore.

The real star, though, was Mantan Moreland, who was cast as an incompetent deckhand, years before *Gilligan's Island*. While Moreland mostly did his standard shtick, his repartee with a young, black female cook on the island featured enough grindhouse double entendres to make me wonder how it got past the Breen Office.

Maybe they didn't bother looking at Monogram films.

Palmer Hanley played Victor's assistant, giving a performance that was lifeless even for a Poverty Row picture. In one scene, Hanley appeared so comatose that Moreland waved his hand in front of his face and then looked into the camera and said, "Welcome to the remake of *White Zombie*, folks," right before the shot faded out.

I had to assume it was an ad-lib left in the picture for kicks. At least it was funny.

Watching the *Kraft Television Theatre* episode proved even more revealing. Hanley had a fairly decent role in it, playing a shady talent agent whose primary client, a beautiful young blonde (played by an actress so obscure even I had never heard of her), turns up murdered.

Jack Warden played a movie studio head and Walter Matthau a detective. Both of them were terrific, as usual, but it was easy to see why a career change was inevitable for Hanley.

While his line readings were adequate, it was like watching a mannequin over which dialogue had been dubbed. His face was expressionless and his body made of oak. He moved from one place to another on the set so stiffly that it appeared he was being pulled around by invisible ropes.

Perhaps radio was the best medium for him as an actor, but by the time he decided to become a mystic, radio drama was in its last days.

I went to bed almost feeling sorry for Palmer Hanley…and faintly craving a Burger Heaven Halo combo.

The next morning I slept in a little later than usual, but it was not like anyone was waiting for me at the office.

Oh yeah; Ricky Sandoval.

After finishing my daily routine I gathered up the DVDs and the videocassette and carried them out to the car; I'd drop them off again on the way home tonight. Only then did I realize that I had left Jack's makeup kit on the seat all night, which was no biggie, but I had also left my corrupted laptop in plain sight next to it, which was.

What if someone had spotted it, broken in to the car, taken it and then had seen what was on it? Grabbing the computer, I ran it back into the apartment and stuck it under my mattress.

If I was playing with the dangerous crowd now, I was going to have to be more careful.

Welcome to the mean streets, kid, Bogart said.

On my way to the office I wondered exactly what I would find there. I assumed that Ricky Sandoval would be sprawled out somewhere, perhaps not quite ready to great the day in such an unusual setting, or maybe he would have gone out again and left a note.

As I pulled into my parking spot I wondered if I wasn't going to look like an idiot presenting him with Jack's Johnny Disguise kit, which in the light of day looked ridiculous.

Then again, maybe it didn't matter, since I might have been a total idiot to simply hand over the keys to my office to someone I still only barely knew.

All those in favor, fart, Mitchum said in my head.

Inside, I was about to shove the key in the lock, like always, when I thought maybe I'd better give a little warning. I knocked loudly a couple times, and heard nothing coming from inside, so I opened up. The place was exactly as I had left it the night before.

If Ricky had indeed stayed here, he had done an excellent job of cleaning up after himself.

The message light on my phone was blinking twice, so I went over and hit the playback.

The first message was from Zareh Zarian, and it had come in at nearly midnight. *Yeah, Beauchamp, I just wanted to tell you that I put a rush on that burger patty you purloined from Burger Heaven, but it came back from the lab clean,* his voice said. *Test revealed nothing in it but beef, pepper and MSG. I guess that kinda kills that story, but not Louie's situation. Have you heard from her? I haven't. Call me if you've got something. And send me your damn invoice.*

The message clicked off. The next one had come in at 7:19 this morning.

Dave, Ricky Sandoval's voice said, *I'm in deep shit! I went out early for a run and they found me! They're coming for me now! I can't get away! Oh, shit...it's not the police! Not the police! But they're armed! Oh, mother...what do you want? Let go of me—*

There was the sound of a struggle and then the call ended abruptly.

I sat down on my chair, shaking. What do I do now? Obviously, the sensible thing would be to call the police. Maybe starting with Detective Colfax would be the best idea. I had the number half dialed when I suddenly hung up, having realized something.

Ricky had been carrying the keys to my office. Whoever it was that had gotten to him would now be able to come in here any time they wanted.

How would they know where the keys go? Edward G. Robinson asked inside my head, but that was an easy question to counter.

Assuming that Ricky's assailants did not simply walk up on the street and kill him and leave the body there, which was a reasonable assumption even for L.A., they had taken him someplace.

And having heard the fear in his voice in that telephone message, I doubt it would have taken much in the way of threats or torture for him to reveal the lock that those keys belonged to.

I had to get out of here. I just wondered if I should put Jack's false beard on to do it.

Oh, that's ridiculous! Vincent Price commented in my head, and I'm afraid he was right.

Leaving the kit on my desk, I rushed out and locked the office back up, then dashed down to my car again.

I had only gotten the driver's door open when it felt like the back of my head had suddenly exploded and my Technicolor reality suddenly went monochrome. I dropped down to the pavement, trying to get my bearings, but to no avail. Then I felt a sharp jab in my butt, like someone had stuck me with a pin.

Or a hypodermic needle.

I felt what little consciousness I had left slipping away.

Why wasch jusht tryna get to my carrrr susch a prrroblem theesch daysh....

CHAPTER THIRTEEN

"Come on, kid, snap out of it," a voice said from somewhere above me. I felt my cheeks being slapped, and not too gently, either.

Opening my eyes, I found myself staring into the face of Humphrey Bogart. He was wearing a fedora and a trenchcoat, collar turned up at the back, a tightly cinched tie, and he smelled of cigarettes.

In person he looked older that I remembered seeing him on the screen. Why was he here?

He helped me get to my feet, which probably wasn't easy since he was very slightly built and a good four inches shorter than I was. I mean, I'd always heard he was small, but I expected more than this.

I was in my office, only it was different. It took me a second to figure out why: just like Bogie, the office was in black-and-white.

"What happened to me?" I moaned as I slumped into my chair behind the desk.

"You got sapped, kid," Bogie told me.

The funny thing was, my head didn't hurt like it should have, particularly since it was the second time I'd been brained in the last couple days. I remembered getting hit, but there was no pain.

"Then somebody stuck a needle in your ass."

"I didn't think the Production Code let you talk like that."

"I could say any goddamned thing I wanted to in the outtakes."

"Makes sense," I said.

As much sense as conversing with Humphrey Bogart, who had died a quarter century before I was born. "You didn't happen to see who attacked me, did you?"

Bogie shook his head. "I didn't see a thing. How about you, Angel?"

Now Lauren Bacall slunk out from my kitchenette. "I saw a shadow, but I couldn't make it out," she said.

"Oh, man, I'm dreaming, right?" I asked.

"Who knows?" a new voice asked, and I looked over to see Orson Welles, the Orson Welles of the 1940s, before he had grown the enormous beard and put on a couple hundred pounds. "Maybe this is reality, or maybe what you're used to is really the dream," he intoned, in the suspicious Irish brogue he used in *The Lady from Shanghai*.

"None of you are being very comforting," I told them. "Oh, god, I'm not *dead* am I?"

"You're not dead," Bogie said. That was at least something. "Let's go, kid, we need to talk."

"Go where?" I asked, but before I could say anything else, my office literally dissolved into the inside of a 1939 Plymouth De Luxe, gray, of course, since it was still black-and-white. Bogie was driving, and the coastline of the Pacific Ocean was visible through his window.

"That was…interesting," I said. "Where are we?"

"Stage 7, Warner Bros.," Bogie answered. "Now shut up and listen. You remember the scene they cut out of *The Big Sleep* to make room for Angel Face?"

I remembered the scene. In the original cut of *The Big Sleep*, which was seen only by servicemen overseas in 1945, there was a long sequence of Philip Marlowe being hauled into the D.A.'s office to explain what he knew about the Sternwood case, which also allowed the confused audience to get up-to-speed regarding the plot.

And if that scene did not conclusively reveal who had killed Owen Taylor, the Sternwood chauffeur, at least it offered a convincing speculation.

But that scene was cut out when retakes and re-editing were ordered so as to beef up "Angel Face" Lauren Bacall's role, and give her more provocative sequences with Bogart, including the infamous "A-lot-depends-on-who's-in-the-saddle" scene.

"What does that have to do with me?" I asked Bogie.

"Recreate it, kid, only with this case you're on. Tell me everything you know about it."

"Well…a young woman came to me dressed as a tomato, because she had been playing an ingredient outside a Burger Heaven restaurant…you don't know what Burger Heaven is, do you, Bogie?"

"I know what it is, but it can't hold a candle to Chasen's."

"Fair enough. Anyway, she was really a newspaper reporter working undercover. She suspected they were putting something in the burger patties that wasn't right, some kind of bad food additive, and she came to me because she began to suspect they suspected her."

"That's a lot of suspicion."

"It gets worse. The tomato disappeared and there was an ominous message on her phone machine. Oh, you probably don't know what a phone machine is, do you?"

"I'm dead, kid, not ignorant. I know what a phone machine is. Go on."

"I get it," I said. "Since I've conjured you up out of my imagination, you know everything I know."

"Next time you conjure me up, make me taller. Now keep talking."

"All right. Louie…Luisa…the tomato vanishes, and her editor at the newspaper hires me to try and find her notes of the case. I try and end up running into the nerd who lives in the apartment next door to her, who's got a crush on her bordering on obsession."

"Now he sounds like a suspect," Bogie said.

"Yeah, except for the fact that he turned up murdered a couple days later. I found the body, and I managed to drop my cell phone in his apartment, where it was found by the police."

I assumed he knew what a cell phone was.

"And now they think you did it."

"I actually worked my way out of that one. At least I think I did. But there's someone else that the police suspect, Louie's dunderhead brother, who ran away from the police and was hiding out in my office. But now he's in trouble, too."

"How so?"

"I'm not sure. He left a call on my machine saying they were after him, but before I could check it out, I got clubbed from behind."

"That it?"

"No, there's also a dancer named Regina who also got herself murdered, though why I have no idea."

"What's her connection to the case?"

"She seems to have been the one who got Louie involved. She also appears to have been Louie's lesbian lover."

Bogie's eyebrows raised and he muttered, "Ohhhhh."

"She also seems to be tied into a pseudo-church called the Temple of Theotologics. There. I think that's everything."

"Mm-hmmm."

"That's all you've got? Just 'mm-hmmm?'"

"What more do you want?"

"Well, you could tell me what, if anything, it all means, and who keeps killing people."

"You sure you don't know?"

"I haven't a clue, and I mean that literally."

"Look at it this way, kid," Bogie said. "You've got a dead dancer, a dead little creep, a dunderhead brother, who by now may be dead for all we know, so what connects them all?"

"Nothing, as near as I can figure, except…oh. Oh, no."

"Mm-hmmm. The thing that connects them all is the tomato, and she's the only thing, from the sound of it."

"I can't believe that," I uttered. "Not Louie."

"You think I wanted to believe Miss Wonderly was behind all the blackbird carnage? Sometimes you have to face facts. Your tomato disappears and people she knows start turning up dead. It wouldn't surprise me if she was the one who sapped you. Kind of poetic, when you think about it: a sap for a sap."

"Have you been talking to Mitchum?" I asked.

Bogie smiled. "I overhear sometimes."

"Okay, there's one thing I forgot to mention," I said, desperately. "Louie's apartment had been ransacked, like someone was searching for something. I assumed it for was her notes on the Burger Heaven investigation."

"So?"

"So, doesn't that exonerate her?"

"She could have turned the place over herself to throw off suspicion."

"Then what about that threatening message on her phone machine?"

"Do you know who left the message?"

"No."

"Do the police?"

"I have no idea. I don't know if they ever heard it."

"So you're the only one who heard the message."

"No, Avery heard it, too. He's the dead little creep."

"Which means he can't confirm your story."

"Right, but…hey, what are you saying? That I imagined hearing the message?"

"Well, kid, you have to admit, you do have a history of hearing voices."

I opened my mouth to protest, but nothing came out. How could I argue with a long-dead movie star that I was not given to imagining things?

Finally I said, "I'm still having a hard time believing that Louie is responsible."

"Suit yourself," Bogie said, pulling the car over to the side of the road. "I've done all I can, kid, so here's your stop. Go on, get out."

I got out of the Plymouth and looked around. To Bogie it may have looked like Stage 7 at Warner Bros., but to me it looked like a real road next to a real cliff that led down to the real Pacific Ocean, but all in black-and-white.

"Do I have to walk now?"

"No, somebody'll be by. Good luck, kid."

With that, Humphrey Bogart drove away, leaving me on the side of the road. He was right, though; several other cars came by. One was driven by no one, but had the Three Stooges in the back seat. That one I let pass. Another one was a Porsche Spyder driven by James Dean, and that one I *definitely* let pass.

Then a convertible pulled to the side to pick me up. It was driven by Ann Savage, the femme fatale of the no-budget noir classic *Detour*. "How far you going?" she asked, a cigarette dangling dangerously from her lips.

"As far as it takes to find the truth," I replied.

"I don't think this heap's got enough gas for that. But get in."

I got in and she pulled back onto the highway. All of a sudden I was aware that it was hot. "I'm glad you came along," I said.

"I'll bet you are," she sneered. "What particular truth are you looking for?"

Since unloading the details of the case to Bogart had resulted in a depressing thought, I didn't want to repeat the experience. So I just shrugged.

Besides, since this was all happening somewhere inside my mind, she must already know.

All happening somewhere inside my mind.

"Mind if I ask you a question?" I said.

"You just did," she replied, her cigarette bobbing, its ash falling on her blouse.

"Right. Well, since you wanted to know what particular truth I'm looking for, here it is. It's not who killed Louie or who killed Regina or what happened to Ricky. I want to know if I'm crazy. I mean, not just a little wacky, but certifiably, lock-him-up insane. So insane that I imagine phone messages. So insane that I talk to dead actors. So insane that I fall for murderers. Am I really that crazy?"

"How the hell should I know?" dead actor Ann Savage, playing a murderer, asked in my imagination.

"Well, because you're me."

She looked over at me, her eyes scanning me up and down. "I may have had some bad mornings, Poindexter, but I never got up looking like you."

"What I mean is, you're in my head. I'm essentially talking to myself."

"No, you're dreaming. There's a difference."

"This is still taking place inside my brain."

"'Bout time something did," she said, turning to smirk at me. "I overhear sometimes, too."

Can't I conjure up anyone who actually *likes* me, I thought, desperately.

Then it hit me. "My god, *I'm* the one who's always insulting me and insisting I'm a failure," I said aloud. "It's *me*. That's my problem."

"Go collect your kewpie doll, Ace," she said, with something that almost resembled a smile.

Then she glanced in the rearview mirror. "We've got a bigger problem, though."

"What?" That was when I heard the siren coming from behind us.

"They're onto us. Cops."

"You sure it's us they want?" I asked.

"You see anyone else on the road? Hang on." She stomped on the accelerator and the car's tires practically left the pavement.

"What are you doing?" I screamed. "You're going to try to outrun the police?"

"Got no choice. They know what I've got in the trunk."

I threw my hands up in the air and began to wonder if I shouldn't have gone with the Three Stooges after all.

The siren was getting louder, more insistent. I looked back and saw that the 1940s-style police cruiser was only about four car lengths behind us. I also saw an officer lean out of the passenger window and point a gun at us.

"Jeez!" I cried as the bullet ricocheted off the side of the car.

Ann Savage, meanwhile, looked unconcerned, like she had done this before. "Gonna let a little thing like a bullet spook you?" she asked.

"It can spook me all it wants, I just don't want it to kill me!"

The second bullet pinged even closer.

"You worry too much."

"Oh, do I? I'll have to bring that up at the next Corpses Anonymous meeting!"

"I think it's cute the way you get so glib when you're scared."

Swell. I hope she found it just as cute that I got so dead when I was shot.

A third bullet whizzed by, but it was the fourth one that put an end to the chase. It hit one of the rear tires and blew it out, and immediately the car began to weave uncontrollably.

Ann tried to bully it back into the lane by wrenching the steering wheel one way, then the other, but it was too late. We were careening off the highway and onto the shoulder.

Unfortunately, it was the shoulder on the cliff side.

We went to the edge of the cliff, and then over, plummeting straight down to the water's edge.

I had seen such a shot a thousand times in a movie or TV show, but never from the point of view of the front seat!

I'm dreaming I'm dreaming I'm dreaming I can't die in a dream I can't be killed in a dream…my brain was screaming. Or maybe it was me screaming. I couldn't tell. All I knew is that we hit the water.

I could feel it on my face…

CHAPTER FOURTEEN

I could feel the water on my face, which shocked me back to consciousness.

I opened my eyes and saw someone standing over me, a big, burly guy holding an empty tumbler.

"Sorry," he said, in such a way that conveyed he wasn't sorry in the slightest and, in fact, had enjoyed throwing a glassful of water into my face. And would like to do it again sometime, only with boiling coffee.

The guy wore a uniform, but it was one I could not place; not quite military, but close, with epaulets on the shoulders of the white, starched shirt. The creases on legs of his black pants could have sliced cheese.

I shook my head, throwing beads of water off in every direction. "Where am I?" I asked.

"The place where bad people go," the guy said.

I guess that meant I was either in Hell or Washington D.C.

"Why am I here?"

"I just told you."

"When can I leave?"

"That's up to you."

"Okay, fine. How about right now."

The guy didn't smile. He looked like he wasn't sure how. "I can't do that," he said.

"Then how about this? Why not tell me what's going on. I assume I've been kidnapped, but why?"

"I'm not at the proper adjustment level to give you information," he said, unlocking the door of whatever holding tank I was in and opening it.

I suppose I could have tried to rush him and get past him, but I was never very good at that sort of thing. Besides, now my head was dully aching.

The bigger truth was, I was disoriented. Maybe this was still part of my dream, but instead of Vera from *Detour*, this time I was in the company of an unbilled extra.

No, 'cause your cranium hurts, kid, Bogart said. *You don't feel pain in dreams.*

Swell.

The guy was out of the room, which gave me an opportunity to inspect it further. It was a regulation prison cell, sized six-by-eight, and came complete with a cot, upon which I had been sprawled prior to being splashed awake, a metal sink and a toilet. The door had a small barred window in it.

Compounding the suspicion that I was in somebody's jail was reinforced by the fact that I was no longer wearing my own clothes, but had instead been changed into an orange prison jumpsuit.

The thing was, I didn't recall any arrest or booking.

There was no need to check for my wallet or keys, since they would have been taken by my captors, and I didn't have to worry about my cell phone, since the police still had it.

My only options at present were to sit down and try to figure out where I was, or wait until someone of a higher "level" showed up to fill me in. Maybe the most surprising thing about this descent into surrealism was the fact that the prison jumpsuit was really comfortable.

With nothing better to do, I sat on the cot, leaned back and closed my eyes, and absentmindedly rubbed my chin in a parody of thought.

And that was when I truly became afraid.

I rubbed my chin again, then my cheeks, my upper lip and my neck. I had at least two days worth of beard stubble.

Going to the small window in the door, I started yelling. I kept it up until someone appeared on the other side, not the guy who had thrown water on me, but someone older, with more pseudo-military decorations on his pristine white shirt.

"What do you want?" he asked placidly.

"How long have I been here?" I demanded.

"Two days, though transporting you here took an additional day."

"And I've been unconscious the whole time?"

"We couldn't very well have you alert during this process. Someone might have gotten hurt."

"Who is *we*?" I shouted, having a terrible feeling that I already knew.

"Things will be revealed on an as-needed basis."

"At least tell me why I've been kidnapped by the Temple of Theotologics," I said, taking a stab at the truth.

"Kidnapped by the Temple of Theotologics," the guy repeated. "That sounds paranoid. Have you been diagnosed as suffering from paranoia?"

"I'll bet you have a program to fix that," I said.

"Oh, many."

"How about murder. Do you have a program to fix murder?"

The man shook his head. "There you go again. Definitely paranoia. We'll have to have one of our adjusters come in to talk to you."

"I'll be happy to talk to anyone," I said. "Ideally someone over your pay grade."

"Low self-esteem, too. You have to try and tear someone else down in order to make yourself seem more important? I'd say we've gotten you just in time."

"Since you've brought the subject up, what time is it?"

The man glanced at his watch and then said, "Five thirty-five. Almost dinner time."

"Great. I'll have a Twin Halo combo."

"A what?" The fellow looked genuinely confused.

"A Twin Halo, from Burger Heaven. The Temple owns Burger Heaven, don't they? That's why I'm here, isn't it?"

"Oh, you mean that fast food chain in California?"

In California?

Wherever I was it was not in my home state. My daylong transport to this charming prison must have been achieved via airplane. "Is that five thirty-five Pacific time?"

The man stared at me, an expression of uncertainty playing on this face. "Five thirty-five is all you need to know."

"How about you go get one of your superiors, of which I assume there are many. Maybe they can tell me where I am."

"You're a very negative person," he replied. "You seriously need adjusting."

With that he scampered away.

Okay, so if I wasn't in California, where was I? A day's transport, he said. If it was by jet, I could be in Europe, though I can't imagine how they would have gotten me through customs.

Where could one build a secret compound within the United States that would be hidden from everybody? My gut told me Colorado, but that might only be because NORAD is situated there.

I started pacing back and forth, trying to think of how I was going to get out of this one.

"Hey, Mitch," I said aloud, "you were in stir. What did you do to pass the time?"

Told myself stories and tried not to think about how I wasn't going to get laid for a while, Robert Mitchum's voice replied in my head. *I was able to make up for it later*.

Fine, I'd try to tell myself stories. I started with the story of a tomato walking into a detective's office, but in the stillness of the cell it did not take long for me to nearly think myself back to sleep.

Maybe there was still some residual knock-out drug in my system, or maybe I was simply reacting to boredom, like the homeless on the streets of Los Angeles, who are seen sleeping most of the day because they don't have any reasons to remain conscious.

I was brought back to alertness by the sound of my cell door being opened.

Two people entered the room, one a middle-aged fellow in what looked at first glance like a full naval uniform…blue double-breasted blazer with epaulets, white slacks and a captain's hat…and a woman I recognized immediately: the security guard from the Sherman Oaks Burger Heaven, whom I also thought I had spotted following me in the grocery store. I had not been certain at the time, but now there would seem to be little doubt. She was wearing a similar uniform to the one the man had on.

"So, which of you is the adjuster?" I asked.

"An adjustment session cannot be conducted here," the man said. "It requires a special room with special equipment." Then, turning to the woman, he asked: "Is this the man, Marta?"

After a second's hesitation, she said, "Yes, that's him."

"You are certain, beyond any doubt?"

"I am indeed the man she met in the Burger Heaven," I said. "Now that we have established that, I have a few dozen more questions of my own."

"You would swear in a court of law that this is the man who raped you?" the guy in the uniform went on.

"Whoa, whoa, whoa, *what*?" I shouted. "*Raped* her? That's bull!"

"You'd swear in court?" he asked again.

"If I had to, yes," Marta replied.

"Very well, you may go."

The woman exited the room, but the man remained.

"Listen, Colonel Klink," I said, "I don't know what you think you are trying to pull here, but I never touched that woman! Good god, even if I had she probably could have killed me!"

"Gordon's judgment was right," he replied with a smirk. "Low self-esteem."

I assumed Gordon was the first one who showed up in the cell, though I also sensed that bit of information was going to do me precious little good.

"So what's the plan? Are you going to charge me with low self-esteem in the first degree? Or just this trumped-up rape charge?"

"We aren't charging you with anything," he said. "We are not a court of law."

"Just a jail."

"A facility."

"I don't know what country you think we're in, but you can't just abduct someone and hold them in a private jail. There are things called laws."

"Funny you should mention country. The Temple of Theotologics is a global entity. We acknowledge that there are countries, but we don't recognize their authority."

Crazy as a bedbug, the voice of Peter Lorre wheezed inside my head, and I had to agree.

"Well, the people outside this facility might."

His smirk widened as he reached behind him to open the cell door and stepped backwards through it, then closed it again. Looking through the barred window, he said: "They haven't yet."

Then he was gone.

How in heaven's name had I gotten myself into this mess? Why was I so dangerous to the Temple of Theotologics?

Cause you know where the bodies are buried, Charles McGraw told me, his sandpaper voice abrading my throbbing head.

But I didn't! I didn't even know *if* they'd been buried yet!

Okay, kid, how about this? the more comforting voice of Humphrey Bogart chimed in. *They think you found the evidence.*

Louie's notes? But I hadn't found them.

But they think *you did, which is good and bad. Bad because you're here, but good because as long as they think you've got the stuff and are holding out on them, they'll keep you alive.*

"So I need to carry on a bluff?" I asked aloud.

You got a better idea? And stop talking out loud, kid. This place is probably bugged, too.

That was a good point.

Okay, fine; I'd bluff and see where it got me, because like Bogie had pointed out, I didn't have a better idea.

Or any idea, for that matter. But what would I tell them? The fact that my clothes were removed while I was unconscious means they must have searched all my pockets, so if I were carrying a flash drive they would have found it.

I didn't want to think about where else they might have checked while I was in forced dreamland. So what did that leave as options? I could claim to have found the stick and mailed it to Zareh Zarian at the *Independent Journal*, stating that at this very moment he was publishing the information and reporting confirming Louie's disappearance to the police.

But if that were the case, there would be no reason for them to keep me alive. They could dispose of me and then go after Zarian.

All right, Fabrication B: I found the stick and hid it. By now, I would imagine, my office, if not my apartment as well, has been completely turned upside-down from a search, and they would have found nothing.

So the hiding place has to be off the premises. A safety-deposit box? Maybe.

But then I could be tortured until I gave up its location, which I would have to make up, because no such safety-deposit box existed.

While that sounded pretty extreme, even for someone with a weekend pass to Kafkaland, I had to anticipate every eventuality, no matter how unreal it sounded. "Flash drive…flash drive…" I muttered, then remembered Bogie's admonishment not to speak aloud.

No, that one was okay, kid, he chimed in. *If they are listening, you've just got them to pay attention.*

That assumption was borne out one long, boring hour later—or maybe it was only fifteen minutes, it was hard to tell—when Colonel Klink came back to the window.

"Good news, Mr. Beauchamp," he said. "You have been granted a shower." He unlocked the door and held it open. "Follow me."

Stepping out into the hallway, I looked both ways and quickly realized there was no use in attempting to make a run for it. Uniformed guards were stationed at both ends.

I followed the man past what appeared to be two other cells before turning a corner and heading down another corridor, which terminated in a large, open shower room, the kind one might find in a public gym.

"You no longer need to wear the orange," Klink said. "Some clothes have been placed on the bench for you. I hope they fit. There is also an electric shaver, should you wish to neaten yourself up a bit."

"Um, no one's going to watch this, are they?"

"What a depraved notion. Are you some kind of kink as well as paranoiac, Mr. Beauchamp?"

"Since you didn't say 'no' to my question, I'll that it as a 'yes,'" I said, and Klink's face soured.

I waited until he closed the door to check out my new clothes—a white shirt and black slacks, of course—and examined the shaver. It was an expensive German one that took care of my stubble in short order, after which I peeled out of the jumpsuit and stepped into the shower.

Soap and shampoo had been provided, and I took ample advantage of soap, and as much advantage of the shampoo as my tender noggin would permit. Having rendered myself as pink and wrinkly as I was able to stand, I shut off the water and reached for the towel that had been provided. Once dry, I checked out the clothes, which, I was pleased to see, included underwear (though they were boxers, whereas I traditionally wore briefs…probably an homage to my days as a lawyer) and socks.

Once I was buttoning up the shirt I noticed there was a word stenciled across the front: *VISITOR*. While a bit stiff, the clothes were not uncomfortable, though the jumpsuit was better. The polished black patent leather shoes were also a bit stiff, because they were new, but they fit well enough, and were in better shape than any of my own shoes.

Maybe if I survived this nightmare I'd get to keep them as a consolation prize.

As I was combing my damp hair with my fingers, Colonel Klink returned.

"Aha," I said, "you *were* watching."

"I don't know what you're talking about."

"How else would you know that I had finished showering and was dressed? You came in the exact moment I was done in here, which means you had to be spying on me."

"You seriously need—"

"Adjusting, yeah, I know. All right, commandant, where to now?"

I was marched by Colonel Klink from the shower area to an elevator, which took us up to a much more corporate-looking floor that came complete with organizational logos on the walls—artfully designed twin "T"s that made the letters look faintly cross-like—and a conference room with a huge table and plush chairs.

I was walked past it and on to a cafeteria, whose presence I detected by the aroma before I ever saw it. I didn't want to admit it to my captors by I was starving and would probably have told them anything for a sizzling grilled cheeseburger and an ice cold root beer.

There were a handful of people inside the cafeteria, each one in a matching white-and-black uniform, though with different levels of bars above the pocket and epaulets on the shoulders.

When I entered, in the company of Colonel Klink, everyone stopped what they were doing to look at me.

"Hi, folks, I'm the new Visitor!" I called out, cheerfully, a move that earned me a strong push over to the food counter.

Whatever else one wanted to say about the Temple of Theotologics, they put on a good spread at meal time. After some deliberation, I decided on the hot roast beef sandwich with what looked like real mashed potatoes and homemade gravy, with fresh steamed green beans on the side. After receiving my plate, and a large glass of (you guessed it) root beer, I was escorted by Klink to a table.

"I hope your opinion of us has altered a little," he said, as I sat down.

"You know, you've never told me your name," I said, as I cut a large chunk of the hot roast beef and bread and prepared to shove it into my mouth.

"Dan," he replied.

After swallowing the mouthful, and finding it almost insanely good, I said, "Well, Dan, I really try to make it a personal point not to diss people who give me food. I'm not going to have to pay for this, am I?"

He smiled. "Not in terms of money, no."

"There you have it then. Once I get out I will tell anyone that the headquarters of the Temple of Theotologics, if that is in fact where I am, has the best chef of any church I've ever been to, and that includes Church's Fried Chicken."

"You enjoy being glib, don't you?"

How strange he should ask. Even stranger was that, thanks to plunging over a cliff with Ann Savage, I could actually answer him.

I swallowed another bite and said, "Well, Dan, it's funny, but I really don't. Since everyone I've met here has taken an interest in improving my character, let me help you by providing a little insight into it. See, some people when they're frightened get nervous or sweat, or maybe begin stuttering, but not me. I become glib. Don't ask me why, because I never knew this about myself until a very short time ago. But thinking back over all the times that I've said the wrong thing in a touchy situation, things I hadn't really intended to, I now have to admit it's true. It's a defense mechanism, I guess. So if you get an attitude from me, that means I'm really scared witless, and since fear is a sensation that I don't particularly care for, I have to say that no, I don't enjoy being glib."

Dan smiled and seemed to puff up a bit, as though my confession of being scared was all the nourishment he required at the moment, like every other psychic vampire.

"*I* make you fearful, don't I?"

If that's what he wants, kid, give it to him, Bogie instructed me. *You can always take it away later.*

"You?" I looked down at my plate and took a big dramatic breath, hoping I wasn't overdoing it so much as to get another critical review from Gary Cooper.

"You make me feel less than comfortable, Dan. I'm sorry. I hope you won't take my food away for saying that."

"Of course not, Mr. Beauchamp," he said, putting his hand on my shoulder. "You can have seconds if you wish."

"That would be outstanding," I replied. I went back to eating and a second later a realization hit me like a fist to the head.

It was something Dan had said repeatedly, and it wasn't so much what he was saying, but the way he said it. It was my name; several times he had called me "Mr. Beauchamp," and each time he had *pronounced it correctly*. To me that strongly implied he had not simply read by name off of my confiscated driver license, but had been instructed in its pronunciation by someone I know.

The list of possible someones was short: Louie, Ricky or possibly Zarian. Zarian was a long shot, frankly, and Ricky had already started to forget how to pronounce my name while still talking to me, which left Louie as the prime suspect.

While that indicated she was still alive and safe, it did not tell me on which side of this abduction was she working?

After finishing my meal, and going so far as to apologize for getting a spot of brown gravy on my pristine white shirt, an act of contrition that also seemed to please Dan, my tray was taken from the table by a uniformed busboy and my guard asked me to follow him out of the cafeteria.

Instead of going back to the elevator to return to my cell, we went down another hallway, this one adorned with photos of Palmer Hanley, both candid shots and stills from the few movies he'd made. There was even one from *Zombie Castle* with him and Mantan Moreland…or what should have been Mantan Moreland. But in this shot while Mantan's body was still there, his head had been replaced by the visage of comic actor Billy Gilbert, who was white! I couldn't even imagine why the Temple authorities deemed that necessary.

"That's our illustrious founder," Dan commented.

"Billy Gilbert?" I asked, innocently.

"Who? Oh, you mean the other actor. How glib. No, Palmer Hanley."

"Yes, I'm familiar with Mr. Hanley's work."

"Really?"

I felt fairly certain he was waiting for me to make a caustic remark about the quality of work (or lack thereof) left behind for posterity by Palmer Hanley, but I restrained myself and simply nodded.

Other photos showed an older Hanley on horseback, on a boat, seated at the head of a conference table, and getting a star on the Hollywood Walk of Fame, which I was pretty sure was also bogus.

At the end of the hallway was a large double door, like you find in a hospital, and going through it led to what looked like a hotel corridor, with numbered rooms. Dan stopped at one labeled "22" and knocked on the door, and then inserted a key and opened it. Inside was a comfortable looking suite, like one might find at any quality Hilton or Hyatt.

Then Dan called out, "I'm not alone."

A second later Luisa Sandoval, dressed in a white "Visitor" blouse and pressed black slacks, walked out from another room.

"I believe you two know each other," Dan said, as Louie stared at me, her mouth open.

"We've met," I said.

"Good. I'll leave you now."

"Wait," she said, as he turned to leave the apartment. "What are we supposed to do in here?"

"Talk things over," Dan replied, exiting the suite and locking the door behind him.

Once he had gone Louie ran up and put her arms around me. "Dave, I'm so sorry I got you into this mess."

"It's okay, Louie."

"It's not okay! You don't know what's going on!"

Putting my mouth close to her ear, I whispered, "Don't say anything else. I'm pretty sure this place is bugged."

She started to say "Bugged?" but I covered her mouth and looked around. Searching for a hidden mic was impractical, as someone would surely come into the suite long before we had checked behind every wall hanging and under every lamp and through every piece of furniture.

"Bathroom," I whispered.

"It's that way," she whispered back, pointing.

"No, I mean let's go there to talk."

She led me to the bathroom, which, as I had hoped, had a switch for a fan. A nice, loud fan, which would obscure anything we said.

Just to make sure, I also turned on the water in the shower. Since we were apparently no longer in California, the drought wasn't a concern.

But even after turning on the faucets I spoke in a whisper. "Louie, they put us together because they think I found your notes on your investigation of Burger Heaven. They think we'll talk about it and reveal where you hid them, and then they can go get them."

"How do you know I hid my notes?" she whispered back.

"Pure surmise. But Zarian thinks you did, too."

"How do you know Z?"

"Technically, I'm working for him. What did you do with your notes?"

"I copied them on a stick."

"Where is it?"

She told me, and I actually hit my head for my own stupidity at not figuring it out, and then regretted it, given my head's other recent abuse. At least I felt certain no one else would ever find it, either.

"Dave, I'm sorry I had to get you involved in this," Louie said.

"Don't stress over it. But I'm afraid I have bad news. It's about Regina Fontaine."

Now she looked wary. "You know Regina?"

"I met her. Louie, Regina was murdered."

She stepped back from me, her face suddenly turning the color of plaster. "My god."

"I'm sorry," I said. "I know how close you two were."

"There was no reason to go after Regina!"

"She became a threat to them. At least they believed so." At this point there was no reason to explain who I thought *they* were.

"Regina was your source for the story about Burger Heaven putting something in the meat, wasn't she?"

Louie nodded. "She contacted the paper because she thought something funny was going on. She didn't tell me at first about her connection with the Temple, but I found out. Then I began to put two-and-two together. Oh, god. Regina never did anyone any harm."

She looked up at me. "Wait a minute, what do you mean you know how close we were?"

"I, uh, found a photo in your dresser."

"You *what*?"

"I'm sorry, but you were missing and I was investigating, and that's what I turned up. I apologize for the invasion of privacy, but I was only trying to find you."

"And now you have."

"And now I have."

"And now I suppose you want me to tell you all about our relationship. Will it turn you on if I do, Dave?"

"You don't have to tell me—"

"It was something that happened, that's all."

"Did you sleep with her to get information from her?"

"I hardly had to. Regina was lost. She was searching for something in her life, anything, and she reached out to me, and then became dependent on me, and…you know, I don't have to tell you anything about this."

"You're right, you don't," I said. "But at least tell me this. Who took the picture for you?"

"What do you mean who?"

"Is there another person involved in this?"

"Like a *ménage à trois*, you mean? This is turning you on, isn't it?"

"I need to know if there's someone else I should be worrying about right now, that's all."

Now she adopted a seductive look. "Sure that's all?" I remained silent and she said, "Okay, fine. No, nobody took the picture. We put the camera on the table and set the timer. Satisfied?"

"Yeah."

"Dave, it was just one of those things. If you play your cards right, I'll tell you all about it sometime. Right now I think we need to figure out how we're going to get out of here."

"I have been thinking about that, and I think I've got an idea."

So much thinking from such a little brain, I heard Robert Mitchum say. Shut up, Mitch.

"It had better be good."

"What if we stage a show for them?"

"What are you talking about?"

"Assuming someone *is* listening, or maybe even watching us through a hidden camera, we start discussing the case and where your notes are hidden, only it's all bogus. We give them false information."

"But if we give them any information, even if it's false, won't we be jeopardizing our lives?"

"They can't do anything to us until they find your notes, and if we keep giving them false information, they won't find them," I argued.

"Maybe you're right," she said. "But what do we say?"

"We'll make something up. If Ricky weren't already in trouble or maybe even captured himself, I'd say you should claim to have given them to him."

"Who's Ricky?"

"Ricky, Ricardo."

She gazed at me uncomprehendingly. "You want me to say I gave my notes to Desi Arnaz? I thought he was dead."

"What? Oh, Ricky Ricardo. I can't believe I didn't realize that before."

"Dave, you're not making any sense. Who is Ricky Ricardo?"

"Come on, Louie, your brother, Ricky. Remember?"

A strange, dark expression enveloped her face and she fell silent.

"What's the matter?" I asked.

"I remember Ricky, Dave," Louie finally said. "I remember him very well. I remember the last time I saw him, too. I was nine."

"Nine? How can that be? The photo of the two of you—"

"It was at his funeral, Dave. My brother Ricky died when he was eleven."

CHAPTER FIFTEEN

"I don't believe it," I muttered, too softly to be heard over the sounds of the fan and the shower.

Unless my schizophrenia, if that's what it really was, had expanded to including completely hallucinating dead people instead of simply hearing their voices, I had been chumped by someone pretending to be Louie's brother, someone who knew enough about her to know that she had a long dead male sibling, and someone with enough smarts to dummy up a photograph of himself with Louie and plant it in her apartment as a proof of his story.

That implied two things: one, that the person that I knew as Ricky Sandoval was nowhere near as stupid as he pretended to be; and two, that he was up to his neck in this mess, if not behind it altogether.

In fact, it had probably been he who had had clubbed me over the head, drugged me, and then brought me here. He certainly looked strong enough to carry my unconscious body.

"Which means he also must have been the one who killed Regina," I said aloud.

"Who are we talking about?" Louie asked.

"The guy who claimed to be your brother. He's probably also the one who killed Avery."

"Hold on a minute. You're not talking about that junior stalker who lives next door to me, are you? You're telling me he's been murdered too?"

I nodded. "What's more, I think I heard it taking place, because that's when I was in your apartment looking around."

"How did you get in?"

"Well, the first time the manager let me in and—"

"He did *what*? Jesus Christ!"

"He only did it once and it took a lot of convincing," I said. "The last time I was there I had a key."

I thought it best not to mention my balcony-to-balcony flying squirrel routine.

"The last time? Am I subletting to you now and don't realize it? Where the hell did you get a key?"

"From Ricky, at least from the guy who told me he was your brother. Now that I think about it, he's probably the one who tore your place apart looking for—"

"Who did *what*?"

"Someone tossed your apartment looking for your notes."

"This just gets better and better!" she cried. "This is starting to sound like a bad thriller movie! I don't believe this shit is happening!"

"I think it's happening because they know you have the power to stop the Temple, or at least make things uncomfortable for them, and they just can't let that happen. Maybe the reason it seems like a bad conspiracy thriller movie is because the guy who founded the Temple only did bad movies, and they're paying homage to him."

"They've known everything all along," she said. "I thought I was uncovering all this groundbreaking information, and they've been ahead of me the whole time, probably laughing. But god, why did they have to kill Regina? And that kid next door? He was a dweeb, but he didn't deserve to die."

Louie's eyes bored into mine. "I'm next, aren't I? They're going to kill me, too, aren't they?"

"Not if I can help it. But what did you discover about the Temple that's so damaging they're going to these extremes?"

"I found out what really happened to Palmer Hanley, the guy who started this operation."

"He's been dead for years. Oh, jeez, don't tell me they killed him too!"

Louie smiled and shook her head.

"They did not, because he's not dead. According to Regina, Palmer Hanley is still alive and being held prisoner by the Temple."

Now that was news. "Are you sure?" I asked.

"I've uncovered enough information to at least open an investigation into it. If I ever get the chance to publish it."

"Where is he?"

"That I don't know, but I was told they're just waiting for him to die, and then they'll quietly plant him somewhere, and nobody will ever know."

"But why bother to fake his death? I mean, if he's still alive, why not use him as the spokesman?"

Crazy, am I? the near-hysterical voice of Colin Clive, "Dr. Frankenstein," crowed in my head.

"Oh, I get it," I said. "He's senile, right?"

"Apparently not," Louie replied. "Apparently he's perfectly sharp and reasonably fit for an old man, but he's repudiated what the Temple has become. If they ever let him out, he'd be the one to blow the whistle for the entire cult."

"So they can't let that happen," I muttered, "and they'll do anything to keep that from happening. Including…"

"We're really in danger, aren't we, Dave?"

"Yeah, I'd have to say—"

"Hold me!" She practically jumped into my arms. Then she started tonguing my nipple through my stiff white shirt.

"Um, what are you doing?" I asked.

"It's the danger, Dave. Being in danger does something to me. I told you if you were lucky, you'd find out about it."

Then she unbuttoned my shirt and started nibbling on my nipple directly. It was getting awfully crowded below my belt.

"Don't just stand there," she panted, pulling off her own shirt, then her bra. "Kiss me back, anywhere you want."

Within about five seconds we were both completely naked.

I can honestly say I have never made love sitting on a toilet before.

I can also honestly say that if you haven't tried it, don't knock it.

After we had finished, both flushed (so to speak), wet, and sticking to each other, she said, "The feeling of danger has been building up for a few days. It just got to be too much. Thanks."

My intent was to be as cool and witty as James Bond in response and say something like, "You're quite welcome," or "Now I'm glad I came," but instead what came out was: "I think I love you."

Louie chuckled, "You don't, really."

"Maybe not, but I'm trying to be a sensitive man. In any event, how about we do this again so I can decide conclusively."

She kissed me on the lips, and until that moment, I didn't think it was possible that there enough respect left in Little Dave to stand up in a lady's presence, but I was wrong.

This time we did it in the shower. Some twenty minutes later I staggered out into the steam-filled bathroom, and said, "Wow."

Louie turned off the water and stepped out, leaning on me for support. "You know, to look at you, you wouldn't think you're that hot."

"Oddly enough, I've been told that once before."

For the record, sport, I'm jealous, I heard Errol Flynn say.

The steam was beginning to abate, but it was still too sultry in the room to actual dry ourselves, so we took our towels out into the hallway, which was much cooler, so cool, in fact, that we had to huddle nakedly together to keep our goosebumps from getting out of hand. Damn.

"Do you really think they have cameras in here?" Louie asked. "I mean, could they see us in action?"

"I wondered about that," I said. "Honestly, it wouldn't shock me, but you know what? I think seeing us doing what we just did would make their day."

"Perverts."

"Yeah, quite possibly," I whispered, "but what I meant was I think they threw us together in here because they wanted us to become lovers. That way they think they've gained leverage over us, by telling us if we don't talk, they'll do something to the other one."

"I wouldn't want that to happen."

"Neither would I. That's why we should talk."

"That show you were talking about?"

"Yeah. Do you, uh, think we should get dressed?"

With a quick, almost sisterly kiss, her "danger jones" as Zarian had described it assuaged (though now I wondered how *he* had found out about it), she pulled away and went back into the bathroom for her clothes. I followed, and found that while our respective outfits were slightly moist from the steam, they were not uncomfortable. In fact, if had softened them up a bit.

Back in the living room, Louie said, "Trashing my apartment like that, I feel so violated!"

She said it loudly enough as to indicate that the curtain had gone up on the "show."

"They really did a thorough job of it, too," I replied.

"They really think I'm so stupid as to leave my research in the apartment? I mailed my memory stick to Aunt Dolores for safekeeping. That's usually what I do for important investigations."

I doubted she even had an Aunt Dolores. "I still can't believe I was so stupid as to buy the story from that guy pretending to be your brother," I said, not only for the benefit of the presumed listeners, but also truthfully.

"Dave, don't beat yourself up over it. These are devious, evil people hiding behind the tax-exempt mask of a church. They are devils. And I have the evidence for that. I just hope they never find out about Aunt Dolores."

I approached her and took her in an embrace, using that opportunity to whisper in her ear: "Don't overplay it."

We separated and she nodded slightly, having gotten the message.

"So, did you uncover proof that the Temple owns Burger Heaven?" I asked.

"Not conclusive proof, no," she said. "I mean, there is no doubt in my mind that they do, as well as dozens of other front businesses, but they are masters at covering their paper trails. Think of the Temple as a modern-day Mafia, investing in legitimate companies for the revenue and to launder the money from their shakier endeavors. And since everybody loves Burger Heaven, there's a lot of money coming in. It's just that all those customers don't realize *why* they love Burger Heaven so much."

Like me.

"Yeah, about that," I said. "I was actually able to sneak a portion of burger out of one of the restaurants."

"You're kidding!"

"No, I managed, and I sent it on to Za…greb, they have a great scientific lab over there in Croatia, but it came back with negative results."

Now she looked genuinely perplexed. "That can't be."

"Sorry, but all the lab found was pepper and MSG."

"That's what…ZZ Top sang to you?"

It wasn't the most graceful code, but it would do. "Yeah. Nothing else."

She stood in thought for a few moments, then said: "How were you able to get the sample out?"

"I just walked out."

"That's all? There was nothing unusual about it?"

I thought back. "Well, the only thing unusual was that it was a freebie."

Her eyes started to sparkle, and a smile crossed her lips, and danged if I didn't want to drag her into the bathroom again and tear that Theotologics uniform off her like husks off an ear of corn.

But we had other things to accomplish.

"A freebie, huh?" she said.

"Yeah, I was given a complimentary coupon because my food from an earlier visit had accidentally been thrown away, and—"

It hit me then, and until that moment I had not bothered to stop and think that maybe that coupon had special significance. What if that coupon was restaurant code for *Give the Bearer of This Paper a Genuine 100% Beef Hamburger Patty*, and handed out only to those who seem to want to take a sample of the food home?

"It was a dummy burger, wasn't it? My god, are they really that diabolically prepared?"

"I think the short answer is yes. The fact that we're both here is a testament to their ability to cover all bases."

"Where is here, anyway?" I asked.

"I'm not positive, Dave, but I think we're in Canada."

"*Canada?*"

"Somewhere in Alberta," Louie said. "The Temple built a complex on the site of an old World War II POW camp."

"Louie, you've got to be kidding me."

"I wish I were. I heard about this place when I was doing my research. It's where they take members who don't conform, or people like us who become a little too troublesome."

"Good lord." I went to the living room and opened the drapes, not knowing if I would recognize Canada by sight or not, but willing to try.

As it turned out it didn't matter; there was no actual window behind the drapes, only a large painting of a landscape behind what appeared to be thick, bullet-proof Plexiglas.

I tried pounding on it, knowing it would be futile.

"Even if you were to break through, it wouldn't matter," Louie said. "It's only a concrete wall behind the artwork. See, Dave, we're I think we're underground."

"Like in a bunker?"

"Exactly."

I staggered over to the sofa and slumped down on it. "It seems like everybody I know told me the Temple was not an operation to mess with, but I don't get it. How can they actually get away with this?"

She sat down next to me and put a hand on my thigh, which I covered with my own. It was not a romantic or sexual signal, it was simply a gesture between two people who shared a big, big problem reaching out to one another.

"They have money, Dave, more than you can imagine," she said, "and when you're that rich, you can do anything you want. Rules and laws don't apply because you can make your own. You can buy government officials and politicians at every level and pay them to either look the other way at all times and make certain you're protected against any and all threats. If the threat seems real, you simply pay whoever you have to make it go away."

Like the theatre critic at the Independent Journal, the one in Chino, I thought. *Like me, in all likelihood, if I didn't have a friend on the force.*

"This sounds like the mob in the thirties," I said.

"It's even worse," Louie said. "The mob dealt in commodities like liquor or cigarettes, even things like magazines and records, any product that people would pay for. But the Temple deals in people themselves. It traffics in souls, particularly lost souls, like Regina Fontaine. She got involved with them through their theatre in Hollywood, which she thought was legitimate at first. It didn't take long for the Temple to size her up and get their hooks into her. Regina was a chain-smoker, and someone from the Temple who was working at the theatre told her he knew of a great program to help her quit. That was the beginning of it. She tried desperately to quit, but she was an addictive personality. If she dropped one addiction, she'd replace it with another."

"So she replaced cigarettes with the Temple?" I said.

"No, she replace cigarettes with Burger Heaven burgers, which she discovered were even more addictive than smoking. That's when she began to suspect there was something extra being put into the meat, and she wondered if it was nicotine, to get people hooked on eating there."

If that was indeed the case, I had to admit that it worked. I also had to admit that in spite of everything I was hearing, I was craving a Twin Halo.

"But whatever it was," Louie went on, "because of all the burgers she was eating she started to gain a little weight, not so much that you or I would ever notice, but the people running the theatre did. They told her she had to go into a diet program, and guess who ran it? She even started sneaking cigarettes again hoping to wean herself off the hamburgers."

"That explains why she nearly jumped out of her skin when I caught her smoking," I said.

"That's the way the Temple operates. They prey on you, beat you down, make you feel like such a loser that you begin to think every basic human requirement is a personal weakness, including hunger."

"And she couldn't simply leave?"

"She fantasized about leaving, but by then she was in to the Temple for tens of thousands of dollars, which is also how the operation works. Once you've signed up they bleed your bank account dry with all their classes and workshops and books and tapes and downloads and programs anything else they can think of, and when they've accomplished that they offer you loans from their own private credit union. Once you're in so deeply to them that there's no way out, you have to go to work for them to pay it off, and if you refuse, they threaten you with legal prosecution." She shook her head.

"A lot of the people working at Burger Heaven aren't working for wages, they're trying to pay off their debt, which they never will. It's a modern form of slavery with the added threat of punishment to anyone who dares trying to approach the authorities with a complaint. Despite that, Regina, had gotten to the point where she was willing to at least try and blow the whistle on them, and rightly or wrongly believing that going to the police or the DA's office was futile, she came to us."

"And paid the price for it," I said.

"God," Louie sighed, shaking her head. "What should I have done differently to protect her?"

"You can't blame yourself."

"Regina was so vulnerable, so completely vulnerable in that artistic way. Every emotion came through her pores. I really wanted to help her, but I think I got too close to be objective. But why am I telling you that? You've seen the proof. I probably should have let her move into my apartment like she wanted. She already had a key."

A bell went off in my head. That had to be where the faux Ricky Sandoval had gotten the key; he took it from Regina right before he killed her.

And...? Bogie prompted.

And while I had suspected Ricky, his possession of the key was absolute proof of his guilt!

Buuuuut? Robert Mitchum's voice said, and yes, even though it was only one long syllable, I recognized it.

"Oh, jeez," I uttered, putting my face in my hands.

"What's the matter, Dave?" Louie asked.

Ricky Sandoval had given me the key, from which I had a copy made, both of which I retained. One, in fact, had been in my pants pocket when I'd been drugged and abducted, and so was now back in the possession of the Temple. So my possession of Regina's key now pointed to *me* the prime suspect in her murder, and even if I ever had the chance to dispose of the copy I'd made, the Temple still had the original and could plant it anywhere they wanted to support the theory of my guilt.

Two steps forward, one step back, straight off a cliff, Fred Astaire sang in my head.

"Are you okay?" Louie was asking.

"Yeah, yeah, I'm all right," I lied. "I just had an idea, but it turned out it wasn't a good one. Not that it really matters, since we're not going to get out of here any time soon."

"Dave, please, we have to remain positive."

"Fine. I'm positive we're not going to get out of here any time soon."

The next sound I heard in the apartment was a knock on the front door, which was unlocked and quickly opened from the outside.

Dan strolled in along with the tall female security guard who was being coerced to accuse me of rape. A third person then entered the suite, one whom I was not particularly surprised to see. In fact, I'd rather been expecting him. Like the others he was dressed in a Temple guard uniform and he waved one beefy hand at me while the other held a police taster.

"Louie," I said, "please allow me to introduce you to your brother, Ricky."

CHAPTER SIXTEEN

"Hi, Sis," he said.

"*Puto*!" Louie screamed, launching herself at him. "I loved my brother!"

I launched myself off the sofa, too, so as to catch her before she fully attacked the man and got herself tased.

"Let me go!" she cried, struggling all the way back to the sofa.

"Louie, honey, don't do it," I said, struggling to hold her. "All you'll do is get hurt. They have the upper hand."

"How gratifying to see you've already accepted the truth," Dan said.

"Speaking of the truth, Colonel, why don't you let us in on Mighty Joe Young's real first name here, since continuing to call him 'Ricky' is only going to give me the runs."

The ape actually looked at Dan as though to see if revealing confidential information was all right, but Dan answered for him.

"This is Alberto, Mr. Beauchamp. You can call him Al if you like."

"I kind of prefer the names Ms. Sandoval came up with."

Dan smiled. "Glibness. Equally gratifying. Now then, it seems we need to talk to the two of you a little more officially."

"Officially?" I asked.

"That means we're going to be hooked up to one of their brainwashing machines," Louie said. I waited for someone to deny that and accuse her of paranoia, but no one did.

"I didn't bring enough quarters for the brainwashing machine," I cracked. "Maybe the braindrying one."

"Very glib," said Dan.

"Very Glib…wasn't he one of the Beegees?"

That one made Louie chuckle, but it seemed to anger Colonel Klink.

"Marta," he barked, and the woman came up behind me and grabbed my arm, twisting it behind me like a pro.

"I don't want to hurt you, Mr. Beauchamp," she said.

"Little too late to worry about that," I winced.

"Okay, *Sis*," Alberto said, holding the taser up to Louie, "we need to talk about our dear Aunt Dolores. Damned if I haven't forgotten where she lives."

"She won't tell you," I panted.

"If it starts to hurt enough, she will," Dan replied.

"You bastards call yourselves a Church?"

"Actually, we don't, at least not beyond a certain level of adjustment. But that is neither here nor there. Marta, take Mr. Beauchamp out."

"What are you going to do with Louie?"

"Not your problem. Get him out of here!"

Marta forced me through the door of the suite. As we marched down the hallway of the bunker, I said, "Jeez, lady, is this strong-arm stuff really necessary?"

"I'm afraid so," she said. "You might try to overpower me."

"Oh, yeah, right! Look what an outstanding job of it I'm doing now. I hope there are secret cameras filming this because if you really persist about this rape rubbish, one look at the footage will make anyone realize I have as much chance against you as Mike Tyson."

"That would be for Judge Maxwell to decide." She twisted my arm a little harder.

"Ow! You mean you already know which judge would…"

I stopped talking, in part because the pain in my arm was taking my breath away, but also because further words were redundant. Of *course* she knew which judge would preside over any potential rape case. It would be the judge who was in the pocket of the Temple.

"In the elevator," she said, pushing me toward the doors at the end of the hallway. "Don't get cute."

She hit the button with her elbow and waited for the doors to open, and once we were in, she let go of my tingling arm and hit the down button.

"How far down does this place go?" I asked.

"To the bottom."

I sighed. And she didn't want *me* to get cute.

When the elevator stopped and the doors opened, she started to take my arm again, but I said, "Look, Marta, you don't have to do that, I promise I won't run. I wouldn't know where to run to."

After a moment's deliberation, she instead took me firmly by the elbow and pulled me down another corridor, this one decorated with photos of celebrity Theotologicians, including movie star Vince Cranna, television actress Katie Laines, and a rapper-turned-actor named Charlie Blue.

Halfway down was the most elaborate carved wooden door I had seen this side of Hearst Castle up the California coast. Set incongruously into the concrete wall, it was enormous and made of what appeared to be mahogany, with intricately carved symbols of the Temple of Theotologics.

Another note of incongruity was the severe looking, lighted security box just under the brass, oval doorknobs.

"What's this room?" I asked.

"I can't tell you," Hannah answered.

I let it go since I was had bigger worries ahead, chiefly being escorted through what looked like hospital doors over which was a painted sign that read, *ADJUSTING LABORATORY.*

Oh, jeez, here it comes.

After going inside I was taken to a dimly-lit room containing a large wall-sized screen, a small table, and in the center a state-of-the-art barber chair. Scattered throughout were a half-dozen machines with dials, buttons, screens and wires. I was instructed to get into the chair and make myself comfortable, which was not easy when I kept expecting Laurence Olivier from *Marathon Man* to come in at any second, carrying a dental drill and asking me, "Is it safe?"

Instead, in walked Helen Mirren, her hair stiffly framing her face, wearing a long white lab coat that ended about a foot above her red pumps. It wasn't the real Helen Mirren of course, but it could have been her stunt double. She was carrying a clipboard and gave me a forced smile.

"Mr. Beauchamp, is it?" she asked, pronouncing it *Bow-SHAWM*.

"BEE-chum," I replied. "I'm not Continental."

"But you are a private investigator."

"I am."

"And it appears you are investigating us."

"I am not investigating the Temple of Theotologics. I was working on a case involving the Burger Heaven restaurant chain, and this is where it has led. You are the ones who brought me here."

"Hmmm, refusal to take responsibility for one's actions," she said to the ceiling, and looking up, I saw a microphone hanging there, with no attempt to hide or disguise it.

"Maybe I should become a politician," I said.

"Thinks he can joke his way out of anything," she announced.

"Has a run in her right stocking," I said, and she immediately examined her leg, but did not find a run. I had just made it up.

When she looked back up at me, irritation marring her face, I said: "Made you look."

"You are *not* funny." At that moment my entire body started to tingle, the same sensation as when one's arm falls asleep, but all over. I didn't like it. I tried to move in the chair, but I seemed to be tied down, which I liked even less.

"What's going on?" I asked.

"What do you mean?" "Helen" replied, sweetly.

"I can't get out of this thing."

"Maybe you don't wish to."

"Like hell." I tried stepping down from the footrest, but could not. The tingling got more pronounced. "What are you doing to me? Why can't I move?"

"Are you experiencing pain?" she asked.

"Not pain…tingling…numbness…discomfort…can't move my body…"

"Where are the notes?"

"What?"

"That woman's notes. Where are they hidden?"

"She sent them to her Aunt Dolores."

"We don't believe you."

The tingling increased. *Why couldn't I move?*

"I'll ask you again. Where are those notes?"

"I'll tell you again…Aunt Dolores…" Not unexpectedly, the tingling became more intense, and while it was still not painful, it was extremely uncomfortable. It felt like every cell in my body was vibrating. That must be it; this chair had to be some kind of vibration device, like those electronic foot massage machines taken to a higher level.

"Turn this off," I demanded, to no avail.

"Not until we get the information we require."

I forced myself to resist, even though it felt like my brain was being shaken to atoms.

"I've always wondered," I said through gritted teeth, "what god do you worship?"

"What?"

"You call yourselves a Temple, a Church, but all anyone hears about are your classes and your betterment programs and your founder, who was one of the lowest of low-rent movie actors. But no one ever hears about any sort of deity. So who do you worship? Yahweh? Buddha? Allah? Cthulu? Who?"

"You are in no position to ask questions!" she shouted.

You're not in much of a position to answer any, either, kid, Bogart added, helpfully. *So just faint.*

"What?" I asked aloud.

Faint, kid. Pretend to faint!

"Where are the notes!" Helen screamed.

"I don't know!" I screamed back, and then slumped over as though I had just died.

Apparently it worked for my tormenter, too, since she suddenly shouted, "Turn off the magnets!"

In an instant, the tingling went away, and so did my attachment to the chair. I started to fall forward and naturally, instinctively tried to prevent myself, but then realized that I had to make this look convincing. So I fell forward out of the chair and landed shoulder-first on the floor, which wasn't pleasant, but was manageable.

I rolled onto my stomach, the position I figured would be the most convincing.

"Dammit!" I heard her cry. "Get in here!"

A few moments later I heard the door open and a couple sets of footsteps come in. I was then aware of being rolled over while something foul-smelling was passed under my nose. I spluttered back to "consciousness."

"He's all right," a voice said, and I recognized it as Dan's. "A weakling is all. And stupid, too, if he thought we were really going to fall for that Aunt Dolores business."

I tried my damnedest not to smile. I may be weak and stupid, but I had duped them all and thus had managed to escape the terrors of the tingly barber chair.

"I don't think he knows where the notes are," my tormentor was saying. "I think he genuinely believes there is an Aunt Dolores."

"Get him back to his room," Dan instructed, and within moments I felt myself being pulled up bodily to my feet. I didn't resist or react much in any way, wanting them to believe I was still groggy from my "collapse."

Once in the corridor, though, I raised my head and saw that my escorts were now a strapping young man and a woman with frizzy red hair who wore a stethoscope around her neck.

They certainly had a lot of staff at this place.

"I guess I didn't pass the test, huh?" I asked.

"We're not supposed to talk to you," the woman said.

"But how is that trick with the chair done? Dr. Mengele's sister said something about magnets, but that doesn't make sense, unless…"

"Hush," she said as we showed up at the door to the suite in which Louie and I had been interned.

"It's these clothes, isn't it," I went on, "these uniforms. They're somehow made with metal, aren't they? Metal wires interspersed with the fabric."

"She said to shut up," the man barked as the woman unlocked the door.

"You're not being very positive, you know," I pointed out, and a second later was shoved into the room so hard I fell on the floor.

"You don't have to be so rough, Dwayne," the woman said, coming to me and placing her hand on my head. "Are you all right?"

"Yeah, I'm fine," I said. "Thanks. So he's Dwayne, what's your name."

"Hannah. I'm a nurse here."

"I would have thought a doctor, given the stethoscope."

"No, just a nurse."

Dwayne stepped forward and said, "Aww, isn't this sweet? Why don't you two go on a date some other time. We have to get back to work."

Hannah's eyes, which were an unusual color of gray, found mine, and I'd swear the look she gave me was that of a dog behind a gate who greeted every passerby with an expression that screamed, *Take me out of here.*

Then she got up and the two of them left the room, locking the door behind them. I got up off the floor and made my way to the sofa. While the experience with the tingly chair had to count as one of the weirdest of my life, I was not hurt.

I could only hope that Louie was receiving no worse treatment.

It would be another two hours before I found out. At least that's what it seemed like. I no longer had any concept of time, and since we were underground, there was no way to use the sun as a gauge.

But at some point, the door opened again and Louie was brought in by Alberto. She looked shaken and exhausted, but unbruised.

"I'll say hi to our cousin for you," Alberto said with a laugh, and then left, locking the door again.

I rushed to her and led her to the sofa, lowering her down and sitting beside her. "Are you okay?"

Louie nodded. "I feel a little numb," she said.

"Did they use the tingly chair on you?"

"Tingly chair? No. I was strapped to a gurney and little sticky electrodes were put on my head that were supposed to read and influence my thoughts. It was supposed to be some kind of lie detector test."

"What's this business about a cousin?"

"Dave, I had to tell them the truth."

"You told them where your flash drive is hidden?"

"Yes," she said. "I told them that I don't really have an Aunt Dolores, and that I really sent all the information to my cousin Tina, who used to be a television news anchor. Oh, god help me, Dave," she said, falling into my arms, and then whispered into my ear:

"The stupid shits fell for it. They really believe this equipment of theirs works."

Then she broke the embrace and asked, "So what's this about a tingly chair?"

I recounted my experience with Helen Mirren's doppelgänger and the weird chair, and my theory as to why I was unable to move when sitting in it, after which Louie said, "That almost makes sense."

"In a Roger Corman film kind of way."

"What do you think they're going to do with us now?" Louie asked, and this question I knew was genuine.

"I don't know," I replied, standing up. "I think we're safe for a while, but once they get that stick with your notes from your cousin... who was it again?"

"Tina. Christina Cordova. She was on Channel Five in the nineties." Louie permitted herself the tiniest of winks to me.

"Oh, I think I remember the name. I guess the real question now is what are they going to do to Tina. I mean, look at what they did to Regina and Avery."

"I don't want to think about it," she said, getting up and embracing me. Then in my ear, she added: "We have to get out of here."

I couldn't have agreed more. If only I knew how.

The girl, stupid, the girl, Robert Mitchum said.

I'm holding the girl, I thought back.

Not that one!

Which one, then? "Ohhhh," I moaned when I finally figured it out.

"Are you getting off just hugging me?" Louie asked.

"Not a bad thought, but no," I whispered back. "I think I might have an idea. Come with me."

Taking her hand, I led her to the bathroom, closed the door and turned on the shower and the tap.

"Okay, there's this girl named Hannah who works here as a nurse. Call it intuition, but I think she might be the weak link in this particular daisy chain because she doesn't seem all too enthused about the stuff they are making her do, which indicates to me that she's doing it out of fear."

"Like Regina was afraid that they were going to find out she had started smoking again."

"Something like that. But if we can figure out what her weakness is, we might be able to use it against her."

"But isn't that the kind of shit they do here?"

She had a point.

"Yeah, yeah it is, but there's one difference: they're not being held hostage."

"But in a way, they are."

"Look, Louie," I said, "do you want to get out of here or not?"

"Of course I do. I just don't want to hurt another woman to do it."

"Neither do I. So maybe we can convince her to take our side in this mess."

"How?"

"By playing on her nurse's training. One of us fakes an illness or injury, and that gets her in here, and then we try to talk to her."

"What, we pretend to have heart attacks?"

"I don't know, exactly, we just have to pretend to have something."

She was silent for a moment, and then said: "Dave, do you trust me?"

"Of course I trust you. Why wouldn't I?"

"Do you love me?"

"Louie…"

"Dave, do you love me?"

"Yeah, Louie, I think I do. You're not going to stomp on my heart, are you?"

"No, but I'm going to remind you that a big part of love is forgiveness." She grabbed my face and gave me a kiss that made my toes curl, and then said, "Trust me, baby."

Then she threw open door of the bathroom and screamed, "You piece of shit!"

I had no choice but to trust her. I ran after her, asking, "What did I do?"

"You know goddamn well what you did!" she cried, then started screaming in Spanish, and while I had no idea what she was saying, I have to admit that it heightened the drama.

"Jeez, what's the problem?" I protested.

"You think just because we did it once as a mercy hump you can have me anytime you want? You're a goddamn rapist, you know that?"

Oh, she was good when she got wound up. I hoped whoever was watching and listening was enjoying the performance.

"Hey, what's the big deal?" I said, attempting to affect a macho-man tone. "You wanted it, you know you wanted it!"

"But not with you!"

"Too bad!" I shouted back. "I'm a guy who likes a little taco meat every now and then. What's the big deal?"

Luisa Sandoval's eyes widened beyond her brows, and I had only a nanosecond in which to realize that maybe I had played the drama a little broadly before she drove her fist into my nose.

After the explosion of flashing lights everything went dark and I went down. The last thing I remember is hearing the voice of Bogart say: *Jesus, kid, why not just pull the pin on a grenade?*

The next thing I heard was a far off voice saying, "It's not broken, but he's going to look like Bozo the Clown for a while."

I couldn't tell if it was one of mine or someone else's voice.

Slowly I opened my eyes and through a sheet of red that quickly faded to pink, then disappeared, I saw Hannah hovering over me.

"You should learn to control your anger," she said to Louie.

"I *was* controlling it," Louie responded.

I tried to talk and became aware of a cloth over my mouth. At first I thought it might have been a gag, but realized it was there to sop up the blood that was still streaming from my nose.

"I'll get some ice," Hannah said, rising. She left the room, locking the door behind her.

Louie took her place, hovering over me.

"How do you feel?" she whispered.

"I've never been hit like that before," I replied.

"I had to make it look good, and I didn't much care for that 'taco meat' crack, either."

"Jesus, Louie, I had to make it look good, too, didn't I? I don't normally say things like that, okay?"

"I'm sorry, baby."

Part of love is forgiveness, a voice said in my head, and it was Louie's. "What do I really look like?" I croaked.

"Ever see a photo of J. P. Morgan when he was old?"

"Great."

I got up off the floor made my woozy way to the sofa, and sat down, still holding the rag to my mouth.

Louie sat down beside me. "So do we try to overcome her when she comes back?" she whispered in my ear.

I shook my head, and it hurt. "They'll see it and stop us," I said through the cloth. "We have to talk to her."

"You know how to play good cop, bad cop?"

Underneath my bloody cloth I was smiling, and that hurt, too. "Trust me, I learned from the best," I said.

Hannah then returned with a large metal bowl filled with ice and a stack of towels. "You stand over there where I can see you," she commanded to Louie, while she took away my reddened cloth and examined my nose. "Wow. I'll try not to hurt you any worse."

"You'd make a great doctor," I said.

"I wanted to be a doctor," she replied, holding, a cold compress to my face. "But I had a drug problem. Most hospitals don't hire doctors with drug problems. The Temple helped me get off drugs."

From across the room, Louie said: "So that's why you're indentured to them?"

"Not indentured, indebted," though the expression on her face did not fully support her words.

"Pay no attention to her," I said to Hannah. "She doesn't understand the way the Temple works."

Glancing up at Louie, I read in her expression that she understood I was about to engage in Act II of this painful drama.

"You must be very grateful to them for helping you," I went on. "So grateful that you work for them in return."

"I am…grateful…in a way, but…"

"But what, Hannah?"

"This isn't like a job, exactly. I'm not getting paid, or anything. My room and board is free, but when I said indebted, I meant I really am. I owe the Temple so much money for classes and adjusting and counseling, that I have to stay here."

"But it's worth it, isn't it?" I pressed. "I mean, you get to act like a doctor, even if you really aren't one."

"And probably never will be," Louie said, sauntering closer to us. "A junkie like you."

"Oh, shut up," I said. "She'll be a doctor, someday."

"Yeah, right."

"You're such a downer!"

"I'm a *realist*!" Louie countered on cue. "And you're nothing but a chump who falls for every pretty face with a stethoscope around her neck!"

"Don't listen to her," I said to Hannah. "I know you're happy here. Who wouldn't be?"

Since I was ad lib phishing for information, I wasn't sure where this line of questioning was going to go. All I knew is that I wasn't prepared for her reaction, which was to completely break down in tears and fold into a near-fetal position.

"Who, *wouldn't* be?" she wailed. "Anyone! I hate it here! I'm stuck here, like a wild animal in a hunter's trap!"

"I had no idea," I lied. "And I'm sure Louie's sorry for what she said. Aren't you Louie?"

Louie rushed over and took Hannah in her arms, and cradled her like a mother comforting a sobbing child. "I'm so sorry, baby. I had no idea, either," she said.

Hannah broke away from Louie and stood up. "I can't be seen doing this. It's a sign of weakness. They'll see. They're watching. They're always watching."

In an instant came the sound of the door being unlocked, and a second later Alberto and Dan came back in.

"Whatever are we to do with you two?" Dan asked.

"Let us go?" I said, and after several seconds' worth of crickets, added: "It was just a thought."

"Until we have all of the information gleaned by Ms. Sandoval here, you two will continue to enjoy the hospitality of the Temple of Theotologics."

"What if I told you I really wasn't able to find anything out?" Louie asked.

Dan smiled. "Frankly, I suspect that *is* the case, but the only way to know for certain is to locate and review your reporters' notes. What was it the man once said? Trust, but verify. Anyway, that is not the issue at present. The issue for you, Mr. Beauchamp, is how we keep Ms. Sandoval from harming you again."

"Put her in a different room," I offered, hoping Dan would automatically reject the idea because it had come from someone who was "unadjusted."

"I actually have a better idea," Dan said, right on cue. "Hannah, prepare two syringes."

Uh oh.

"What are you going to do?" Louie demanded.

"Don't worry, you won't feel a thing. You didn't when you were brought here."

"He's going to keep us drugged, Louie," I said, "probably until they find your cousin Tina."

Turning on Hannah, Dan said: "You were given an order, private. What are you waiting for? Get the syringes."

"Yeah, make tracks," Alberto said. "Get it? *Tracks*?"

Then he laughed while Hannah crossed her arms over her chest, as though trying to hide the evidence of intravenous drug use. The gesture came so automatically that it must have been reflex, and the look of pain on her face spoke volumes.

Hannah glanced up at me with an inscrutable expression, and then dashed out of the room.

"I must say, Beauchamp, that you have taken your sock in the nose with equanimity," Dan was saying.

"I provoked her," I responded.

"Still, I would think you'd like to settle the score."

"I don't hit women," I said.

"Turn the other cheek, is that it?" Dan sneered. "Or in your case, the other nose? Admirable."

He then lashed out and backhanded Louie so forcefully she flew across the room before colliding with a chair and going down.

"*Hey!*" I shouted, charging him, but Alberto stepped in between us and shoved me back. I nearly went down on my butt, too, but I fought to retain my balance. I stared at Dan. "Big man, huh?" I said. "I'll bet you'll jack off tonight to the memory of that."

"And I'll bet you'll shut your mouth unless you want to see me give it to her worse."

My mouth opened and then closed again. I wasn't about to risk having Louie hurt again. And I had to assume that was the point. I was being broken down.

"Big men," I said again, impotently. "Big, big men."

"I'm okay, Dave," Louie said, getting up and wiping the blood from her mouth. "Don't make it worse."

We were at a four-person stand-off, like the bridge game from hell, when Hannah returned, holding two syringes.

"You might need to hold them," she said.

"Quite right," Dan agreed. "Alberto, you take the woman."

Alberto violently dragged Louie over to the sofa and threw her against it, and then pressed his forearm against her throat, while Dan—who was stronger than he looked—did the same for me.

I don't know how much pressure was being applied to Louie's windpipe, but mine was near collapsing. Alberto and Dan were standing side by side over us as Hannah approached and took the caps off the needles of the syringes and plunged one each into the butts of both Alberto and Dan.

Clearly shocked, they dropped their chokeholds on us and staggered backwards. Hannah leapt back as the two tried to charge her, but they got only halfway across the room before faltering, weaving, swearing, and ultimately falling down on the floor, making futile attempts to rise like the cows in those "give-now-to-stop-this-barbaric-practice" PSAs.

Finally, the two stopped moving.

"Good god, you didn't poison them, did you?" Louie asked.

"No, but I made the shot super strong," Hannah said. "They'll be out for a long time. Now let's go."

We followed her through the door and into the hallway. "There are cameras all over this place," I said. "They're probably watching us right now. How far can we get?"

"There's one place where there are no cameras of any kind," Hannah replied. "We'll go there for the time being."

"Where's that?"

She didn't answer but forced us to hurry along the corridor, and then stopped in front of the enormous door of the Master Suite. Pulling out a key card and putting it into a very well disguised slot on the door, she pushed it open and hustled us in, closing the door behind us.

A cynical whistle (if whistles can be so characterized) coursed through my head, followed by Bogie's voice saying: *Get a load of this!*

Even in the dimness of the suite it was possible to make out its ornate luxury, like a room in a European palace, not that I'd been in many. Or any. The ceilings were high, at least a storey-and-a-half high, and made of paneled wood, from which hung a crystal chandelier.

The walls were covered with a deep-red wallpaper that reminded me of the décor of an old Southern California restaurant chain called Joanne's Chili Bordello, which had a place in Long Beach for a while.

The enormous stone hearth and fireplace that was cut into one wall was large enough to stage a Shakespearean production in, though if we were really as far below ground level as had been indicated, I had to wonder how they managed the chimney.

"That's just for show," Hannah said, seeming to read my mind. "This place has central heat and air."

Over the fireplace was a oil painting, lit on all sides by track lights. It was no surprise that the subject of the painting was Palmer Hanley as he must have looked in the mid-1960s, his head tilted up slightly and his eyes gazing into the distance, revealing a masterfully-rendered expression of optimism and wisdom. It was more expression than I had ever seen on the man's face from any of his film appearances.

"What is this place used for?" I asked.

"What do you mean?" Hannah said.

"Well, is this the VIP suite or something? The honeymoon suite? What?"

The woman looked and me like I was an idiot. "It's the Master's suite," she said.

"I get that, but how does one earn a night in the baroque presence of the worst actor in the history of Hollywood?"

From behind me a somewhat squeaky voice said, "By being a rude jerk, that's how."

Turning, I saw an elderly man.

It was clear he had once been fairly tall, though now he was stooped and remained upright only through the aid of a silver-headed cane, which he grasped in his gnarled right hand. His hair was white and thin, but still there, for the most part, and his face had more lines than the Thomas Guide page showing downtown.

Even though his eyes showed a liveliness and intelligence that was never revealed on film, he remained recognizable.

"Who are you anyway?" demanded Palmer Hanley.

CHAPTER SEVENTEEN

"What is all this, Hannah?" the old man asked.

"I'm sorry, sir. I thought you'd be sleeping," she replied.

"Um, Mr. Hanley," I began, "I think I owe you an apology."

"Everybody does, why should you be any different? Who did you say you were?"

"My name is Dave Beauchamp. This is my friend Luisa Sandoval, and obviously you know Hannah."

"What are you doing here?"

"Well…we've been kidnapped."

"Okay, but what happened to your nose?"

"My nose? Oh, right."

I had managed to get so used to the throbbing ache in my face from Louie's punch that I'd forgotten I looked like W.C. Fields at five in the morning.

"Yeah, I got hurt in the struggle."

"You should be more careful," Hanley said. "You say you owe me an apology?"

"Yes sir. I'm sorry I cast aspersions on your acting. I'm sure you were doing your best."

"You said your name was Dave?"

"Yes sir, Dave Beauchamp."

"Well, Dave Beauchamp, you and everyone else in Los Angeles cast aspersions on my acting. I did fine on the stage, you know. I played Happy in *Salesman* in New York and nobody got sick. But I never had that magical quality that you need in Hollywood, the one that makes the camera love you. Truth is, the camera hated me. It somehow sapped my energy, like a vampire. My face turned into a mask and my voice became a dial tone. Why that was, I've no idea."

He appeared lost in thought for a moment, then continued:

"Now you take Marilyn…I knew Marilyn, you know, poor little mouse…on stage she would have been an ice box, a piece of furniture. But on camera, well, the camera loved her. *Loved* her, more than

Romeo loved Juliet. Me, on the other hand? The camera hated me just as much as it loved her. Ah, that's old history now."

He made his way to the expensive sofa and fell back on it, almost in slow motion, like a feather falling from a height.

"But as for you, Dave Beauchamp," he went on, "you're about the only person I ever met who had the good manners and class to stand up and look me in the eye and apologize for dumping garbage on my head, so your apology is accepted. You're all right."

He thrust a birch twig arm out at me and I walked over to the sofa to take his hand, which was surprisingly strong, and shake it enthusiastically. At that moment I decided I liked Palmer Hanley, no matter what he had done in the past, and would do whatever I could to help him.

"I'm ninety-four years old, Dave Beauchamp, did you know that?"

"No sir, I didn't."

"Well, now you do. Now that that's settled, what are two you doing in my rooms?"

"At the moment, we're hiding," I said.

The old man gave a wheezy laugh. "Well, you've sure as hell come to the right place, then. I've been hidden away here for thirty years."

"This is incredible," Louie said.

"I'm sorry, dear, what was your name again?"

"Louie."

"Louie...like Louie Calhern? You sure don't look like Louie Calhern. Well, call it incredible if you want, but I've been tucked away here because they don't want me shooting my mouth off about how they turned my dumb little money-making idea into a criminal's paradise."

"Who, exactly, are *they*, Mr. Hanley?" Louie asked.

"I'm getting tired. I don't get visitors often, not since… Christ, I don't even remember."

He turned and hobbled to an overstuffed sofa and plopped down in the middle of it.

"Honey, could you bring me something to drink?"

"Of course," Hannah said, leaving the room.

"Now, what were you asking? Oh, right, *them*. You sure you want to hear all this, Louie?"

She slid onto the sofa next to him. "Positive."

"Suit yourself."

Hannah hustled back in with a glass of ice tea, which Hanley took from her.

"You two want any?"

"We're fine, thanks," Louie said.

"Bottoms up."

He took a healthy chug that half-emptied the glass, and then said: "Do either of you know what a Mason is?"

After ridding my head of the voice of Raymond Burr, I said, "You mean the secret society?"

"Well, it's about as secret as an earthquake, particularly in Hollywood, but yeah, the society. Back in the day all the studio heads were Masons, and so were most of the big guns in town. Hope, Autry, the Duke, DeMille, even old Roy Rogers, all Masons. And Harold Lloyd was Mason in chief. But you're probably too young to know who Harold Lloyd was."

"He was right up there with Chaplin and Keaton," I said.

Hanley's face registered surprise.

"A young kid who knows Harold Lloyd. Maybe there's hope for the world yet."

"What about the Masons?" Louie prompted, ever the reporter.

"Well, as you probably know my career in Hollywood was totally in the jakes by the late fifties. I already told you why. By then I wasn't even successful enough to get in trouble with HUAC! I could've marched up and down Hollywood Boulevard wearing a union suit with hammers and sickles all over it and nobody would've cared. You had to be famous to be blacklisted. At least working."

He finished his tea and handed the glass back to Hannah before continuing.

"Anyway, the point came where I was so broke I was living in a friend's guest room. He was a Mason, and was working on me to try and get me to join, or apprentice, or however it was you became a member, saying it might lead to something. I guess the idea was that if you put on a robe and skipped around a Pentagram with Walt Disney, he'd put you in one of his movies."

While I doubted that was what really went on in the Hollywood Masonic Temple, I didn't call him on it.

"But laying there in that borrowed bed, in that borrowed room, I thought I had a better idea," Hanley continued. "I'd start my own club and charge people to be in it. But then I got the brainstorm to not just settle for a club, an organization, or even a secret society. You still have to pay taxes on those. So I decided to start a church. I got a guy I'd done a television show with to write up a half-assed bible for it, based on some baloney we concocted, and put out the word that I was holding spiritual cleansing sessions, and the suckers took the bait."

"So you never actually believed any of what you created?" Louie asked.

"Miss Calhern—"

"Just call me Louie, okay?"

The old man shrugged. "All right, Louie. Have you ever seen a picture called *House of Wax*?"

"Yes. A long time ago. Why do you ask?"

"I had a scene in the movie that got cut out. But if you look at the wax figure of John Wilkes Booth real closely, he might look a little familiar."

"You modeled for Booth?" I asked.

"I had a short scene where I got killed by the monster because I looked like Booth, but they cut it out."

"Guys, this is fascinating," Louie said, "but why are we talking about an old movie?"

"I'm getting to that as a way of answering your question, young lady," Hanley said. "Do you believe Vincent Price really killed those people and then coated them in wax?"

"Of course not. It's a movie."

"Right. Ol' Vinnie, God bless him, was just an actor working for a paycheck. He didn't believe any of the rubbish the studios hired him to do, but he managed to make the audience believe that he was an insane murderer, and believe it so completely that they got scared."

With some effort, Palmer Hanley leaned forward.

"That's what it's all about, young lady. It doesn't matter what *I* believe. It only matters what I can make others believe. And a lot of them believed that I somehow had discovered the secrets of life and could pass those secrets on to them. They believed it so completely they paid money just for the chance that they might learn what they believed I knew."

"What was that?" I asked.

"Well, what I came to know is that most people just want to be relieved of the onus of having to make their own decisions. They'll pay good money not to be in charge of their own lives. That was the idea behind the Temple of Theotologics. My idea, anyway. Then the boys got involved."

"The boys?"

"Organized crime. They were already out here because of the film and music business, and once they smelled the kind of money I was starting to make, they moved in.

"I didn't realize what I was getting into at first. I just saw a bunch of golf shirts and dark glasses offering to capitalize my venture. Before I knew what was happening the mob was in charge of the whole shebang and using the Temple to launder money from their other pursuits. Theotologics was a godsend for them because there are only two kinds of schemes where you don't have to worry about taxes. They already had one, the black market, and I had the other, religion."

"That sounds rather cynical, Mr. Hanley," Louie said.

"Honey, I'm ninety-four years old, and anything good that ever happened to me over that long, long time has been taken away again in one fashion or other. I think I've earned the right to sound cynical."

"That's the lead!" Louie cried, jumping up off the sofa.

"Lead for what?" I asked.

"My article! Maybe even a book! Don't look at me that way, Dave. You don't seriously think I'm going to walk away from the story of the decade, do you?"

"But we have to get out of here before you can write it."

"Then let's get out of here," she said, just like that. "Hannah will help us, won't you, Hannah?"

The nurse nodded tentatively.

"That's it then."

"Louie, I'm for getting away from this prison as much as any-one," I began. "But think about it for a minute. Let's say we actually are able to escape from this building. We're still stuck somewhere in the middle of Canada. How do we get back to L.A.? I don't have any cash. They took my wallet, so I'm assuming they took my ID as well."

"Did you say Canada?" Hanley asked.

"We're all in a bunker somewhere in Alberta, aren't we?"

"Where did you get that idea?"

Louie and I exchanged looks.

"I heard about this complex from the members of the Temple I spoke with for my article," she said.

"I don't know who told you what, Miss Calhern, but we're not in Canada."

Having appeared perfectly lucid up to this point, I had to assume that Palmer Hanley did not even know where he was being held. It's not like there were any windows out of which he could look. I had to side with Louie's source, who had also been correct about Hanley still being among the living, but under the circumstances decided it was best to humor the old guy.

"Where are we then, Mr. Hanley?"

"Hollywood."

"Sir, how can we still be in Hollywood?" I asked gently. "How could you build a place like this in plain sight?"

"You put it in a movie studio, that's how," he replied.

"A movie studio," I repeated dumbly. Then I looked at Hannah, who had reddened.

"My god, he's telling the truth, isn't he?"

"This is Windsor Studios on Santa Monica Boulevard," she confirmed. "They tell the people who are brought here that they are in the wilds of Canada somewhere, deep underground, as a way of dissuading them from even thinking about breaking out. It's a very effective. Those of us who are allowed to come and go are sworn to secrecy, or else."

"Or else what?" Louie asked her.

"They have information on all of us that they will use against us if we ever talk," Hannah whispered. "In my case it's my drug use."

"And they make you stay here and work for them under the threat of releasing that information?"

Hannah looked pleadingly at Louie. "I could go to prison if they got the information to the right person in the D.A.'s office."

There it was again: the *right* judge; the *right* person in the D.A.'s office. How far did the tentacles of the Temple extend?

The organization had to be brought down. The question was how.

Unfortunately, I seemed to be the only one at present who was actually taking the time to ponder the details of our escape.

Louie was pacing the living room, dictating her story out loud to herself and getting more and more excited with each word, while Hannah was staring self-consciously at her feet like a little girl forced by a teacher to stand in the corner.

What's more, my usual mental cheering squad were uncharacteristically quiet.

"Mr. Hanley," Louie said, stopping her pacing, "you don't happen to have a tape recorder in here anywhere, do you? Something on which I could record an interview and take with me?"

The old man looked at her.

"You really are planning to break out of this place, aren't you?" he asked.

"Yes, as soon as possible."

"And you really think you can make it?"

"Or die trying, and I don't intend to die."

"Well...well...well."

The old man's fingers went to his shirt, and he struggled to undo two of the buttons. Reaching in, he pulled out a small medic alert device attached to a chain.

"You know what this is?"

"Your call button," Hannah said. "Do you need medical attention? Is there something I can do?"

"No, no," he said, struggling to rise to his feet, and leaning heavily on the cane. "But if I press this, within about thirty seconds a small army of people will come rushing through that door there. Some of them will be concerned for my safety, like Hannah here, while a few others will be hoping this is finally my last call, so they can have the pleasure of watching me croak."

"Mr. Hanley, nobody wants that," Hannah said.

The old man smiled.

"If you say so, honey. The point is, if I press this button, none of you has a snowball's chance in hell of leaving this building, or even this room, without being stopped."

"Why would you do that?" Louie asked.

"He's concerned about us," Hannah replied for him. "He thinks we won't make it, and he's trying to save us."

"Sorry," Hanley said, "but that's not it at all. The truth is, I have a feeling that you will make it. You've made it this far, after all. No one else has ever managed that. But unless you do one thing, right here and now, I'm going to press this button and nobody's going anywhere. And believe me, I'll do it, because I've got nothing left to lose."

"Mr. Hanley, I don't want to be rude," Louie said, "but any one of us could take that thing from you before you had the chance to do anything with it."

"I won't let you harm him," Hannah declared, stepping in front of Louie.

In the interest of preventing a cat fight over the welfare of a ninety-four-year-old man, I said: "Let's hear him out at least. Okay, Mr. Hanley, what is it you want?"

He mumbled the words so much that I wasn't sure I had heard him correctly. A moment later I realized that his voice had become indistinct because he had choked up and was crying.

The cries became sobs, the desperate sobs of a prisoner.

Turning to Hannah, I asked, "Did he say what I think he said?"

She was beginning to tear up as well, but her voice was clear. "Yes, he did," she said.

"Well, I didn't catch it," Louie said. "What does he want? Whatever it is, let's do it so we can get out of here."

"He said that he would turn us all in unless we promised to take him along with us in our escape," I told her.

CHAPTER EIGHTEEN

"That's wonderful!" Louie was shouting. "He'll be able to tell his own story to everyone on camera!"

"Cameras hate me," Palmer Hanley blubbered.

But Louie wasn't listening. She had already made plans in her mind for a media blitz, a book, a shot on *60 Minutes* and a feature film, and we had not yet left the living room of the Master Suite.

"Louie, I hate to be this kind of person," I said, "but before you can accept your Pulitzer we still have to get out of here."

She stopped pacing. "Okay, what do you suggest?"

I turned to Hannah. "Do you have any ideas? You know this place better than we do."

"There are secret exits, but opening the doors set off alarms," she said.

"I have a feeling the general alarm was set off as soon as you drugged Dan and Alberto. We'll have to run for it."

"We won't get very far. There are security cameras everywhere. No matter where we went, we'd be seen."

"Why are there no cameras in here?" Louie asked.

Hannah looked down at her feet again.

"They don't want images of Mr. Hanley ever leaking out, so they make sure there are no images of him."

"Here's what they don't want a picture of," the old man said, giving the finger to the ceiling of his apartment so strenuously he nearly lost his balance and fell over, cane and all.

"I'll take a picture of that!" Louie laughed. "We'll run it with the story! God, Dave, we have to get out of here. We have to! We have to leave right now. I need this story!"

Yeah, we had to leave right now, but how?

I was still trying desperately to think of a way of breaking out of this maximum security church camp when a voice broke into my head. It was Moe Howard saying, *Lady, if you don't leave now, you're not going to miss anything.*

Anyone who has seen that particular Three Stooges short (and really, who hasn't?) knows that a moment later, one of the most titanic pie fights in the history of Hollywood breaks out.

Pies.

"Oh, my god!" I said, starting to laugh.

"You okay, Dave?" Louie asked.

"Mr. Hanley, do you shave yourself?"

The old man's eyes narrowed as thought it was a difficult question. "Yeah. Why?"

"Electric shaver?"

"No, I'm too damned wrinkled for an electric shaver. I do it the old fashioned way. If you're looking for a straight razor, son, forget it. I used one of those three-blade plastic things."

"What I'm looking for is the shave cream."

"What are you up to?" Louie asked.

"Hannah, you know where these cameras are located, right?" I asked.

"Well, yeah, they're all over, and they're not that hard to spot. Little black half-circles. on the ceiling. Why?"

"Folks, we're going to give the communications room of the Temple of Theotologics pies in the face. Where's your bathroom, Mr. Hanley?"

He pointed behind him, and I dashed in that direction, finding several other rooms, including an enormous walk-in closet, before getting to the palatial bathroom. The toilet wasn't made of gold, but that was just about the only economizing in sight.

I might be able to stand being a prisoner in this kind of environment.

On the marble counter I found a can of Gillette Foamy and was delighted to find it was nearly full. Rushing back out, I looked back and forth between Louie and Hannah, trying to guess their weights. The difference between the two was probably negligible.

"I need a volunteer, and you're it," I said, pointing to Hannah. "Get on my shoulders."

"What?"

I crouched down.

"Hurry, get in my shoulders, like we're at the beach or something."

"I don't want to."

"You know where those cameras are, now come on!"

With a great show of distaste, she straddled my head, and I struggled to stand up, nearly throwing her off behind me in the process.

"I didn't realize you were into this sort of thing," Louie said.

Ignoring her, I made it to my feet and handed Hannah the shaving cream.

"Squirt a blob of this in your hand," I instructed. "When we get in the hallway, tell me where the closest security cameras are and I'll run you there, and you smear it all over them."

"This is really stupid," Hannah said.

"Yeah, I know. It's my specialty. Now come on."

I started for the door while she maintained her balance by holding onto my hair. I would have to crouch a little to get through, and I only hoped my legs were strong enough to not collapse out from under me.

Louie rushed up to open the door, which fortunately was taller than the standard size, since this was the Master's Suite.

"She's right, Dave," Louie said, "this is stupid, but I wouldn't miss it for anything."

"Hang on, Hannah," I said, easing through the door, and then shouting. "Okay, where to first?"

"Turn right, about fifteen feet," she said, and I started jogging. I could hear her filling her hand with shave cream, followed by her shout of "Stop!"

I stopped, and she slathered the first camera with the Foamy.

"About face, past the door, and another fifteen feet," she commanded, and we repeated the action.

Within a minute we had "pied" five cameras up and down the corridor.

"Okay, that's that, now let me down," she demanded, and I was only too happy to get her weight off of my shoulders. I didn't even mind that she wiped her hands clean on my shirt, since it wasn't really my shirt. It belonged to the Temple.

We ran back to the Master's Suite and I said, "Okay, everyone out and hide somewhere."

"How about the room where they held us?" Louie asked. "Hannah has the key."

"Good idea. We can do the pie trick in there, too. Mr. Hanley, could I have that thing around your neck?"

"My alarm?" he asked.

"Yes. We're going to have a little diversion."

He lifted the device off and handed it to me.

"Okay, all of you go to the other apartment, I'll be there in a second."

They took off down the hallway. I pressed the button, threw it into the now-empty Master Suite and closed the door until it was just slightly ajar. Then I took off after them.

By the time I got back to the apartment, Hannah was already on Louie's shoulders and soaping up the visible cameras, while the unconscious forms of Dan and Alberto continued to sleep on the floor.

"What did you do?" Palmer Hanley asked me.

"I hit the alarm button."

"But that's going to bring every damn guard in the building down here!"

I smiled. "Yeah, I know. Hannah, when you're done with the foam I'll need your card key to the suite."

Louie let her down and practically beamed when Hannah cleaned her soapy hands off on her shirt.

As Hannah gave me the card key, the first sounds of approaching guards were heard in the hallway. I counted to five, and then crept out.

"Where are you going?" Louie asked.

"Back to the suite. If I'm not back in sixty seconds, you guys are on your own."

"Shit, Beauchamp!"

"Sixty seconds," I reiterated, then crept down the hallway, and saw the last few guards of what I presumed was a small army of uniformed guards flooding into the Master's Suite.

When the last one had disappeared inside, I ran down, slammed the door and locked it from the outside. The chorus of cries coming from the other side of the door was sweeter than the Andrews Sisters on their best day.

Running back to the apartment, I said: "Okay, I think we've got a chance now. But Hannah, do you think you could get some more of that knock-out juice, just in case we need it?"

She nodded. "All the drugs are kept in the lab."

"Lab? On what are they experimenting?"

"Well, we call it the lab, but it's more like an infirmary," Hannah said. "Though there is some sort of laboratory in the back. Even I'm not allowed in there. It's top secret."

"Why would they need a top secret lab? Louie asked, then got it. "To make whatever shit they're putting in the hamburgers! Hannah, we need to see inside that laboratory."

"I told you, I don't have access," Hannah replied.

"But you can get us to the infirmary, right?" I asked, and she nodded. "Okay, do that, and I'll figure out the rest."

Hannah sighed. "Elevator. This way."

She led us to the elevator, and after a fraught minute of waiting, at any moment expecting another army of angry, probably armed Theotologicians to come swarming over us, the bell dinged and the door opened.

The elevator car was blessedly empty and we leapt in (well, Hannah, Louie and I leapt; Palmer Hanley shuffled). Hannah hit the button marked *U2*, which I took to mean either we were headed up toward the second underground level, or Bono was a member of the Temple.

The doors opened and we stepped out into an empty hallway.

"Luck's with us," I said, which of course signaled Luck to run out faster than a tank of gas in a Hummer.

The hallway was suddenly filled with an ear-splitting alarm, which I could only presume was meant to alert the uniformed herd that we had escaped. Glancing up, I could see the security cameras dotted along the ceiling.

There was no hiding now.

"They're watching us," Hannah said. That was when I had an idea. "Mr. Hanley, give me your cane," I said.

"But I can't walk without it," he replied.

"Louie, help him. Carry him if you have to. But try to make it looking like you're forcing him."

"What are you up to?" she asked.

Taking the cane from the old man, I held it like a rifle and pointed it at Hannah.

"If they think Louie and I are taking the two of you hostage and forcing you to come with us, they might stop to ask questions before opening fire. That's at least something. Hannah, put your hands up and get us to the lab."

"All right," she said, and I wasn't sure she fully understood what I was attempting, but she went along with it.

As for whoever might be watching us, I could only hope that the resolution of the security footage was low enough to mistake a cane for a gun.

The laboratory was at the end of the hallway and was protected by the kind of metal door that wanted to be part of a bank vault when it grew up. Hannah produced the cardkey from her pocket and quickly opened it, and as soon as we were in, I waved the cane around and shouted: "All right, everyone, get down, now! I have a gun!"

Hannah immediately dropped to the floor, even though she was not the one I was addressing; instead it was the four people in white lab coats and masks amidst the tables filled with machinery and medical apparatuses, who were startled by our sudden appearance.

Whether genuinely frightened or simply so used to following orders that it was second-nature, they all hit the linoleum.

Nudging Hannah with my foot, I whispered: "You get up and get the knock out shots."

While she did I continued my act. "Don't anyone move, or you'll get it in the back of the head!" I shouted.

The only reply came from Bogie: *Jesus, kid, who writes your dialogue?*

"Don't hurt me!" one of them cried.

"Do as your told and you won't get hurt," I replied.

It took only a few seconds for Hannah to stick each of the prone scientists in their butts.

"Thanks for cooperating, folks, and nighty-night."

When they were all under, I asked Hannah to show us the door to the secret lab, but to my surprise, she hesitated.

"What if I get in trouble?" she asked.

"Hannah, we're a little beyond that now!" Louie cried.

"I'm not supposed to enter the lab."

"Hannah, look, you still don't have to enter it," I said. "Just show us where it is."

"Even if I show you, I told you, I don't have a key."

"No, but one of them might," I said, pointing at the four prone figures on the floor, now stripped of their lab coats and masks.

Practically leaping to the closest one, Louie shoved her hand in his trouser pocket. Finding nothing, she tried the other pocket, then rolled him over and tried his shirt pockets.

"Help me!" she called, and I went to another of the lab workers, but after examining him, I could only find an ID tag and a handful of change. Louie was already onto the third one when it hit me.

"Look in the lab coat pockets," I said, and she dashed over to the pile of coats that had been draped across a table. Three of them yielded nothing but a used tissue, but from the fourth she pulled out a keycard embossed with the word *RESTRICTED*.

"Bingo," Louie crowed, and then she returned to Hannah. For a moment I was afraid she was going to use force on the poor girl to get her to show us to the lab, but instead, she smiled and lightly traced Hannah's face with her hand.

"It'll be fine, baby," she whispered. "I promise."

That worked (and someday, if we were all lucky enough to get out, I knew I'd have to ask Louie where you go to learn knowing exactly what to do to get what you want).

The lab door was at the very back of the infirmary, and unlike the door we had come through, it was nondescript to the point of being invisible. It did not even have a knob, just a push plate and a key slot.

Louie slid in the keycard and a green light appeared, followed by a buzz signaling that the door was ready to be opened.

"I hope no one's inside," Hannah whispered, though we didn't have to worry. The large room was empty of people but contained enough tubes, flasks, piping, wads of steel wool and Bunsen burners to fill a dozen Dr. Frankenstein laboratories.

"Oh, my god, I don't believe it," Louie said. "They're not putting nicotine into the burgers, they're putting methamphetamine!"

"Are you sure?" I asked. "How do you know what a meth lab looks like?"

"Didn't you ever watch *Breaking Bad*, Dave?"

Running to the closest table, Louie began searching through the flasks.

"Whoa, whoa, whoa, what are you doing?" I said.

"Looking for a sample to take with us," she said. "We'll need the proof for the story."

"Louie, even if we make it out of here, which is a big if, neither of us has any ID. They've taken it. So should the police show up—"

"Why would they show up?"

"Because the Temple has called them, maybe? You're the one who claimed they have influence within the police department."

"Okay, so they catch us without ID. Is that a crime?" she said.

"No, but walking around carrying methamphetamine, or whatever it is they make here, is. Do you really want to take that chance?"

She fell silent for a second, which I took as the acknowledgement of my argument.

"But we have to get proof."

"We'll come back," I said. "First we get out of here, then we get the police and ideally a search warrant, and we come back for the proof. Now let's go."

Reluctantly, Louie agreed. Back in the infirmary I instructed Louie and Hannah to remove the lab coats and masks from the four prone figures, while Palmer Hanley watched with amusement from a stool.

"You're pretty clever, young fella," he said.

"Only on my good days," I replied.

"I take it that we're going to wear these outfits to get out of here," Louie said.

"That's the plan."

"But I don't think any of these coats are going to fit Mr. Hanley," Hannah said. "They're too big."

"That's all right," I told her. "Mr. Hanley isn't going to walk out with us."

The other three shouted in unison, "But you said—!" and I merely held up my hand for silence.

"Why should he walk when he can ride in style?"

Then I pointed to a folded-up wheelchair that was leaning against one wall. It took Hannah less than thirty seconds to unfold it and roll it over, but a bit longer for Palmer Hanley to settle himself into it."

"Now come on. Let's get these coats on and get out of here."

We were just about to leave when Louie said, "Wait, why don't we take their IDs with us, just in case?"

"Good idea," I said, picking the pockets of one of the unconscious lab workers, taking not only his Temple ID, but his wallet as well.

"All right, folks, here we go. If one of us gets stopped, the others keep going. Agreed?"

Louie, whose face was now obscured by a medical mask, nodded, while Hannah said, "I'll stay by Mr. Hanley's side no matter what happens."

As for Hanley, he merely smiled and said, "I'm ready for anything."

After leading everyone to the lab door I took a deep breath and then threw it open as though I owned the building, and stepped out into the hallway. Two uniformed guards were running the opposite direction, and one of them stopped.

"Everything okay?" he asked.

"Yes," I said through the mask, "though the Master has had a…a seizure. We need to get him up top."

Upon recognizing the man in the wheelchair the guard's mouth fell open and he practically genuflected.

"Master, this is an honor," he stammered.

"Thanks," Hanley replied, though I could see him mouth silently, *for nothing*.

"Do you need any help?"

"We're fine, but we are in a hurry," I said. "You wouldn't want to be responsible for the Master not getting the care he requires, would you?"

"No, no!" the guard screamed. "Go on!"

We dashed to the elevator and waited nervously until the car arrived, and once inside, rode to the top level. When the doors opened again, we looked out onto pandemonium. All manner of people were running around as though there was a fire, and confusion reigned.

"This is bad," Hannah said.

"No, it's good," I countered. "Mr. Hanley, keep your head down, okay?"

Lowering his head, he placed a bony hand over his brow and balanced that arm with his other hand.

"Hannah, take the lead and run us to the nearest exit, and I mean run. I'll push the wheelchair."

She dashed out of the elevator with the rest of us following and weaved her way through the stampede of Theotologicians, none of whom appeared to give us any attention at all, which was what I was hoping.

We soon came to an exit door marked *Emergency*.

"There's an alarm on this," Hannah said, stopping before it.

"Good," I said, "more confusion can only help us."

Since it appeared as though she was deliberating whether to actually go through, Louie charged the door and pushed it open. Immediately, a siren sounded. She held it open so I could get Palmer Hanley through. But Hannah remained where she was.

"Coming or going?" Louie shouted.

"I...I...I don't think I can leave," Hannah said.

"Nothing's going to happen to you out here," I said.

She shook her head. "What if I go back on drugs out there? The world is a dangerous place."

"Hannah, it's time to stop believing your indoctrination," I said.

"It's not that, it's...look, the security tapes show you appearing to hold me at gunpoint to get you out, so let me stay here and confirm that's what happened. I'll be okay."

Yeah, okay like Regina Fontaine, okay like Avery Klemmer, the cynical, wheezy voice of Elisha Cook, Jr. said inside my head.

But there was nothing more I could do.

"Mr. Hanley is in good hands now," she said. "He doesn't need me anymore."

There was no time to argue. "Be careful, Hannah, and thanks," I said, pulling Louie away and letting the emergency exit door close on the young nurse.

Hopefully that's all that would be closing on her.

Looking around, I had to smile in spite of myself. We were indeed on the lot of a film studio, having just emerged from what appeared to be an administration building. A soundstage stood to our right and another one in front of us, and just beyond it I could see a parking lot.

"This way," I said, pushing Palmer Hanley down the narrow street that separated the stages.

For those who have never actually been on a movie lot, they are a lot like a city whose buildings are shaped like enormous airplane hangars, only taller. A grid of streets run between them, which are reserved mostly for pedestrians, bicycles and golf carts, with very little vehicular traffic. It is extremely hard to get inside your average movie lot unless you have official clearance, but not that difficult to leave.

Here at Paranoia Pictures, however, it was clearly different. Having made it as far as the parking lot, I could see guards stopping everyone, those coming in and going out. To make matters worse, it was probably us the outgoing guards were looking for.

"What do we do now?" Louie asked.

"I tell 'em who I am and we get the hell out of here!" Mr. Hanley said, squirming in his wheelchair.

"I'm afraid that wouldn't work, sir," I told him. "You'd be back in the Master's Suite before you knew it, and we'd be…well, I don't know what they'd do with us."

The old man shook his head. "Why couldn't I have become a bank robber all those years ago instead?"

As we sat there—well, Palmer Hanley sat; Louie and I crouched— I tried to figure a way out of this. Then the solution came rumbling toward us. It was a "greens" truck, a flatbed with high sides containing potted trees used for filming, and it appeared to be leaving the studio!

"That's it, right there," I said. "Louie, take Mr. Hanley. When I stop the truck, get him onto the flatbed and then you jump up there and both of you hide in the plants."

"What about you?" she asked.

"I'll be right behind you."

"How're you going to stop the truck?" Mr. Hanley asked.

"Watch. And get ready."

The greens truck was not moving very fast which made it easy to jump out in front of it without fear of getting run over.

"Hey! Hey!" I shouted, waving my arms, bringing the truck to a halt.

"What do you think you're doing?" the driver bellowed through the window. "God, buddy, you look like you've already been hit by a truck."

"What? Oh, right, my…uh, makeup," I said, acknowledging my swollen nose. "I'm sorry to bother you, but do you know where Stage Six is?"

"What?"

"Stage Six. I'm supposed to report there to play a doctor for a training film, but I can't find it."

Peripherally I could see Louie pushing the wheelchair containing Palmer Hanley past the other side of the truck.

"All the stages are that way," growled the driver growled, a burly, Teamstery looking guy with sunglasses and a ball cap, and arms of such size and thickness that I hoped I wasn't making him too angry.

"That way?" I pointed aimlessly.

"*That* way!" he shouted.

I was already sprinting away when I shouted, "Okay, thanks!"

As soon as I saw him face forward again in the truck cab, I darted around behind and grabbed onto the wooden-slat gate over the end of the bed and held on as the driver threw the truck into gear again. I was praying that Louie had been able to get over the gate and had managed to get Hanley in, when I noticed their faces peeking out from between the potted trees.

I had to wait until the driver had stopped at the gate before I was able to completely pull myself up and over, and join them.

"I had to pick him up out of the wheelchair and lift him over the tailgate," Louie whispered. "It's a good thing I work out."

Yeah, great, my nose said.

Moments later the truck was cleared to leave and we were out of the studio. As we bumped down Santa Monica Boulevard Louie asked: "Now what? Where do you think we are going?"

"I don't know," I replied, "but as soon as it's convenient, we'll get out."

That convenience came about three minutes later when the truck stopped at an intersection that I knew from experience had very long lights.

Rushing to the back, I leapt over the gate, careful not to land on the car that was stopped directly behind us.

"Hi," I said, smiling and waving to that car's driver. Louie brought Palmer Hanley to the back and between the two of us we lifted him up, down and out, after which Louie easily vaulted over the gate.

Weaving our way through the stopped cars, and carrying Palmer between us, we got to the sidewalk a full minute before the light changed and the greens truck drove off to its destination, wherever that was, its driver completely oblivious that he had facilitated the escape of three wanted fugitives from a cult.

"Whoo-ee!" Palmer Hanley exclaimed, looking exhausted, but also beaming. "That's the most action I've had in three decades. But I need to rest before the next lap. Can we find a place where I can get something to drink?"

"You mean a bar?" I asked.

"Just water. Or maybe some coffee."

With Louie on one side of him and me on the other, we managed to get him to a fifties-style diner that was a half-block up the street.

Seated at a table away from a window, just in case, we looked over the menus, while Palmer Hanley drained the glass of ice water the waitress had brought for him.

"That's better," he sighed. "When you get to be my age, a little bit of excitement goes a long way."

"Leaping in and out of a truck isn't exactly commonplace for me, either," I told him.

The waitress returned and took an order for coffee and a piece of strawberry pie from Hanley, an ice tea from me, and a kind of *cerveza* called Victoria from Louie.

"I've earned it," she said.

Surreptitiously inspecting the wad of cash I had lifted from the unconscious lab technician back at the studio, I was gratified to see that I could afford anything on the menu.

The Temple must pay their drug cookers well. I had even stopped worrying about getting in trouble over the theft, having realized that the victims' statements to the police would be, *Yes, officer, I was minding my own business at the meth lab like usual when these three broke in...*

After our drinks and Palmer Hanley's pie arrived Louie took a long swig of her beer and said, "I have to hand it to you, Dave, we're out. So what's next?"

"I'd say we get word to someone to come and get us. We need to get hold of a phone, since ours are still back in the studio-prison, along with our ID."

"Who would you call?"

"Detective Dane Colfax in robbery-homicide."

"Why him?"

"Because I trust him."

Sure, Colfax tended to play things a bit aloof, to the point where it was hard to imagine him in any kind of personal relationship, but I did trust him.

"I'm not as trusting when it comes to the police," Louie said, looking behind us. "But I think I've solved the phone problem."

Sliding out from the booth and taking off her lab coat, which she deposited on the seat, she straightened the shirt of the Temple uniform and headed straight for a young Chicano busboy.

Walking to him she started talking in Spanish, which I did not understand, but there was no mistaking her body language. It read, *I'm in trouble and I need your help, please oh please oh please oh pleeeease*!

Now grinning broadly, the busboy pulled his cell phone from his pocket and handed it over to her. Louie smiled back, making me suddenly wonder what the Spanish word for "dimples" was, and kissed him on his cheek, which made the kid blush.

Then she ran back to our booth.

"You're shameless," I told her.

"Hey, you do what you have to do to get the story," she said, punching a number into the phone.

After a second, she said, "I need to talk to Z, it's Louie Sandoval."

It appeared to take no time at all for Zareh Zarian to come on the line.

"Z! Yeah, it's me. I'm fine. Safe. Dave Beauchamp is here with me and you're not going to believe who else. I'm not going to tell you until I'm guaranteed a cover."

I could hear yelling coming from the other end of the line, and saw Louie smile triumphantly.

"I've got the story of the decade," she went on, "maybe the quarter-century. But right now we have to get to you, and we have no means of doing so. You have to come get us. We're in a diner on Santa Monica Boulevard. No, I don't know the address."

Holding the phone away, she asked: "What's the address here?"

Getting up and trotting to the front window, I peered out and took note of the cross-street. Coming back, I said, "Corner of Santa Monica and Ogden Drive."

She repeated that into the phone, then repeated: "Yes, we're fine. I told you."

"Can I talk to him?" I asked, and Louie handed the cell phone over.

"Hi, Zarian? This is Beauchamp. Everything Louie told you is true. This really is the story of the quarter-century. But we're kind of in trouble, too, so if you could call Detective Dane Colfax at the LAPD, he's in the robbery-homicide division, and a good guy. Just let him know that I need to talk to him as soon as I can. No, I don't have his number, but his office is downtown at police admin center. Yeah. Okay, thanks."

I held the phone out to Louie but Palmer Hanley said, "Wait, if he's rescuing us, I want to talk to him, too."

After exchanging glances and shrugs with Louie, I gave him the phone. "Hurry up, I don't have unlimited time!" the old man said, and then handed the phone over.

"Who was that? It's a long story," Louie told her editor. "See you soon."

She cut off the call slid out of the booth again, returning it to her new friend.

When she came back, I asked: "How long will it take for Zarian to get here?"

"It's in his best interest to get here as soon as possible," she replied.

"As long as we're stuck here waiting," Hanley said, "how about ordering me another slice of pie?"

I wouldn't have believed it, but the former actor turned phony religious guru was on his third piece of strawberry pie when Zareh Zarian walked into the diner.

Making a bee-line for our table, he lifted Louie out of her seat and bear-hugged her. "Goddamn, girl, you don't know how worried I was about you!" he said.

"Z, how many times do I have to tell you that I can take care of myself."

I helped a little, *don't you think?* a voice said inside my head, and it was *my* voice, but I decided to leave it where it was.

"Hi, Beauchamp," Zarian said when he was through groping Louie. "What the hell happened to your face?"

"Like Louie said, she can take care of herself."

"Christ, you hit him? What'd he do to you?"

"We had to stage a little pretense for our captors, and it had to look convincing," she replied.

"It's going to keep looking convincing for about a week. Does it hurt, Beauchamp?"

"Oh, only when I breathe," I said.

"But look who else we brought with us," Louie went on, ignoring my battered nose and instead turning Zarian's attention to the other person seated in the booth.

The editor's face betrayed confusion for a few seconds, then the fog lifted.

"Holy shit, Sandoval," he said, "are you telling me this is—"

"Palmer Hanley," the old man said, spraying pie crust crumbs across the table.

"I don't believe it."

"They were so desperate to get my research information," she went on, "but look what I took from them. This is better than any reporter's notes."

"But you still have the notes, right?" Zarian asked.

"Safely hidden."

"As we need to be," I broke in. "When we were guests of the Temple they emptied our pockets. Wallets, IDs, cell phones, keys, everything was taken from us. Even if I can get back to my apartment or office, I have no way of getting in, not that it matters, most likely, since I'm sure both are being watched by members of the Temple. The same probably goes for Louie's place."

Across the table, Louie suddenly tensed. "They're here, too," she said, nodding toward the front of the diner. "They've found us."

Cheating a look back, I saw two strapping men in the quasi-military uniforms of the Temple guard standing in the doorway and looking around. "I don't think they've spotted us yet, but it's only a matter of time."

"Is there a back way out of here?" Zarian asked quietly.

"There must be," Louie said.

"Then you three go find it and get out. I'll pay the bill and meet you outside, somewhere. I'll cover your exit. Go."

It'll never work, a voice said in my head, and I didn't even care who it was. That line had been spoken in so many movies by so many actors and actresses that it hardly mattered. What mattered was that I fully agreed with the speaker, this plan was doomed to failure.

Unfortunately, I didn't have a better idea at present. As Zareh Zarian stood up, keeping his back to the door of the restaurant, Louie and I slid out from the table, pulling Palmer Hanley with us, and crouched our way to the restrooms.

"I wasn't finished," the old man protested, but we ignored him. If we didn't get out of here, we'd all be finished.

"There," Louie said, pointing to the emergency exit at the end hallway in which the bathrooms were located. "Let's hope it's not alarmed."

"Even if it is, that's too bad," I said, rushing to the door and pushing it open. No sirens or bells when off, so we ran outside into the parking lot.

"What do we do now?" Louie asked.

"Wait for Zarian, I guess, and hope nobody from the Temple shows up."

"Bastards," Hanley muttered. "All of 'em."

For some reason that made me laugh, a reaction I attempted unsuccessfully to stifle.

"Don't get hysterical on me, Dave," Louie cautioned.

"I'm not hysterical, it's just that. All of a sudden this seems kind of funny."

I was still chuckling when I saw Louie tense again.

"Uniform coming up behind you," she whispered.

Then I heard a voice at my back say: "Okay, let's go."

I stopped laughing then, and concentrated my efforts on trying not to wet myself.

CHAPTER NINETEEN

Slowly I turned around, and when I saw the short Hispanic man in the parking attendant's uniform, which in Louie's defense did resemble a Temple of Theotologic's guard uniform fairly closely, my legs nearly buckled.

"Come on, buddy, let's go, I've got other customers waiting," he said. "Give me your ticket and I'll give you your keys."

"I don't have a ticket," I exhaled. "We're not parked here."

"Just here for the scenery, huh?"

"No, my…uh…father suddenly felt ill, so we came out here for some air."

"Who's father?" Palmer Hanley said.

I silently mouthed *senile* to the attendant, whose demeanor suddenly changed to one of concern. "Is he okay? You need me to call an ambulance?"

"No, but if there's somewhere to sit down…"

"Yeah, sure, come to the booth."

As I half-dragged the still-oblivious Palmer Hanley to the guard booth, which had two chairs inside, another customer came up waiving his ticket at the guard.

"Hold on," the guy said, "this is an emergency." Ushering us in, he said, "He can sit there. I'll be back."

After the guard had gone to deal with his impatient customer, Hanley asked, "What's going on, anyway?"

"We're hiding," I told him.

He looked around at the well-lighted, windowed guard booth.

"Not too well, we're not."

He had me there.

Then I heard a car horn and through the window of the booth spotted a beat-up looking minivan on the street, with Louie Sandoval hanging out of the window, beckoning us.

Grabbing the old man up again, I dashed toward the vehicle as the guard called out behind us. I ignored him. Practically throwing

Hanley inside the minivan, I jumped in after him and Zareh Zarian peeled away from the curb and onto the street.

"You know, Dave Beauchamp," Hanley said, "being chucked around like a sack of potatoes is getting a little old. How come I couldn't keep that wheelchair? I kinda liked traveling that way."

"I'll try to get you another one," I said, then asked Zarian where we were going.

"To a safe house," he called back, running a red light.

The *Los Angeles Independent Journal* utilized a safe house? Who knew?

I had barely finished wondering how safe it was when the voice of Dustin Hoffman entered my brain saying, *It's so safe you wouldn't believe it.*

Thirty-five minutes later, we pulled into the Ali Baba Motor Hotel located in one of the more scurrilous sections of southern Hollywood.

Bette Davis's voice provided the commentary: *What a dump*!

At first glance it was hard to tell if the place was even open for business or not.

"*This* is a safe house?" I asked, getting out of Zarian's van. "It doesn't look safe enough to spend the night in."

"That's the entire point," Zarian replied. "Would *you* look for somebody important here?"

"How long did it take you to find this little bit of heaven on earth?"

"My cousin owns it."

"Swell."

"Oh, stop grumbling, Beauchamp and get your ass inside."

Zarian led us into the lobby, where a bored-looking woman sat behind the counter.

"Is Antran here?" he asked.

The woman looked up at Zarian and rolled her eyes.

"He's in the back," she offered, before turning to the room behind her and shouting, "Antranig, your cousin!"

Moments later Antranig came out.

"Zari!" he cried, embracing his cousin. "Who are we hiding this time?" Then looking at me, he added: "And what the hell happened to you?"

"Picked a bar fight with a midget," I told him. "Never do that. They're short, but they're mean."

"Okay."

"I worked with Billy Barty once," Hanley said. "He was nice as all get out—"

"I believe you, sir," I said, cutting him off.

"Antran, you're not going to believe it," Zarian broke in, "but this is Palmer Hanley. You know, the Temple of Theotologics Palmer Hanley?"

The manager looked the old man up and down. "You're joking."

"I'm not."

"He's right, he's not," Hanley added.

"Why is he here?"

"They're looking for him."

"Who's looking for him?"

"The entire Temple," I interjected.

"So who are you, midget-puncher?"

"My name's Dave Beauchamp, I'm a private investigator."

"Like Magnum with a purple nose?"

"Yeah, just like. Except I don't have a stunt double like Tom Selleck does."

"You should think about getting one. I am Antranig Bedekian. I don't have a stunt double either."

He laughed heartily.

"Look," Zarian said, "I need two, maybe three rooms. Do you have them?"

"Well, I don't know, we're pretty booked…" Antranig said.

Sure. The empty parking lot told how booked up the place was.

"The usual safe house rate."

"For family, I always have room."

"Two should be sufficient," I offered. "Louie and I can stay in one room."

The proprietor looked at us. "Are you married?"

I was about to lie to him and say yes when I heard Louie say instead: "I'll stay in one room and the boys can stay in the other."

"Fine, two rooms," the proprietor said. "Ten and twelve, next to each other."

"That will be fine," Zarian said.

"How long will they be here?"

"That I can't answer. Tonight, obviously, maybe another night."

Well, if I had to be stuck in a room in a fleabag hotel somewhere on the bad side of town, at least I'd be with someone to whom I could talk about the old days of Hollywood, if Palmer Hanley was up for it.

Then another thought struck me. "Did you ever get in touch with Detective Colfax?" I asked Zarian.

"Just got his machine and left a message. I'll try again when I get back to the office."

"If we can get him involved, I'm sure we can get out of here and back to our own places."

"I don't have a place anymore," Hanley said.

"Don't worry," Louie chimed in, "when my story breaks, you'll be able to stay anywhere you want."

Bedekian now handed us the keys to our respective rooms. "If you need anything, call the desk," he said.

"I don't suppose you have breakfast, do you?" I asked.

The proprietor laughed. "Anything you can catch, you can eat."

I hoped he was kidding.

As the four of us stepped out of the office, Louie said to Zarian: "I need to go back to the Temple complex, you know. I have to get absolute proof regarding that meth lab."

"But it has to be done the right way," the editor argued.

"Z, if we wait too long, they'll dismantle the lab and hide all the evidence!"

"And if we fly off the handle and don't do things exactly by the book, whatever you do find will be tossed out of court. You don't want that, do you?"

"What I want is to lie down," Palmer Hanley said. "Think we could go to the room?"

"Sure, come on," I said, "but you two come with us."

We walked to Room Ten and opened it, and at least bats didn't fly out. The place was actually relatively clean, though there was only one bed. It was probably technically big enough to hold us both, but I wasn't particularly looking forward to finding out.

Sometimes ya gotta do what ya...gotta do, John Wayne helpfully intoned inside my head.

Sure, Duke, like you ever bundled with Walter Brennan.

While Louie and Zarian continued to argue about the best way to storm the movie studio that was the Temple of Theotologics' fortress, Palmer Hanley crawled onto the bed and in less than a minute began to snore, and I doubted he could be awakened even by the rising volume of Louie's voice.

"Guys, can we have a truce here?" I asked, and the two stopped arguing. "I really think I can make everything a lot easier by involving Detective Colfax. Zarian, you must have a cell phone. Let me try calling him again."

"All right," he said, pulling a smart phone from his pocket and handing it over. Since I didn't have Colfax's number memorized, and I didn't have my wallet, which probably wouldn't have mattered, since I don't think I put his card in it, I dialed 4-1-1…and then handed the phone back.

"This is out of juice," I said. "I thought I was the only one who forgot to charge his phone."

"That's not like you, Z," Louie added.

"It blipped earlier to tell me it was hungry, and then you guys called, and I forgot all about it," he protested.

"Okay, fine, I'll call from the room," I said. "There is a phone in here, isn't there?"

"On the desk."

Desk. That was a creative name for the rickety pile of wood that was pushed against one wall of the room. But it did hold a phone.

"Z, at least take me back to the office," Louie was saying. "I can make some calls there."

"Look, kiddo, I can't risk losing my best reporter," Zarian replied. "You stay here tonight. The world won't end in one night. I'll go back and call my shysters and get some advice from them on how to proceed. Okay?"

Louie didn't like the arrangement, but she finally agreed.

"Good. I'll be back in the morning. Until then, don't do anything visible."

"In this neighborhood?" I said. "I don't think I'll be taking any long walks."

After a quick hug of Louie, Zareh Zarian turned and headed out, leaving her, me, and a snoring nonagenarian to the delights of the Ali Baba Motor Hotel.

"God, I hate this!" Louie said. "I hate just sitting around and waiting!"

"Hanley's sawing some pretty big logs," I said. "Maybe I could just leave him here and come over to your room…"

"Nice try," Louie said, smiling warmly and revealing those dimples again, "but I need to think, and make some notes."

Seeming to read my expression (which, if on the outside it looked anything like I was feeling, I could have taken the Gold in Pathos), she put and hand on my shoulder and added:

"Aw, turn off the hurt puppy look, okay? I like you, Dave, I really do, but we're no longer in enough danger."

"I could run with scissors," I argued.

"Or you could hotwire a car and drive me back to that movie studio so I can get my evidence. That would be dangerous!"

Suicidal was my word for it. I shook my head.

"Even if I knew how to hotwire a car, I wouldn't do it," I told her. "You're going to have to go with your boss on this one."

"He's never going to follow up on it," she said. "He's terrified of the Temple."

"You still have Palmer Hanley, live and in the flesh, to tell his story. Shouldn't that be enough to get the DA's office interested?"

"I know you're trying to help, Dave, but…shit." She gave me a chaste peck on the cheek. "That's for trying to help."

Then she went out and unlocked her room, Room Twelve. I heard her moan, "Oh, god, what a pit," right before the door closed behind her.

Fine, I thought, *I'll call Colfax on the house phone.* If there was a charge for it, Zarian would be paying anyway.

Maybe I should call my cousin in Cleveland while I was at it. I went to the parody of a desk and picked up the phone and hit the "O" button.

Antranig answered a second later: "Yes?"

"Hi, it's Beauchamp in Ten."

"My cousin's friend?"

"Yes. I need to get an outside phone line."

"Hang up, hit star-nine, and that will take you out. It will be put on your bill."

"Your cousin is paying, remember?"

"Of course," he laughed, "but I hope you know better than to try to fuck with him regarding money. I've known him longer than you."

This was followed by another laugh, which I did not respond to, because I had suddenly turned colder than young Charles Foster Kane sledding down the hill.

"Right…thanks," I said, putting the phone receiver in the cradle on the second try.

I'm wrong, I thought; *I have to be wrong.*

You're not wrong, kid, Bogie told me.

I must have made a mistake.

No mistake, Duke Wayne chimed in.

"What do I do now?" I said aloud.

Well, stop shaking like a leaf, for one thing, Lauren Bacall admonished.

That was easier said than done, because listening to Antranig Bedekian on the phone just now, I thought I recognized his voice, and hard as I tried to tell myself I was being ridiculous, I knew I had heard it before.

And I knew where.

Furthermore, because I spend so much of my time hearing and placing disembodied voices, to the point where I could even tell those of Gene Kelly and John Garfield apart (and if you think that's easy, try it blindfolded sometime), I was confident in my identification of Bedekian, the manager of the ten-cent hotel and the cousin of Louie Sandoval's editor and friend.

It was his voice on the threatening message that was left on Louie's phone machine in her apartment.

CHAPTER TWENTY

Antranig Bedekian was one of *them*, and we had just been delivered into his hands. Did that mean Zareh Zarian was *also* a Theotologician? That made no sense whatsoever.

Are you certain about that? the skeptical voice of Edward Everett Horton asked.

"Yeah, I am," I told the room, which contained only me and the sleeping form of Palmer Hanley. "He's a crusader for the truth, at least in his own mind."

Or is he someone who uses his position to make certain that the truth never actually emerges? This time the questioner was Spencer Tracy.

Was that possible?

It still didn't scan, but even if Zarian was an innocent bystander, the fact that his cousin was not only involved in the Temple but at a high enough adjustment level that he could leave threats against people suddenly made Zarian untrustworthy.

I had to let Louie in on this.

Dashing out of the room I practically pounded on her door.

Opening the door, she said, "Look, Dave, I told you once—"

"We're in dan…trouble," I blurted out.

"What kind of trouble?"

I told her, and her first reaction was to tell me I was wrong, then that I was crazy, but I persisted.

"Louie, think. Did Zarian ever act as though he didn't want you to follow the Burger Heaven story?"

"Hell no, he made it easy for me."

Then she stopped and her face became thoughtful.

"Oh, Jesus Christ, Dave," she said, finally. "He made it *too* easy. He let me have *carte blanche*, never questioned any of my decisions or actions, the way he normally would when I'm on a story. I assumed it was because he was as excited about the outcome of this one as I was, but now…oh, god, do you think he was playing me? What an idiot I've been!"

"Louie, we don't have time for recriminations. We have to get out of here, and we have to take Hanley with us."

"You make that sound like it's a problem."

"Go next door. He's snoring so loudly I doubt you could roust him if you lit a fire under him. I guess we could try calling for a cab, if Antranig isn't listening in on the phone, but I wouldn't bet against that. If it was just you and me, we could simply leave and start walking."

"Dave, you're not working yourself up into leaving him here, are you?"

"No, of course not."

"Because I need him for my story."

"I know, and I'm not so heartless as to abandon an old man who's been held captive for thirty years. I just don't know what to do."

If anybody inside my head has a wizard idea, this would be an excellent time to say so. No? It figures.

But Louie, for some reason, was smiling at me.

"You know, Dave, you can be a genius at times."

"Thanks. What did I say?" I asked.

"You said you could only get Hanley up if you lit a fire under him. So, we'll light a fire."

"Louie, that's an expression."

"Think about it, though," she said. "We set a fire, the fire department comes, we ask them to call your friend with the police, and we get out of here."

"Arson is illegal, you know."

"Only if it's proven."

I looked at her, hoping to find some indication she was joking, and finding none.

"Have you ever thought about going into politics?"

"Occasionally, but that's no matter. We have to start a fire."

"This place will go up like tinder!"

"Not if we start a small one."

"Okay, fine, all right, let's say we agree to start a fire. How do we do it? I don't smoke. Do you smoke?"

"No," she said. "I wish Regina was here. She smoked like a chimney. Do you think Hanley smokes?"

"I didn't see him with a cigarette. Hey, maybe Bedekian in the office has matches?"

That's good thinking, kid, Bogie piped up. *Go borrow matches from the manager right before a fire breaks out.*

"I have an idea, Dave," Louie said, taking off her shirt and then her bra.

"Louie, please don't tell me that your ultimate danger jones is to make love in a burning building," I moaned.

"Sounds kind of sweet, but this isn't for you," she replied, then she put her Temple shirt back on, but only fastened the bottom button, which made her look like the cover model for the *Theotologics Today* swimsuit issue.

I couldn't help it; I was getting hard. Louie didn't notice, however; instead she stepped to the window of the room, slid open the curtains, and peered out.

"What are you looking for?" I asked.

"A smoker."

About three minutes later, her face broke into a grin and she turned around, winked at me, and then went outside. Barely a minute later she returned with a lit cigarette.

"What did you have to do for that?" I asked.

"Less than you think," she said. "Now, get that wastebasket over there and find some paper."

The ancient L.A. city phone book on the desk made the most obvious paper source, so I started ripping out thin pages and dropping them in the basket. She then took the lit cigarette and held the end to them, and in no time, we had quite a little camp fire going.

Picking the basket up carefully, Louie carried it over to the window and stuck the bottom of the curtains in the blaze, igniting them. Then she threw the burning basket on top of the bed and opened the door of the room.

"Next door, hurry. We have to wake the old man up."

Palmer Hanley proved so hard to awaken that, if not for his snoring, I might have assumed he'd at last reached the final fade-out while we were gone.

Finally he opened his eyes. "I was dreaming," he muttered.

"Sorry, sir, but we have to leave," I said.

"Again? How this time, another flatbed truck?"

"Nope," Louie said. "This time by fire engine."

Hanley shook his head.

"Thirty years you sit in a room and read and watch TV, and then you get a lifetime of adventure in one day. All right, let's roll. Wait… I smell smoke."

"That's why the fire truck's coming. We'll explain later."

The three of us ran outside and watched as smoke billowed out from under the door of room twelve. A few moments later, Bedekian came running out of the office, his arms waving.

"What the hell did you do to my motel?" he screamed.

"We didn't do anything!" Louie lied. "It must be the crappy wiring in this place."

"Wiring my ass! I'm calling the police!"

"The fire department might be a better choice, don't you think?" I asked.

"Shit!" Bedekian cried, running back into the office and the fire in the room grew larger.

The first siren was heard off in the distance about three minutes later. Meanwhile the woman at the motel, presumably Mrs. Bedekian, ran out with a bucket of water, which she threw through the door of the room onto the flames, then ran back to get more. By the time the first fire engine had shown up, flames were largely out.

Add a successful arson fire to the list of things I can't do.

Even though there was little left of the blaze but smoldering blankets, the firefighters were too busy to be pulled aside. I thought Louie might have a little more luck gaining their attention, but even she was not able to distract them. I was starting to think that this whole, dangerous adventure was so much wasted effort, when another vehicle with a siren arrived.

It was an unmarked police car which screeched to a halt in the Ali Baba's parking lot, and at first sight it filled me with hope. Then I saw the driver get out.

It was Detective Hector Mendoza.

"Oh, holy Mother of God!" he said upon seeing me.

"You know, Hector, I understand that the LAPD is understaffed for a city of this size," I said, "but isn't there anyone else?"

"This is my turf, asshole," he replied. "Manager called me. Said he had a firebug. So are you into arson now, Beauchamp?"

"It was the wiring in this garbage hotel. Just look at the place. Hey, where's your new helper?"

"Back at the station."

Louie came up and asked, "Are you LAPD?"

"Yeah, who are you?"

"Luisa Sandoval, *L.A. Independent Journal*, and I need you to take me back to Windsor Studios."

"Louie, don't!" I cried.

"Windsor Studios…what the hell are you talking about?"

"Hector, look," I broke in, "take us back to the stationhouse. I promise I'll explain everything there. I'll even tell you who killed Regina Fontaine."

"What the hell do you know about that?" Mendoza shouted. "Oh, I get it, you did it, that's how you know."

"Stop being such a Mexican moron, would you?" I yelled, and while I would have loved to blame that one on one of the regular voices in my head, I'm afraid it was original.

But I was beyond caring. "Take us in, book us if you must! It might prove to be the only place we're safe!"

Mendoza shook his head. "I really don't get it," he said, "but I'll be happy to book you, Beauchamp. Get in the car. You too, lady."

"And the old guy, he goes with us," I said.

"Fine, whatever."

We started to pile into Mendoza's car when Palmer Hanley said, "You promised me a ride in the fire truck!"

"Sorry, but this is the best I could do," I said, pulling him onto the seat beside me. Louie got in next and closed the door.

"Whatever all this is, it better be good," Mendoza said as he drove out of the parking lot.

"When we get to the stationhouse," I said, "I want to call Colfax."

"What's Colfax got to do with this?" the detective asked.

"For one thing, he's investigating another murder related to the same case."

Mendoza suddenly pulled over to the curb and stopped the car.

Turning around to us, he said, "Another murder? All right, I want to hear what this is all about, and I want to hear it right now, and I don't want to hear it from you, Beauchamp. I want to hear it from real people. You, *Independent Journal*, what's this about?"

As though she were dictating copy for a news story, Louie related the case cogently, intelligently, and most impressively, grammatically.

When she was finished, Mendoza said, "You're telling me that old dude is Palmer Hanley?"

"Ninety-five next August," Hanley offered.

"And the Temple of Theotologics is putting crystal meth in the hamburgers?"

"*Some* kind of meth, is my guess," Louie responded. "We need to get a sample to be sure, but now that the police are involved, that shouldn't be a problem."

"And two people were murdered to keep everyone from finding out about the drugged burgers?"

"Two at least, that we know of," I said.

"And you knew about this and didn't come to the police until now," Mendoza snapped.

"It's a little hard to contact your friendly neighborhood patrolman when you've been kidnapped and are being held against your will. I asked Mr. Zarian, the guy who runs the *Independent Journal*, to contact Colfax, but he didn't. That was before we realized Zarian was in on all of this."

"I still can't believe that," Louie said.

"Now that you know everything, Hector," I said, "you can call Colfax."

Mendoza snorted. "That's not going to happen."

"Why? Oh, I get it. You want all the glory for cracking the case yourself."

"If I can get it, yeah," Mendoza said. "But even if I don't, I'm not talking to Colfax. That asshole could've helped me when my fitness for this job was being questioned, but he didn't. So fuck Dane Colfax."

"I think you're being unfair," I said. "He still keeps tabs on you."

"I don't give a shit what you think or what Colfax does. We're playing by my rules now."

"What does *that* mean?" Louie asked, her earlier bravado having dropped.

She actually looked frightened, though if the danger she felt was great enough to have that aphrodisiac affect on her, it would probably be Palmer Hanley who was the lucky man, since he was sitting in between us.

"Here's what's going to happen," Mendoza said. "I'm going to take the three of you into the station, not as suspects, but as witnesses. We'll get everything you said here down on paper. Then I'll let my superiors decide what to do with you."

"All right," Louie said, relieved.

"Fair enough," I added.

"By the way, shithead," Mendoza said, pulling away from the curb, "I like your new look. I only wish I'd done it."

Since the three of us were in the back seat of the car, I reached across Palmer Hanley and took Louie's hand. She didn't pull it away. Then Hanley put his gnarled hand on ours, and there we were: the Three Musketeers. All for one and one for all, riding to the Palms police station.

Somehow, we'd get through this.

My first thought that something might not be right was when Detective Mendoza pulled into a parking garage.

"Is this the station?" I asked. Mendoza didn't answer. He drove the car down, down, down into the lower levels of the parking garage, until we came to a solid wall. There were empty parking spots all around us, but he took none of them.

"What's going on?" Louie asked.

"Special parking," the detective said, and holding up a sensor of some sort, pointed it at the concrete wall and pressed the button. The wall began to slide to the side. Louie and I looked at each other, and I sensed we were both feeling danger.

"What is this?" I asked, but the opening in the wall was complete, and we drove through.

"You think you're so fucking smart," Mendoza commented.

"I don't, actually, but where are we going?"

"Where no one can help you."

We drove further down and then came to a stop. This had to be the deepest parking garage I'd ever encountered.

Mendoza pulled into a space and stopped the car. "Okay, Beauchamp, get out," he said. "The other two of you stay where you are."

I looked at Louie who was breathing hard.

"I said move, Beauchamp," Mendoza shouted, and this time he produced something that strengthened his argument. It was a gun, pointed directly at my chest. I got out of the car, and so did he.

Suddenly I felt the uncontrollable urge to pee.

CHAPTER TWENTY ONE

So here's where you came in.

LAPD Detective Hector Mendoza, a man with whom I already had a rocky professional relationship, was pointing a gun at my heart in some kind of secret underground bunker several levels below the ground, while my two companions, Louie Sandoval and Palmer Hanley, remained in the back of the police car, peering through the rear window, and I was about to wet myself.

At the moment, there was only one part of this situation I could explain: Hanley and Louie were locked inside the car and couldn't let themselves out. They looked at me helplessly through the rear windshield, which was quickly steaming up from their breath.

"Hector, I really have to pee," I told Mendoza.

That made him laugh. "Aw, is little baby gonna piss himself? Go ahead."

My bladder didn't even wait for his permission. I don't recall having wet myself at any point in my adult life, but I simply couldn't stop it. The feel of the hot liquid running down my leg was one I didn't want to re-experience any time soon, either.

"I wish I had a camera," Mendoza said, grinning, as the reek of urine filled the stifling bunker.

When I was finished, he asked, "Better?"

"Hector," I said, refusing to let him see the tears that were threatening to form in my eyes, "even you can't be so blinded with hate for me that you'd simply kill me because you've gotten the chance."

"Oh, how much you don't understand," Mendoza replied.

That was when I had the epiphany. "Oh, my god. What an idiot I've been."

"I won't argue."

"Cable ties."

"What?"

"Cable ties." Jack Daniels had said it; some cops use cable ties instead of handcuffs, and Avery Klemmer had been strangled with nylon cable ties.

"You killed Klemmer, didn't you?"

"See? Even you're capable of figuring things out when a gun's pointed at you."

"And Regina. You killed Regina, too?"

Mendoza nodded.

"Why?"

"She was catching on, that's why. She thought nicotine was being put into the food, so I proved to her she was wrong. That black bitch found out the hard way what an injection of pure nicotine can do to a person."

"My god, you really are a maniac, aren't you?"

"Fuck yourself, asshole. As for that pussy Klemmer, he saw me going through your girlfriend's apartment, so I had to improvise that one. That's why I used the zip ties. Normally I try to make my actions look like the work of amateurs."

"Like the break-in and bugging of my office looked like the work of an amateur."

"You know a better way to disguise the fact that you're a professional than to look like an amateur? Hell, why am I asking you? Like you'd *know* the difference."

"But why, Hector?"

Then another epiphany hit me. *She was catching on, that's why*, he had said. Regina Fontaine had been discovering, or at least suspecting the truth about the addictive Burger Heaven burgers, truth that the Temple could not risk being exposed. She had to be silenced.

"You're part of it, aren't you?" I said. "You're in the Temple."

"You say it like it's a bad thing," Mendoza replied.

"That's why Bedekian called you, not because the Ali Baba was in your turf. Your turf is Hollywood. He called you because you're one of the cops the Temple has bought-and-paid-for."

"Pretty well, too."

Behind us, Louie Sandoval was pounding her fists on the rear windshield, indicating that she was either trying to break out or she and Hanley were running out of air.

"You know, the guy that started this precious Temple of yours is suffocating in a car," I said. "Lot of respect you're showing him."

"That old shitbag? Sure, he started Theotologics, but as a joke. I don't know why they've kept him alive, frankly, but it's not my decision."

"Oh? You're not going to kill him down here?"

"Nope. Not the girl either. We still have to find out from her where she stashed all her notes on her investigation, after which both of them will be taken back for safe keeping. Hanley goes back to his happy home until he has the good sense to die, and the cunt gets sent to a place we have for people who prove particular difficult."

"And where is that?"

"The Temple owns several mines in Africa. They always need new workers. People keep dying."

"God," I muttered.

"Hey, look at it this way? She'll spend the rest of her days surrounded by diamonds."

"You're insane, you know that, Hector?" I said.

He leveled the gun at my head, which would have scared the piss out of me had I any left.

"Don't ever say that to me."

That struck a nerve! said the voice of William Powell inside my head. *Keep it up.*

"They're going to come for you, Hector, and put you away in a padded room."

"Shut up!"

While he wasn't lowering the gun, his grip on it was so tight his hand was starting to shake. Continuing with this strategy was a risk, but I didn't have any other options.

Behind me I heard Louie continuing to pound on the glass, as well as her muted cries from the car.

"I get it now," I went on. "You joined the Temple because you couldn't accept the fact that you were crazy, and they told you they had an alternative treatment for insanity. Is that it? It all goes back to your mother screwing a private eye, doesn't it?"

He fired at me, but he was shaking so much that he missed. I heard it whiz past my right ear. I forced both my legs—the dry one and the pee-soaked one—to remain upright.

"That must have scarred you for life, the thought of dear old Mommy doing the Chicago shagnasty with a twenty-five dollar a day man. You're so crazy even the Temple can't fix you. They can only use you to do their dirty work."

"You're a dead man, Beauchamp," he cried, now holding the gun with both hands. "But before I kill you, maybe I'll beat the shit out of you, just for fun."

I think you should let him, Bogie said. *I mean it, kid. Dare him to fight you. He can't shoot you if he's punching your lights out.*

It was such an idiotic idea, that it almost made sense. And I didn't have any better ideas at the moment.

"You're going to beat me up, Hector? Get real," I said, fighting to keep my voice from shaking.

"Oh, you don't think I will?"

"I don't think you *can.* Oh, sure, you can shoot me, because I'm unarmed. I hear they teach a special class in killing unarmed suspects at the Police Academy."

"You are so fucking asking for it, man," he said, dangerously.

Taking a deep breath, I said: "But you don't have the *cojones* to fight me, and I know you don't have the *cojones* because yours were driven up into your frontal lobe last year by a woman at the stationhouse, right in front of all your cop buddies, who think you're the wuss of the galaxy. I've heard how they laugh when you're not around."

Whatever dungeon we were in wasn't very well lit, but even so, I watched Mendoza's eyes turn crimson. Maybe he'd have a stroke right now and I wouldn't have to worry about his pummeling me into corned beef hash.

No such luck.

Tucking the gun in his coat pocket, he charged me, grabbed me by the shirt collar, and threw me a car length across the bunker, like I was a medicine ball. I hit the concrete and rolled, and he was on me again, wrenching me up, and this time driving his fist into my cheek. The world went orange and the next thing I knew I was being slammed into the concrete wall.

Bogie, maybe this wasn't such a great idea.

Mendoza hit me in the face again and I thought that punch would be the one that sent me under, but somehow I remained conscious, barely, just enough to hear the lugubrious voice of Alfred Hitchcock say in my ear: *Have I ever shown you how to strangle a man with one hand? It's quite amusing.*

Yeah…I remembered that I had seen Hitchcock do that trick on a television show. It was apparently one of his favorites at parties. While he didn't actually strangle anyone, he demonstrated how you could grab another person by the side of the throat, with your fingers in back and your thumb on their Adam's Apple, and squeeze…

Mendoza hit me again, this time in the gut, hard, knocking the wind out of me.

Then he stepped back and smiled. "No balls, huh?" he said. "If I'm the one with no balls, how come you're not fighting back? Go ahead, Mary, try and hit me."

I looked up at him, gasping for air, lurched over and put a hand on his shoulder, an almost friendly gesture that made him laugh.

Then I patted his cheek, like he was a good boy, which made him laugh even harder.

Then with every ounce of strength I could muster, tempered by desperation, I grabbed his throat and squeezed as hard as I could, driving my thumb into his trachea, trapping that laugh in a crushed windpipe.

He began to shake and then broke out of my grip, wheezing and gasping. He went down on one knee, doubled over, fighting for air intake.

I used the opportunity to haul back and kick him in the face as hard as I could. He was spluttering now, and I sensed that if he'd had enough wind to form words, he'd be calling me every name he'd ever heard.

His hand started to go into his pocket, the one containing the gun, and I stomped on his elbow before he could reach it. Then *I* went for the gun.

Sure, I could have shot him, but then I'd be just as bad as him.

Instead I went to his car and motioned for Louie and Hanley to get their heads down and shot out a window. Even at that the doors refused to open, so Louie instead crawled through the broken window, managing to avoid any damage from the glass shards, after which the two of us then pulled Hanley through.

"My god, Dave, you were unbelievable," she said. "But your face looks even worse now."

"I love you too, honey," I replied.

By now Mendoza had enough breath back to cough and enough strength to rise to all fours. I stood over him and pointed the gun at his head.

"You don't fight fair," he wheezed.

"Sue me," I replied.

Louie walked over to us. "Even though I couldn't find the car door release, guess what I did find?"

She held up a pair of steel handcuffs.

"Nice. No cable ties for you, mister," I told Mendoza, as Louie went around behind him and kicked him prone then roughly cuffed him.

She was so quick, efficient and brutal about it that I wondered how much experience she'd had at it. I'd put off thinking about that until later.

"Smells like someone took a leak in here," Palmer Hanley said, his face registering offense. "Damned hoboes."

"Yeah, they ruin everything, don't they?" I muttered. "Let one into an underground bunker and there goes the neighborhood."

"Damn straight!"

"Speaking of underground bunkers, does anyone have any idea how to get out of here?"

"That thing he used to open the door must still be in the car," Louie said, rushing back to look.

"This looks like it," she told us, and half-crawled back into the car to get it, yelping once out of pain from having found a bit of the broken glass. She came back with what looked like a television remote in one hand and a growing drop of blood on the other, which she sucked away.

Then she pointed the device at the seemingly solid wall and started hitting buttons until it began to slide. It had opened nearly all the way when I saw someone on the other side.

As soon as he stepped into the light, such as it was, I whimpered, "Oh, no…"

It was Detective Dane Colfax, his right hand clamped around a gun.

CHAPTER TWENTY TWO

"Is the Police Protection League a wholly owned subsidiary of the Temple of Theotologics?" I cried.

Colfax lowered the gun. "What are you talking about, Beauchamp? And what the hell happened to you?"

Only then did I notice that there was an entire phalanx of uniformed officers behind him.

"Your friend Mendoza expressed his displeasure with me," I said. "And be straight with me, Dane. Are you in the Temple?"

"I'm not even Jewish."

"Oh, god." For the second time in the last quarter hour my legs gave out and I sank to the floor of the bunker. "Why are you here? Not that I'm not happy to see you. I'm thrilled, in fact. But why are you here, detective?"

He didn't answer at first. Instead he walked over to the prone, cuffed figure of Detective Hector Mendoza.

"Hi, Hector," Colfax said.

"Fuck you," Mendoza spat back.

Turning back to me, Colfax asked: "Did you do this?"

"It was a joint effort between this lady and myself."

"Jesus, Beauchamp, you sure have a taste for tough women."

Welcome to the club, the voice of John Garfield said inside my head. Or maybe it was Gene Kelly.

Detective Colfax motioned for two of the uniforms to come and pick Mendoza up off the floor, and for one horrible moment I was afraid he was going to release him.

Instead he instructed the cops to Mirandize him and put him in the back of a cruiser. Then he started examining the opening wall, and said, "I've never seen anything like this in my life."

"Colfax, please, why are you here?" I asked.

"I've been working with internal affairs regarding Hector," he replied. "I've been following him. The brass thought he might be hinky. I didn't want to believe that at first, but you do what you're assigned. I figured this was a chance to exonerate him. The more I tailed him, though, the more suspicious he started looking. When I saw him coming out of that apartment building in Palms, right before the murder of that kid Klemmer was reported, I had to admit something wasn't right."

Dane Colfax; master of the understated emotion.

"And you know, Dave," he went on, "if you hadn't told me that cell phone of yours we found by Klemmer's body had been lifted, I might have suspected Hector of taking it and planting it to frame you."

"Oh…yeah. Lifted. Right."

"Are you trying to tell me something, Dave?"

"Me? No, I've just been through quite a lot in the past week. I'd almost forgotten about my phone."

"Yeah, you do kind of look like dog crap—pardon my honesty."

That seemed to be the prevailing opinion. I guess if Jesus' face can appear on a piece of toast every now and then, mine can appear on a turd.

"As to why I'm here," Colfax went on, "we were tailing Mendoza because he got a call on his cell, and then ditched his new partner Willford and took off."

My own guess was that call was from Antranig Bedekian at the Ali Baba Motel, summoning Mendoza to take care of the people his cousin had been brought to the "safe" house.

"We followed him into this structure," Colfax continued, "and then he just disappeared. We couldn't figure it out. We were going nuts, to be honest about it. It just didn't make any sense. And then all of a sudden, the wall opens up and there he is and there you are. What is this place, anyway?"

"I don't know exactly, but I'm pretty sure it is owned by the Temple of Theotologics," I said.

"That's the second time you've mentioned them. What have they to do with all this?"

"Detective Colfax, take us out of here, get that old gentleman over there to a nice bed, get the young woman he's with to a phone so she can call the Associated Press, and if it's not too much trouble, take me to the nearest emergency room, because talking has suddenly become quite painful, and in return I will tell you absolutely every-thing I know."

Right then, I'm told, is when I passed out.

CHAPTER TWENTY THREE

Remember those 1970s and 80s youth comedy films, like *Animal House*, that would always end with a segment under the credits telling you what would happen to the characters in the future?

Well here goes.

The story of what was in the beef at Burger Heaven became the biggest media circus since the O.J. trial, and Luisa Sandoval was smack in the middle of it. Hardly a day went by when she wasn't on television or in the newspapers talking about her involvement in it, and she has just signed a contract to write a book about the case, which has already been optioned to the movies.

We still see each other every now and then. A few weeks ago I picked her up to go to a movie, but before driving to the theatre I put a blindfold on her that I'd gotten at a magic shop on Hollywood Boulevard, one that allowed for complete vision, even though it didn't look like it.

She didn't know it was a trick, particularly since I managed to pull off a couple of near-misses with parked cars. We never made it to the movie, and instead pulled into the first motel we saw.

And for the record, I can now reveal that her hotly sought-after notes were on a flash drive sealed in a Baggie and hidden inside the ballcock of the toilet tank in her apartment—the same toilet in which I had flushed the bug found in her apartment.

So close, and yet so far.

When the police raided Windsor Studios it actually resulted in a standoff with Temple security, which the police won.

Among those arrested, I'm happy to say, were Dan, Arturo, and Marta. Inside, the authorities found enough of the secret lab intact to discover that the stuff that was being added to the Burger Heaven patties was indeed a new form of methamphetamine that was slightly more benign than the standard drug. That hardly mattered to the FDA, however, and every Burger Heaven restaurant was closed immediately, never to reopen.

I didn't feel all that bad for the employees who lost their jobs, because most of them weren't being paid anyway. Maybe this was what they needed to get right again.

What I do miss is the taste of those Twin Halos, even knowing that they were tainted.

Hannah, whose last name turned out to be Skaal, turned state's evidence and testified before a grand jury about what she knew regarding the Temple and its drug operation. She is also now working full time for Palmer Hanley as his assistant, chauffeur, and general protector.

Investigation into the fire at the Ali Baba Motel revealed that the dump's storeroom held several dozen party-sized packets of cocaine, with a combined street value of about three-million.

Antranig Bedekian had disappeared into the night, along with his wife, and remains at large. The motel itself is an abandoned, slightly charred wreck, into which several homeless people have moved.

Unfortunately, my good friends at the LAPD (who know of my involvement in the "mysterious" fire but have been instructed by the DA's office not to pursue it further) have dubbed the place the Beauchamp Arms. On the street, moving out of a cardboard box and into a room at the Ali Baba is known as "spending a day at the Beauchamp."

At least they're pronouncing it right.

If there is a true victim to this story, it is Zareh Zarian.

His involvement with the Temple had begun when his cousin encouraged him to attend a meeting after a bad relationship break-up. Zarian subsequently joined the Temple and grew to trust his Theotologic masters to the point where during one of his sessions, he revealed a past incident that involved underaged girls, which nobody had known before.

From that moment on, Zarian was the Temple's property, and forced to do their bidding under the fear of having his secret their revealed to the authorities. Their bidding primarily consisted of his using his position as a newspaper editor to do everything he could to keep damaging stories about the Temple out of the press, which included Zarian's complicity in framing his own theatre critic, Jonathan Greene (who has since been exonerated and released from prison) by planting child porn on his computer.

Upon being contacted by Regina Fontaine, Zarian had assigned Luisa Sandoval to the story with the intent of killing whatever she discovered, which resulted in the killing of Regina Fontaine.

Here's the tragedy: unable to face both the public repudiation of his journalistic integrity and the revelation of his past peccadilloes, not to mention his complicity in the death of Regina and Avery Klemmer, Zareh Zarian hanged himself with an electrical cord.

Louie Sandoval wept upon hearing the news.

Detective Hector Mendoza I'm happy to say is currently sitting in jail, awaiting trial on eighteen counts of murder. Not only was he a problem eradicator for the Temple, he did some freelance jobs as well. Remember that big music company exec who turned up dead last year? That was Hector's doing. A sign of the amount of trouble he's in can be gauged by the fact that no celebrity lawyer, the sort who would have defended Osama bin Laden for the publicity alone, has offered to touch his case.

While I'm of the opinion that Hector should get everything he deserves, and then some, Dane Colfax remains a bit shaken by the revelations about his former partner. From my standpoint his loyalty, while admirable, is a bit misplaced.

Incredibly, despite everything, the Temple of Theotologics is still in business, fighting back against the arrests, lawsuits, indictments, loss of tax-exempt status, and waves of bad publicity with a media blitz of their own.

It's hard to turn on a television for five minutes without seeing the rugged, smiling face of Vince Cranna telling everyone that it's all a misunderstanding, and that the Temple, while not perfect, is "adjusting" itself. It would be nice to report that the Temple will eventually be brought down like the walls of Jericho, but I know better.

You're sounding a little cynical, kid, Bogie was telling me.

Yeah, well, maybe that's because, my contribution to bringing down the Temple of Theotologics earned me nothing that I could put in the bank. I was even out a laptop and a cell phone, though on the asset side I now had a dopey disguise kit with a beard that looked like a Davy Crockett hat stapled to my chin.

My real reward was having my bruised nose fully recover, having the DA's office clear me of any involvement with anything untoward, and seeing at least a few of the good guys win.

Chief among the good guys is Palmer Hanley, who is having the time of his very long life. He's been interviewed by everyone from Jimmy Fallon to some nine-year-old on a PBS edutainment show, and he's signed with ICM and is acting again. He's become the star he always hoped he would be, and he's loving every minute of it.

The legal team for the Temple is doing its best to paint him as a senile, lying, ungrateful old goat, but their arguments are facing nonstop objections in the court of public opinion. Whenever Hanley does exhibit a senior moment on camera (and interestingly, today's digital cameras like him far more than yesterday's film cameras), it becomes beloved and goes viral.

I was thinking about Palmer Hanley this very morning, when to my surprise, the door of my office opened up and he rolled in in his motorized wheelchair, which he doesn't really need, but loves anyway.

Hannah Skaal followed him in.

"Hey, Dave Beauchamp," Hanley said, reaching out his gnarled hand for me to shake.

"How are you, sir? Hi, Hannah."

"Hey," she said, smiling.

"I couldn't be better, Dave," the old man said, "really, I couldn't. Say, you think you could do something for me?"

"If there's ever anything I can do for you, you know that I will."

"Are you familiar with the Hollywood Celebrity Show?"

I was. I called it the Hollywood Has-Been Show, but I wasn't about to refer to it as such to Hanley. It was a bi-yearly event in which the movie and TV stars from your childhood, no matter how old you are, collected together in a hotel ballroom to meet and greet fans and sign photos for twenty-five dollars a pop. I had gone to one years ago, and despite the obvious attraction for a film buff I had come away depressed at seeing so many people who had been so large a part of my childhood virtually begging me to buy their signature so they could make the mortgage.

"Sure, I know about it," I told him.

"Well, they want me to do the next one coming up, and that's fine with me, but I'd like you to come with me."

"Well, I'm flattered, Palmer, but why?"

"'Cause Miranda Love is also going to be there. Do you know Miranda Love?"

I knew she'd been a Universal starlet in the late 1940s and went on to a career in low-budget films and television through the 1970s. I didn't think she had done anything since.

"I've never met Miranda, but, yeah, I know who she is," I answered.

"Never met her, huh. Well, you're lucky. I worked with her once and I said if the two of us ever got together again, someone was gonna die."

Oh, how I wish he had not been so prophetic.

ABOUT THE AUTHOR

Michael Mallory is the author of the "Dave Beauchamp" and "Amelia Watson" mystery series and the horror novel *The Mural*, as well nine nonfiction books, 125 short stories, and some 600 magazine articles. A recognized film historian and occasional TV actor, he lives in the Los Angeles area.